"I want you,"

J.D. whispered, his voice low and husky. "I want to take you somewhere where no one will interrupt us."

Liza wasn't sure she could speak. "But I…"

He took her mouth then. She opened to him. And he drank from her.

Liza felt as if she'd just leapt onto a hurtling train. The rush, the power, the beauty of the race tugged at her senses. Needs she couldn't put a name to made themselves known. Desires clamored to be recognized. She'd found someone who could unleash her wildness.

But her life was so disorderly right now—her heritage unknown, her plans up in the air.

Yet, awash in unfamiliar pleasure, Liza made her decision.

She would let the hard-driving sheriff of Pine Bluff, Arizona, take her where he would….

Dear Reader,

Special Edition's lineup for August will definitely make this a memorable summer of romance! Our THAT SPECIAL WOMAN! title for this month is *The Bride Price* by reader favorite Ginna Gray. Wyatt Sommersby has his work cut out for him when he tries to convince the freedom-loving Maggie Muldoon to accept his proposal of marriage.

Concluding the new trilogy MAN, WOMAN AND CHILD this month is *Nobody's Child* by Pat Warren. Don't miss the final installment of this innovative series. Also in August, we have three veteran authors bringing you three wonderful new stories. In *Scarlet Woman* by Barbara Faith, reunited lovers face their past and once again surrender to their passion. *What She Did on Her Summer Vacation* is Tracy Sinclair's story of a young woman on holiday who finds herself an instant nanny to two adorable kids—and the object of a young aristocrat's affections. Ruth Wind's *The Last Chance Ranch* is the emotional story of one woman's second chance at life when she reclaims her child. Finally, August introduces *New York Times* bestseller Ellen Tanner Marsh to Silhouette **Special Edition**. She brings her popular and unique style to her first story for us, *A Family of Her Own*. This passionate and heartwarming tale is one you won't want to miss.

This summer of love and romance isn't over yet! I hope you enjoy each and every story to come!

Sincerely,

Tara Gavin, Senior Editor

Please address questions and book requests to:
Silhouette Reader Service
U.S.: 3010 Walden Ave., P.O. Box 1325, Buffalo, NY 14269
Canadian: P.O. Box 609, Fort Erie, Ont. L2A 5X3

PAT WARREN
NOBODY'S CHILD

Silhouette®

SPECIAL EDITION®

Published by Silhouette Books
America's Publisher of Contemporary Romance

To Joey, Stephanie, Leah and Angie,
my special little ones—
"No one's going to harm you, not while I'm around."

 SILHOUETTE BOOKS

ISBN 0-373-09974-6

NOBODY'S CHILD

Printed in U.S.A.

Books by Pat Warren

Silhouette Special Edition

With This Ring #375
Final Verdict #410
Look Homeward, Love #442
Summer Shadows #458
The Evolution of Adam #480
Build Me a Dream #514
The Long Road Home #548
The Lyon and the Lamb #582
My First Love, My Last #610
Winter Wishes #632
Till I Loved You #659
An Uncommon Love #678
Under Sunny Skies #731
That Hathaway Woman #758
Simply Unforgettable #797
This I Ask of You #815
On Her Own #841
A Bride for Hunter #893
Nobody's Child #974

Silhouette Romance

Season of the Heart #553

Silhouette Initimate Moments

Perfect Strangers #288
Only the Lonely #605

Silhouette Books

Montana Mavericks
Outlaw Lovers #6

PAT WARREN

mother of four, lives in Arizona with her travel-agent husband and a lazy white cat. She's a former newspaper columnist whose lifetime dream was to become a novelist. A strong romantic streak, a sense of humor and a keen interest in developing relationships led her to try romance novels, with which she feels very much at home.

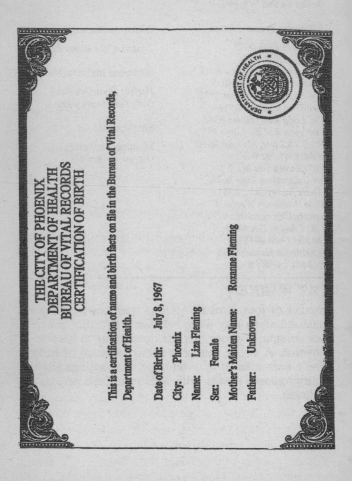

THE CITY OF PHOENIX
DEPARTMENT OF HEALTH
BUREAU OF VITAL RECORDS
CERTIFICATION OF BIRTH

This is a certification of name and birth facts on file in the Bureau of Vital Records, Department of Health.

Date of Birth: July 8, 1967
City: Phoenix
Name: Liza Fleming
Sex: Female
Mother's Maiden Name: Roxanne Fleming
Father: Unknown

Prologue

Abby Thatcher laid her head on her folded arms and tried not to cry. Winthrop hated tears, though God knew he'd handled enough weeping women during the forty years he'd practiced law in this small office in downtown Phoenix.

Exhaustion combined with sorrow had her feeling numb. But the numbness didn't make the ache in her heart go away. She raised her head and, taking a deep breath, straightened her thin shoulders and patted her salt-and-pepper hair. Indulging her grief wouldn't get the work done, and now, on top of everything else, she had to deal with the ineptitude of the temporary help she'd just dismissed. In two days, the silly girl hadn't been able to follow the simplest directions.

It had been only three days since Winthrop's funeral, but with all Abby'd had to cope with since his fatal heart attack last week, it seemed more like three years.

She opened a file on her always organized desk, wishing instead she could give way to her grief for the man she had loved for over four decades, the man who'd seen her only as his dedicated, organized and ever-so-dependable secretary. There had never been any hope for her. Winthrop Ames, Esquire, had been married to the law.

Her last official duty would be to close his office. Before she could, she had to make arrangements for his pending cases and dispose of a lifetime's accumulation of files, since he had no partners.

The half-dozen cartons along the oak-paneled wall of the small library would be picked up this afternoon by a messenger from the law firm the client had asked to have assume the case. Yesterday, she'd directed the temp to mail several files. Abby was still waiting to hear from other people she'd spoken with regarding their cases, and she had letters to write to Winthrop's remaining clients.

But before another sheet of paper left the office, she needed to tend to the special files, those that had been so dear to Winthrop's heart.

With a sense of purpose, she crossed the room to the cartons she'd filled herself. Large manila envelopes, along with a stack of typing paper the temporary had failed to put away after mailing the real-estate files, were on the desk next to them.

Abby stopped in front of a yellow carton. A small smile touched her lips as she looked fondly at the folders inside.

The babies, she thought, a rush of warmth suffusing her.

Winthrop's practice had been varied, but his favorite cases were the adoptions. He loved little children. Three cases in particular had been special to Winthrop: Shaw, Russell and Parker.

It was with that thought that she noticed the first folder wasn't the one she'd placed there yesterday. She was certain she'd left the Shaw file in front. She specifically remembered putting it there after instructing the temporary to mail everything in the carton next to it.

Perplexed, Abby removed the box of stationery and mailing labels the temporary had left on the box and searched through the remaining folders. The Parker and Russell files were there, but where was Shaw?

She went through the box again slowly, carefully checking each folder. Fifteen minutes later, she admitted defeat. The Shaw file was nowhere to be found. Deeply troubled, she picked up the Russell file.

Russell, Janice, Abby thought, reading the name on the folder tab.

She sat down at her desk, frowning as she glanced through the papers in the file.

She'd never approved of Janice Russell's decision. It just wasn't right that the young man had never been told he was a father. He should know he had a child.

Abby reached for the mailing envelope.

After the Russell file was out of the way, Abby opened the Parker file, the very first adoption Winthrop had handled twenty-eight years ago. She'd actually seen this baby—a little girl—because the papers had been signed right here in the office. The adoptive parents had been so thrilled with their daughter.

Such a long time ago. Abby wondered how they were all doing as she addressed the mailing envelope to Mr. and Mrs. Ralph Parker.

Twenty-eight years earlier

Ethel Bisbee paused in the hallway outside the law offices of Winthrop Ames, Esquire, feeling tense and hes-

itant. The hour she'd spent driving south on I-17 from
Pine Bluff, Arizona, hadn't calmed her nerves one bit.
Having lived all her life in the small Western town, she
had to admit that the bustling city of Phoenix with its tall
buildings and heavy traffic wasn't her cup of tea.

But that wasn't entirely the cause of her unease.

Ethel glanced down at the infant snuggled in a soft
pink blanket and instinctively tightened hold on the
child. Such a beautiful baby with reddish blond fuzz for
hair and big blue eyes, her skin flawless, her features
delicate.

A few years ago, Ethel would have given everything she
owned for a little girl like this one. But when her husband, Herman, had been killed in a railroad accident ten
years ago, a week after their fifth anniversary, Ethel's
dream of raising a family had died with him. The big
three-story stucco house she'd inherited from her parents would have been perfect for raising hordes of children.

Fate had chosen to leave her alone with little money,
few marketable skills and a large mortgage to pay off. A
short, energetic woman with thick brown hair and kind
eyes, Ethel had never wanted to depend on anyone.
Which was why, after Herman's death, she'd turned the
family home into Bisbee's Bed & Breakfast. Since there
was no hotel in Pine Bluff, she'd done fairly well. Keeping busy had also meant she had less time to miss Herman and the children they'd never had.

Adjusting the blanket around the dozing infant, Ethel
felt a pang of envy for the couple who would have the
privilege of raising this sweet girl. At age forty, with a
business to run, she couldn't see herself taking on the
additional responsibility. It wouldn't be fair to the baby,
either.

The child had been given to her by someone who trusted Ethel to do the right thing, to make sure the little girl would have a better chance at a good future than she'd have faced in Pine Bluff. They'd also paid her a generous sum to keep the details private. That's why Ethel had phoned Abby Thatcher, knowing that her cousin worked for an attorney. Mr. Ames had speedily arranged for a private adoption, assuring her that the adoptive couple were very fine people.

Reluctant to let her go, Ethel gazed at the child's face, watching the tiny features wrinkle into a baby frown. Her heart ached for the mother who'd had to give up her infant daughter. From within the blanket folds, she removed a black lacquered box that she'd been given along with the child. Inside, she'd found some things that the child's relatives had apparently wanted the little girl to have.

Overcome with emotion, Ethel reached into her purse and extracted a tiny gold heart hanging from a delicate chain. It had been hers as a baby. Since she had no children of her own to inherit it, she added the small gift to the box. For luck.

The girl would undoubtedly need it.

The baby sleeping so innocently in her arms had already had a shaky beginning to her life. Ethel touched a brief kiss to the sweet head, silently wishing her well.

Then, squaring her shoulders, she opened the door to the office of Winthrop Ames, Esquire, hoping that Abby was waiting for them.

Chapter One

Liza Parker sat in her father's favorite chair, gazing at the three cartons of papers in front of her, and struggled with a fresh rush of tears.

It seemed as if she'd been crying for the entire five days since she'd gotten the fateful phone call telling her that her father had suffered a massive coronary and had died within minutes. Thoroughly shaken, she'd jumped into her blue Mazda RX-7 and driven from Tucson to Phoenix in record time, later scarcely able to recall the trip.

The funeral had been yesterday and now she faced the oppressive chore of going through his things, deciding what to keep, what to sell, what to give away. Times like this, she wished she'd had a brother or sister to share the decisions, and that her mother, Blair, had lived.

Needing to get to it, Liza leaned forward and picked up an expandable folder marked House Papers. As she opened it, the ringing of the doorbell startled her enough to cause her to drop the folder. Her nerves were on edge, she decided as she rose.

A shadowy figure stood on the front stoop shaded by the generous overhang. Peering through the screen, Liza saw that the man holding a clipboard and a large manila envelope wore the uniform of a mail-delivery service. She pushed open the door.

"I'm looking for Ralph Parker," he told her. "I was here yesterday, but no one was home. We make two attempts to locate, then return the package to sender. Would Mr. Parker be home?"

"I'm afraid not," Liza answered. "Mr. Parker passed away a few days ago. I'm his daughter."

"Oh, I'm sorry." The tall man frowned as he gazed down at the large manila envelope. "I don't know. Says here I'm to deliver to Ralph Parker. Maybe if Mrs. Parker was at home..."

"My mother died a long while ago." Liza squinted, trying to make out the name of the sender. "Who sent the package?"

"Some law office in Phoenix." He swiped at his sweaty brow. "Mind if I use your phone? I'd better call my supervisor."

"Not at all. If you'll wait here, I'll bring it out." Liza walked inside to the end table where she'd left the portable phone and took it out to him. "I'll get you a cold drink while you call," she said, wondering if by chance the package had been sent by her father's attorney and contained his will, which she hadn't yet run across. Of course, she was Ralph's only legal child and heir, but he might have made some special bequests that she'd like to honor.

Giving the man some privacy, she went to the kitchen to get his ice tea and took her time returning. He finished his call as she walked back out and handed him the frosty glass.

"Thanks a lot. It's really hot out there." He took the drink. "My supervisor says if you can show me some ID, you can sign for the package."

"Fine." Liza went to get her driver's license and the obituary that had been in the newspaper naming her as Ralph's only surviving relative.

The man drained his tea thirstily, then checked both pieces. "Looks okay to me. Sign here." He held out the form attached to the clipboard. As soon as Liza finished, he tore off his copy and handed her the envelope. "Thanks again."

"You're welcome." Inside, Liza locked the screen, then walked slowly back to the leather chair as she ripped open the envelope. Sitting down, she withdrew a packet of papers clipped together and read the cover letter first.

Her interest increased as she saw that the material had been sent by Abby Thatcher, the secretary to Winthrop Ames, the attorney who'd arranged her adoption as an infant. She'd been told the story as a young child about how she'd been a special chosen child. Even after Blair Parker's untimely death leaving him with the overwhelming task of having to raise an active little girl all alone, her father had never shown signs of regretting the adoption.

Reading on, Liza discovered that Mr. Ames had died recently and Ms. Thatcher was cleaning out his files. Apparently the lawyer had handled several adoptions and his secretary was releasing the files to the appropriate parents.

Only, both her parents were gone.

Her excitement mounting, Liza slipped off the paper clip. Despite the fact that Ralph Parker had been wonderful, she'd had a normal curiosity about her birth parents and a secret desire to look them up one day. But she hadn't wanted to hurt her father's feelings so she'd never pursued the matter.

Maybe these papers would show her the way.

But as she quickly scanned the pages, she was disappointed to discover that there was no information on her birth parents whatsoever. However, there was a black-and-white Polaroid picture of a baby wrapped in a blanket and lying on a huge four-poster bed. Her heart suddenly fluttering, Liza wondered if that picture was the first ever taken of her.

Undaunted by the skimpy material, she decided to call the secretary to see if she could learn more. Taking the number from the letterhead, Liza dialed with nervous fingers and was pleased when Abby Thatcher herself answered. Quickly she explained herself to the woman who listened quietly.

Abby drew in a calming breath as Liza Parker finished, hoping her annoyance wouldn't be detected in her voice. "That file wasn't intended for you, Miss Parker."

Though the woman sounded stiff and somewhat haughty, Liza pressed on. "I realize that. However, as I explained, both of my parents are dead. I have no relatives left on either side as my father's family was from Canada and my mother's from Florida, all long gone. In view of that, you can understand my interest in trying to locate my birth parents, I'm sure."

Abby was not unfeeling. But this situation was clearly out of the realm of her experience. What would Winthrop have done? she asked herself. "There isn't much I can do to help you, I'm afraid," she answered vaguely.

Liza struggled not to sound impatient. "Perhaps you can. For instance, I can't understand why the Consent to Adopt form has Father Unknown marked on it and the line for mother left blank. Surely Mr. Ames, who handled my adoption, knew the names of my biological parents."

Wearily, Abby removed her glasses and wished she'd never answered this call. "Yes, the birth mother would likely have signed the consent form. However, the original is locked in court records and cannot be obtained without a court order. The copy I included in the package, which I intended for your adoptive parents, is always left blank to protect the anonymity of the biological parents."

Liza caught the note of reprimand and ignored it as she tried to absorb the information, her mind filling with questions. "Did my father also have to sign?"

"Sometimes fathers sign also. In cases where the mother doesn't know who the baby's father is, we type in 'Unknown.'"

Feeling her knees weaken, Liza sat down. "Are you saying that my mother didn't know who fathered me?"

Abby closed her eyes. "I'm not saying that was the case with your adoption. This office handled many adoptions through the years, so naturally, I can't recall each specific case." Which wasn't exactly true. The Parker case had been Winthrop's first and Abby remembered a great deal. However, she was ethically bound not to reveal too much. "I'm merely informing you that usually, when Father Unknown is typed in, the father either declined to admit to paternity or the mother refused to name him, or in some instances, she didn't know who he was."

Everything in Liza fought that possibility, dismissing it. As a teenager, she'd often fantasized about her birth mother, imagining her in several tragic scenarios that caused the poor woman to give up the baby she'd most certainly wanted. But never in her wildest imaginings had she even considered the possibility that the woman who gave birth to her didn't even know the name of the man who'd fathered her.

Aware that Abby was silently waiting, Liza decided to try another tactic. "If I were to hire an attorney to petition the court, would I possibly be able to obtain the original consent form?"

Abby was more comfortable discussing legal questions than conjecturing about who did what twenty-eight years ago. "Doubtful. The birth mother would have to be located and her permission obtained. Even if the court had the manpower to accomplish that, I doubt any judge would grant your request."

Liza felt a flash of temper. "Why not? Maybe my birth mother would be glad to hear that I want to find her."

"If that were the case, she could have and would have started her own search for you." Then, wanting to soften the blow of her words, Abby went on. "Perhaps you could check with some of those agencies that work to put adoptees in touch with birth parents."

Liza's anger disappeared, replaced by a wave of discouragement. "Thank you, Miss Thatcher."

The disappointment in the young woman's voice got to Abby. She felt genuinely sad for Liza Parker, with no relatives left from her adoptive parents and the means to locate her birth parents denied her by legalities. "I'm sorry I couldn't be more helpful."

So much for that, Liza thought as she hung up and reached for the manila envelope. As she did so, a piece of paper she hadn't noticed before fluttered out. She picked it up.

The single yellow sheet appeared to have been torn from a legal pad and contained notes in a bold handwriting. Had Winthrop Ames written them? she wondered as she noticed the Parkers' name and address in one corner, the date at the top and a reminder of the court date when the consent form was to be presented.

Near the bottom was the notation that the child had been brought in by an Ethel Bisbee of Pine Bluff, Arizona, at one o'clock on Tuesday. Though she'd never been there, Liza knew that Pine Bluff was about an hour's drive north of Phoenix. Fighting back her rising excitement, she saw that written in the opposite corner was a list of items that appeared to have come with the child. A pink blanket. A white crocheted dress and booties. And a black lacquered box.

The last item had Liza frowning thoughtfully. Earlier today when she'd been going through her father's dresser drawers, she'd noticed a black lacquered box. Because she'd been looking for papers, not mementos, she'd ignored it. Maybe it was worth a second look. Setting the legal packet aside, she went to her father's bedroom.

The box was in the corner of his top drawer. With a trembling hand, she picked it up and saw that there was an envelope underneath with her name written in her father's precise handwriting. Sitting down on his bed, she unfolded a white sheet of stationery.

Her eyes widened as she read. Her father wrote that a woman named Ethel Bisbee had given the box and its contents to the Parkers at the time of the adoption, telling them to give them to her if she ever asked about her birth parents. Since she'd never asked, he'd kept it for her.

Ralph went on to say that after her mother had died, he'd gone to Pine Bluff to try to locate Liza's biological parents, thinking it only fair that she know them. From the outset, the townsfolk had been unfriendly to him, rebuffing his questions, and some people had been downright rude. Even Ethel had refused to talk with him, which had been a shock.

That night, at the motel on the outskirts of town where he'd registered, someone had slashed his tires and bashed in his side windows. The note left on the seat had read "Go home where you belong."

Her father went on to say that he hadn't been frightened so much as dismayed. Apparently there were people in Pine Bluff who were very protective of her birth parents. Not wanting to cause trouble, he'd left and never returned.

However, Ralph added, he knew that Liza was not only spunky and persistent but also lovely and charming. If anyone could win them over, it was her. *If* she even wanted to try. He ended by giving her his blessing to go for it, but warned her to use care. It was entirely possible that someone in Pine Bluff had it in for the Parkers.

Liza folded the sheet, wearing a puzzled frown. Why had they treated her father like that without hearing him out? Surely they hadn't feared a man as mild as Ralph Parker. What were they afraid of? Who were they protecting and why? And what had made Ethel Bisbee change in four short years?

Returning her attention to the lacquered box, she took off the lid. Cautiously, she held up a small gold heart on a delicate chain, obviously meant for a child. Next, there was a small circlet, like a ring, and it looked as if it had been carved very beautifully from an acorn. She slipped it onto her ring finger and found that it fit. Who had carved the ring and for whom? she wondered, her imagination picturing a handsome young man presenting it to a beautiful woman with long auburn hair like hers and deep blue eyes that matched her own.

Wishing she weren't quite so fanciful, Liza removed the last item from the box. It was a green leather diary. As she opened it, a dried and faded rose that appeared to have been pink at one time dropped onto her lap. Who had picked that flower and where? If only she knew.

Carefully thumbing through the brittle pages of the diary, at last she found a page that contained an entry. The date was June 8, the handwriting small and feminine. "I met him today and it promises to be the most exciting summer of my life." Nothing was written on any of the other pages.

Liza swallowed around a dry throat. Had her mother written that? Had the man she referred to been her father? Why had the woman who'd given her up for adoption included these particular items? Had she perhaps been forced to give away her baby against her wishes, for whatever reason? Had she sent the lacquered box containing a few precious items along with her baby daughter in the hope that when the child was grown, they'd offer a clue as to how to find her?

If that was true, the clues were too vague for Liza to comprehend.

She rose and returned the contents to the box. Back in the living room, she picked up the sheet of yellow legal paper again. Pine Bluff, Arizona. Was Ethel Bisbee still living there? Liza badly wanted to know.

Her nerves jumpy, she gathered her heavy auburn hair off her neck and hastily improvised a ponytail with a piece of blue yarn. It was mid-September but still quite warm in Phoenix, and her father had neglected to get the air conditioner repaired. She wished he were here so she could talk this over with him.

Thoughtfully, Liza stared at the phone, then quickly dialed Information before she could change her mind. Moments later, she hung up, a satisfied smile on her face. There was a listing for Ethel Bisbee in Pine Bluff, she'd been told. Phoning her was too impersonal and would give the woman too much opportunity to snub her if she was still protecting someone.

Or was Ethel Bisbee her mother?

Unlikely. She was probably only a messenger. Or her mother's mother. Or an aunt, perhaps. Maybe she had several relatives in Pine Bluff. Waves of excitement skittered along her spine. Liza knew she wouldn't rest until she found out.

Could she afford to take more time off from work? Actually, she was in a better position to go now than she had been in ages. Things in Tucson had been going better than usual lately after long years of struggle. After graduating from the University of Arizona with a degree in fashion design, she'd worked for two years with Carmella Jones, a well-known Southwest designer. Then, with her father's encouragement and backing, she'd taken a big risk and opened her own studio.

Success hadn't happened overnight. She'd worked hard, long hours and weekends. But finally, three months ago, she'd sold her new women's casual sports line exclusively to a major Tucson department store. At last she'd been able to hire a full-time assistant, Marianne Webster, who was bright and talented. With Marianne's input and the continued assistance of her part-time helper, Tina Larkin, the studio was finally moving into solid black ink.

Her career off to a flying start, Liza had moved to a sunny, well-located apartment that she could finally afford alone after her closest friend, Dawn Myers, had moved out recently. She'd been feeling good about her life.

Then the doctor had called about her father.

She glanced again at the yellow legal sheet and the other papers. Maybe this was just what she needed to get over her father's sudden death, to focus on something positive, the challenge of locating her birth parents. Coming to a decision, she picked up the phone again.

Later, after Marianne's assurances that she and Tina could handle the studio for a little while longer, Liza sat back. She'd set her plan into motion. Methodically, she considered what else she needed to do. First, she'd call Dawn and ask her to keep an eye on her apartment a while longer. As an obstetric nurse at Community Hospital, Dawn worked odd shifts, but she'd manage to pop in, water her plants and pick up her mail, Liza was certain.

That left Tony.

Dr. Tony Hilliard, the handsome pediatric surgeon Dawn had introduced her to six months ago. He'd been a dream date with his all-American good looks, his caring nature and quiet sense of humor. He was fun to be with and supportive of the things she wanted to accomplish. He'd even hinted once or twice that he wanted to settle down soon. But something was missing.

At twenty-eight, Liza had never been in love, at least not in the way she'd dreamed about. She'd come to that realization when Dawn had met and moved in with a local sportscaster recently. Every time Liza saw the two of them together, she could almost feel the sizzle of their intense attraction to one another. Infantile as she often told herself it was, she wanted to experience that intensity.

Unfortunately, Tony seemed unable to make her sizzle.

She'd call Tony, and he'd probably be annoyed at the delay in her return. He'd just have to be patient, that's all. This was something she simply had to do.

She looked again at the boxes waiting to be sorted through. They would wait until she returned. A Realtor friend of her father's was coming this afternoon to put the house on the market. She'd already called the church and made arrangements for his clothes to be picked up. She'd make a few calls, pack her own clothes and be ready to leave in the morning.

Feeling better than she had in days, Liza reached for the phone.

The next day, seated in her Mazda with a map spread out beside her, Liza approached the intersection of the main road leading into Pine Bluff. Stopping at the light, she noticed a motel up a ways and across the street, and wondered if that was where her father had stayed years ago when his car had been vandalized. Sleepy little towns didn't change much, so the possibility existed.

The string of tired-looking rooms badly in need of paint didn't look appealing, so she decided to drive into town and see what else she could find. It wasn't even noon yet, she realized, glancing at her watch. A truck pulling a horse trailer on the opposite side of the four-lane divided highway was the only other vehicle in sight.

Just as the light changed, she heard a siren moving closer from behind and glanced into her rearview mirror.

A red Toyota was hurtling toward her at a crazy speed. As Liza shuddered, the driver swerved around her Mazda into the left-hand lane and zoomed past. Startled, she saw the Toyota barely pause as it sprinted through the intersection and kept going. Her heart slammed against her rib cage as she again raised her eyes to the mirror and saw a silver van with its red dome light flashing and siren blaring also heading straight for her. The driver leaned on the horn, as well, but she was frozen in place.

Liza braced herself for the crash, but the driver managed to swing the wheel to the right and come to a jarring stop in a ditch.

As the dust settled, Liza looked out and saw a tall man hurry over to the driver's side of her car. She reached to lower the window, but he jerked open her door before she could.

"Get out," he ordered. "I'm seizing your car for official police business."

Liza's grip on the steering wheel tightened. "Oh, no, you're not!"

Chapter Two

J. D. Kincaid narrowed his gaze as he frowned at the woman. He was not used to his orders being refused. "What did you say?"

Liza's glance skimmed over him, noting that he was quite tall, several inches over six feet, with broad shoulders and big-fisted hands. From the rolled-up sleeves of his blue cotton shirt to his faded jeans and dusty boots, his body looked lean and hard. She had a quick impression of strength, impatience and more than a touch of arrogance. She was probably foolish to challenge him, especially on this lonely stretch of road with the traffic so light as to be nearly nonexistent. But she didn't like bullies or being ordered around, and she wasn't about to hand her car over to a stranger who claimed to be an officer. "I said, you're not taking my car. You don't look like any policeman I've ever seen."

Swearing under his breath, J.D. groped in his pocket for his badge. Gray had often told him he ought to wear it always, but usually, it wasn't necessary. Every one of the nearly two thousand residents of Pine Bluff knew him by sight and sound. He thrust the shield at her. "I'm the sheriff around here. Now, get out of the damn car."

Just his luck, J.D. thought, running into a stubborn woman wearing designer clothes and driving an expensive sports car instead of a local in a fast truck. He could see no cars he could flag down coming in either direction. He'd been on his way to Gray's ranch to spend his day off when his radio had picked up the call. He'd quickly notified Richie White, one of his deputies, that he was closer and would take up the chase. He'd have closed in, too, if it hadn't been for the Mazda blocking his path, forcing his van into the ditch to avoid hitting her. By the time this little package stopped arguing with him, Gonzo would be at the Utah border in his souped-up Toyota.

Liza didn't move, carefully looking over the badge. "How do I know you didn't steal that and the van from the real sheriff?" She'd read stories like that, where the bad guys masqueraded as good guys. He didn't look all that law-abiding with his dark windblown hair worn kind of shaggy and his angry eyes. "There's no name on this shield."

His patience, never his strong suit, was being strained to the max. "That did it," J.D. said. Reaching inside the vehicle, he slipped the gearshift into Park, hit the lever and slid back her seat, then scooped her into his arms. Ignoring her shocked protests and the sweet female scent of her, he maneuvered her over the console and deposited her in the passenger seat. Quickly he climbed behind the wheel, shoved the seat back as far as it would go, shifted into Drive and stepped down hard on the gas.

"You can't do this," Liza yelled at him, rubbing the top of her head where he'd caused her to bump it on the dome light.

In moments he had the needle up to seventy, yet he saw no sign of the red Toyota. In another couple of miles, the road would narrow into two lanes, J.D. knew, and he'd probably have to slow down in the face of heavier oncoming traffic. He'd been after the wily petty thief known as Gonzo for months and he didn't want to lose him now.

Furious that he wasn't answering her, Liza glared at him. She should probably be more frightened than angry, but she'd made only two payments on her car and the maniacal way the big bully was driving, he'd surely slam it into the side of a mountain. "Kidnapping's against the law, you know."

He shot her a fierce glance. "I *am* the law, lady." To shut her up, he reached into his shirt pocket for his ID and tossed it to her. "Now, will you pipe down so I can concentrate on catching this guy?"

Liza read the card issued by the Department of Law Enforcement. Sheriff Jonathan David Kincaid was typed under the blurred picture of an unsmiling cowboy wearing a Stetson. She supposed there was a tiny resemblance to the big galoot racing her car around a curve on two wheels. Holding on for dear life, she frowned at him. "Do you always drive like this?"

"Only when I'm trying to catch a criminal who just robbed a convenience store back in Pine Bluff, leaving the owner beaten and bleeding," J.D. answered through clenched teeth. Squinting through the windshield, he thought he spotted a red vehicle some distance ahead of them as they rounded the bend.

"Beaten and bleeding?" Liza's conscience kicked in. She certainly didn't want to be responsible for preventing a lawman from apprehending a dangerous criminal. "Why didn't you say so in the first place? It looked as if you were simply chasing a speeder."

J.D.'s hands curled around the steering wheel as he prayed for patience and tried to tune her out. She was as annoying as she was attractive. He hadn't been too preoccupied to notice her thick auburn hair and huge blue eyes, to say nothing of how soft she'd felt in his arms as he'd moved her. She smelled good, too, in the enforced intimacy of the small car, or was it just that he hadn't been with a woman in such close quarters in a while?

The highway changed to two lanes, one in each direction, and it straightened somewhat, stretching ahead as far as the eye could see. He caught sight of the red Toyota and nearly cheered when he saw that Gonzo was stuck behind a slow-moving truck hauling logs against a sudden rush of heavy traffic. If only he had his Bronco with its siren.

Expertly he streaked around a station wagon with only inches to spare and saw that his suspect had little to no chance of passing the logging truck. He downshifted, moving so close to the older-model Chevrolet in front of him that the driver began to wobble nervously in the lane. Only two cars separated the Mazda from Gonzo now.

"It's that red Toyota you're after, right?" Liza asked, fumbling with her seat belt. If there was to be a sudden stop, which seemed highly likely, she thought she ought to be prepared.

"Yeah," he muttered, concentrating.

Her mind searched for a way to help him, thinking that if she did, he'd march out of her life as quickly as he'd rushed in.

Just then, the Chevrolet that had been kissing his front bumper swerved off onto the very narrow shoulder, taking a chance on sliding down the grassy embankment rather than having the Mazda wind up in its trunk. J.D. moved up. Only a gray Ford Pinto separated them from Gonzo's Toyota.

The legal term "obstruction of justice" flitted across Liza's mind's eye and she stole another glance at the formidable sheriff who loomed so large in her small car. He was grim-faced, tight-jawed and unsmiling, but surely he wouldn't arrest her for preventing him from catching this guy if he got away, would he? He was also very attractive in an earthy sort of way, which was beside the point. Why on earth had she questioned his credentials, anyway? she asked herself. After all, she'd heard his siren and seen his Bronco land in the ditch.

Because everything wasn't always what it appeared to be, that's why. And a woman alone in an unfamiliar area couldn't be too careful. At the first calm moment, she'd explain herself to Sheriff Kincaid and dare him to find fault with her reasoning.

Up ahead on the right, she spotted a truck stop and gripped the door handle nervously, wishing she could get out and go inside. She wanted nothing more than for this whole nightmare to be over. The thought had no sooner formed than the Toyota suddenly left the highway and bounced along the narrow path leading to the restaurant. Liza peered through the dust cloud and sent up a silent prayer.

J.D. swung the wheel sharply to the right and followed Gonzo, hoping the desperate little man wouldn't do anything stupid. There were half a dozen cars in the parking lot of Ernie's Place and any number of people inside, he was certain. He'd need to grab the little creep outside to prevent others from getting hurt.

"He's going around back," Liza said, unable to keep still. "Why is he doing that?"

There was a large thicket of evergreens behind the eatery, looking dense and shady even in the sunlight. "He might think he can outrun me in the trees," J.D. conjectured.

"Escape on foot?" From what she could see of the fugitive, he looked to be much smaller than the man beside her. "His chances were better on the highway. Coming here was a mistake."

J.D. watched as Gonzo reached the same conclusion and frantically circled to the front again, his tires squealing as he jerked his car around the corner. "That's what we wait for—the criminal to make a mistake."

Gonzo's eyes must have been on the rearview mirror for he miscalculated the second turn and lost control of the Toyota. It spun around crazily before crashing noisily into an outside phone booth. As red clay dust swirled upward, J.D. stopped the Mazda directly behind, blocking Gonzo's exit.

But the nervous fugitive decided to make a last-ditch effort. Shifting into Reverse, he stepped on the gas and the Toyota slammed into the Mazda, smashing the right front fender and grille. The red car let out a final wheeze before its motor died.

His hands braced on the steering wheel, J.D. had only been jarred, but he'd heard the woman's head crack against the side window. "You all right?" he asked hurriedly as he shifted into Park.

"Yes, but look what's happened to my brand-new car!" Liza moaned.

He didn't have time to worry about her car just now. J.D. jumped out before Gonzo could open his door. Tucked into his waistband at the small of his back, he had the .38 he'd grabbed from the seat of his van. But he didn't think he'd need it. He jerked the smarmy little man out, shoved him against the car, propped his hands on the roof and spread his legs for a quick body search.

"Hey, man, I'm clean, you know," Gonzo sniveled. "I don't carry no piece."

Only, Kenny Brown, the owner of the convenience store, had told the deputy that he'd thought Gonzo had a gun. Which meant that somewhere along the way, Gonzo had shed his piece or it was concealed within the damaged Toyota. If that was true, they would find it eventually. Silently J.D. reached for his handcuffs, placing one bracelet on Gonzo's wrist and securing the other to the door handle of the Toyota.

"What are you doing, man?"

J.D. stepped back, trying to keep the disgust he felt from showing as he read Gonzo the Miranda.

"You got nothing on me," Gonzo whined.

"I say I do. Armed robbery, assault and battery, flight to avoid prosecution. That's for starters."

"You got it all wrong, Sheriff," Gonzo complained, slicking back his straggly hair. "So I took a couple of six-packs. Big deal. But I didn't hit nobody and I don't have a gun."

"You'll get your chance to tell it to the judge, Gonzo." Two burly truck drivers and a portly bald man in an apron came hurrying toward them from the diner.

"What's going on?" Ernie asked.

J.D. hauled out his badge and ID again and explained the situation. Satisfied that things were under control, the truckers moved off.

Ernie sent Gonzo a disgusted look. "Lock him up and throw away the key, Sheriff." He wiped his hands on his apron, eyeing the damaged telephone booth. "Want to use my phone inside?"

"Thanks. I'll be there in a minute."

"If you're hungry, we've got chili cooking." Ernie made his way back to his restaurant.

"Hey, you just going to leave me here?" Gonzo complained. "It's hot and I'm thirsty."

"You'll live. Sit tight. I'll have my deputy come for you." He walked over to the Mazda and saw that the woman had gotten out and was examining the damage to her car. With the adrenaline rush over, J.D. drew in a deep breath. "I'll get that fixed for you in Pine Bluff," he told her.

After an emotional five days coping with her father's death and arranging his funeral, Liza had set out this morning in a state of excitement over the possibility of finding her birth parents. But from the moment she'd stopped at that light, she'd been alternately angry, frightened and worried. Gingerly touching her cheek where it had slammed into the side window, she realized she was still having trouble handling the conflicting emotions buffeting her.

As she looked up at the tall sheriff, she decided there was no one else around to take the flak except the big jerk who thought his badge gave him the right to push people around. "Do you do this a lot—get ordinary civilians involved in your frenzied chases, manhandle them, risk their lives and finally trash their cars?"

Manhandle! J.D. jammed his hands in his pockets as he swallowed an oath. Apologies weren't something he had to hand out on a regular basis. Truth be known, he was usually on the receiving end of one. It grated on him, but he forced himself to remember that she was one of the citizens he'd sworn to protect, even though she wasn't from his town. "I'm sorry that you were inconvenienced. I said I'd see to it that your car is repaired, and I will."

She just stood there looking up at him, her wide blue eyes angry and demanding more.

"Damn, but you're an exasperating woman!"

"Damn, but you're a bossy man!"

He shuffled his booted feet, his temper rising. "Listen, I had no other choice. Did you see another vehicle around I could have used instead of yours?" He motioned toward Gonzo with his head. "I've been after that dude for months. Did you think I should let him get away so you wouldn't miss some fancy luncheon date?"

"Fancy luncheon date?" She narrowed her eyes. "For your information, I just buried my father two days ago. I was on my way to Pine Bluff to...to get away from things for a while. But if everyone in your precious town is as sweet as you, I might have to rethink my plans."

Chagrined, J.D. ran a hand over the back of his neck. "Look, I'm sorry. Really. Could we start over here?"

Liza's annoyance fled at the conciliatory expression on his face. She had no business taking out the week's emotional frustrations on this man. "It wasn't your fault. I didn't mean to give you a hard time."

She watched a slow smile appear and realized it held considerable charm and changed his whole face. Where before he'd looked rugged and somewhat forbidding, he now seemed, well, more approachable, at least. Not exactly friendly, but not off-putting, either. His eyes were a deep brown with tiny lines at the corners, though she doubted that he laughed all that much. He didn't seem the type.

Her near apology relaxed J.D. Now that the creep was handcuffed, he took a moment to study the woman whose car he'd confiscated so unexpectedly. The sunlight had streaks of red shimmering in her long hair. Her skin was like pale gold, as if she didn't care for the sun or didn't have time to sit out in it. She wore yellow slacks made out of some soft material that showed off her long, long legs, and a matching top with a small parrot embroidered on one shoulder. Designer duds, he was certain. Even her strappy white sandals that seemed so out of place here in the desert looked expensive, to say nothing of her pricey sports car.

No question about it, she wasn't a country girl.

Aware of his scrutiny, her eyes locked with his and her mouth returned his smile. Full and pink and wet, her lips had his gut tightening as he incongruously wondered what she would taste like.

J.D. cleared his throat and took a step back. What the hell was the matter with him? He didn't even know her name.

"You have me at a disadvantage," he said, realizing that his voice was a shade deeper than usual. "You know my name, my job and that I'm from Pine Bluff, but I know nothing about you except that you're not from around here."

"I live in Tucson. My name's Liza Parker."

He held out his hand, inexplicably wanting to touch her again. "Nice to meet you, Liza. They call me J.D."

She placed her hand in his ever so briefly. Yes, just as soft as he remembered.

His hand was big, rough and callused, yet it spread heat through her with a surprising force. Liza pulled back, frowning at her surprising reaction.

With a glance at the hot noonday sun, J.D. beckoned toward the restaurant. "I have to call my deputy to come get our suspect. Let's go inside while we wait."

Liza decided she was probably stuck for now. Trying to avoid looking at her crumpled fender, she grabbed her shoulder bag and let the sheriff lead her into Ernie's Place.

Ernie's wife, Rita, was Mexican and made the best green chili north of Acapulco, or so Ernie announced as he placed two steaming bowls on the table, insisting that lunch was on the house. Liza squeezed lemon into her ice tea, surprised to find her mouth watering.

"Hope you like it hot," J.D. said after a small taste, "'cause this just might send smoke pouring out your ears."

Liza dipped in her spoon, her curiosity almost as aroused as her appetite. She'd watched J.D. make his call after he'd ushered her into a booth by the window, then noticed that he'd paid a waiter to take a tall, cold drink out to the handcuffed culprit. A man who had compassion for a suspect who'd beaten an innocent storekeeper warranted a deeper look, she decided.

She drew in a quick, shocked breath as Rita's secret spices slipped down her throat, then blinked as tears sprang to her eyes. "Whoa, you were right." She dipped her spoon into the bowl again. "It's wonderful. I love good Mexican food."

J.D. found himself reluctantly impressed. If she could down Rita's chili and go back for more, maybe she wasn't a piece of dainty fluff, after all. Asking questions was second nature to him, by personality as well as profession. "Are you a native Arizonan?" he began.

A good question, Liza thought as she took her time chewing a mouthful. Her father had told her that she'd been four days old when they'd picked her up. She had no actual knowledge as to where she'd been born, just some vague clues she'd picked up from the attorney's packet that had brought her to this area. She wasn't about to reveal to this stranger that she was on a mission to discover her background. A little improvisation was in order. "Originally from Phoenix," she answered. "But I went to college in Tucson and liked it so well that I stayed. How about you?"

"Borderline, I guess you'd say," J.D. answered. At her puzzled look, he went on. "I was an only child born in the back of a truck somewhere near the New Mexico and Arizona border, so my mother told me. My father was a ranch hand with wanderlust and a fondness for booze. He'd work at a place for a while, then move on. The fact that my mother was about to go into labor didn't stop him from changing locations when the urge hit him." He didn't add that their moves were usually caused by Roscoe Kincaid getting into another of his frequent drunken brawls and getting himself fired, which meant that his little family would get tossed out regularly. "We lived in a dozen different cities before I was ten."

She heard a hint of bitterness he seemed unable to hide completely. "That must have been awfully hard on both you and your mother."

He turned from the quick sympathy in her huge blue eyes, shrugging in a false show of nonchalance. "Ah, it wasn't so bad. Great way to learn your way around the Southwest."

Liza took another swallow of ice tea in a vain effort to douse the fire in her mouth, then set down the glass as a waitress came by to pour refills. After the girl left, Liza picked up the conversation, wanting to know more, not buying his breezy explanation of enjoying his geography lesson. "Did things change later?"

A muscle in his jaw tightened. "Yeah. My father left for good and my mother got a job as a cook on the Flying D Ranch in Palo Verde. You familiar with the area?"

"I saw it on my map, but I've never been there. Not far from Pine Bluff, right?"

He nodded toward the highway they'd just left. "About ten miles farther north. Nice town. My mother loved it there after all the moving around. Now *there's* a lady who knew her way around a kitchen."

The affection for his mother came through loud and clear, in sharp contrast to the disdain when he'd mentioned his father. But he'd spoken in the past tense. "She's no longer around?"

"She died about five years ago."

"I'm sorry." Essentially, he was as alone as she, parents gone and no siblings. Liza looked up as Ernie sent over another bowl of chili for J.D. before she'd finished even half of hers. It was apparent that the man loved to eat.

"I was headed there to the Flying D today."

"Is it a big ranch?"

J.D. dug into his second bowl with gusto. "About a hundred acres. The original owner was Mac Duffy who started out with a handful of purebreds years ago. That was back in the days when Arabians were commanding the high dollar, and he made a killing. But Mac was smart enough to diversify, opening a store that sells ranch supplies, then starting a business that handles Jeep tours into the desert, and later conducting hiking expeditions. I'd be there now if it weren't for that creep out there. It's my day off."

Which explained his casual clothes. Finishing, Liza wiped her mouth and sat back. "Occupational hazard, I guess, your work interfering with time off." Across the Formica-topped table, she had the opportunity to study him closer. He had a battered look, his nose looking as if it had been broken more than once, but it only added a rugged aspect to his face. His mouth was full, his teeth very white against the deep tan of his skin. Life, she thought, had left marks on him, as if hard lessons had been hammered into him since his unusual birth. He seemed perfectly suited for his role as sheriff of a Western town. "How long have you been a lawman?"

"I was a deputy for two years. When Sheriff Ambrose Finney retired six years ago, I ran for the office and got elected."

She wondered how long Sheriff Finney had been around. Back as far as the year she'd been born? Was he still alive and living in Pine Bluff? Liza wanted to ask J.D. questions along those lines, but remembering the reception her father had received, she decided to go slowly. "Do you like police work?"

J.D. scooped up the last bite and washed it down with cold tea. "Yes, I do. I suppose, living in a bigger city like Tucson, you probably think there isn't much going on in small towns. But Pine Bluff keeps me busy. Any particular reason you picked our town, or are you visiting someone there? I guess I know most everyone for miles around."

What a wealth of information he had inside his handsome head, she thought, wishing she could ferret some of it out. But she decided that it was wiser to be cautious. "I'm on vacation and thought it would be restful to spend some time in a small town. After the emotional turmoil of my father's funeral, I felt the need to re-group, you know?"

"You mean you just picked Pine Bluff at random and decided to stay a while?"

She frowned at him, realizing she was not a good liar. "Why? Aren't strangers welcome in your town?"

"Sure they are, though there's not a lot to do around here, unless you're a horse person." Which he seriously doubted, by the fashion plate look of her.

Crossing her arms on the table, Liza leaned forward, amused at his tone, which clearly indicated that she was anything but. A lock of dark hair had drifted onto his forehead. She struggled with a ridiculous urge to reach up and smooth it back. "Actually, I love horses. My father had a friend who owned a ranch in north Phoenix. I learned to ride before I started school. I often go hiking, too." She saw the astonished expression on his face and almost laughed out loud. "I see I've shocked you."

"Yeah, you could say that. You don't look like you'd enjoy the country."

She smiled. "I'm not sure what someone who enjoys the country is supposed to look like. Should I have come wearing spurs and a Stetson?"

She was making fun of him, and perhaps he deserved it. "Okay, you got me. What do you do down in Tucson when you're not riding horses?"

"I design clothes." She pointed to the small parrot on her shoulder. "Papagayo, Inc. That's me, my studio. The parrot's my logo and it appears somewhere on all my designs. Since you're from the Southwest, I'm sure you know that *papagayo*'s the Spanish word for parrot. Now it's my turn to stereotype you and say you don't look like the type who'd read fashion magazines, so I don't imagine you've seen my work."

"You're right about that." She had a nice smile. A knockout of a smile, actually. J.D. wasn't one to trust strangers easily, perhaps because of his background combined with his police training. He rarely responded to fleeting attractions to women he scarcely knew, either. Yet, he had to admit to a surprising interest in Liza Parker, and more than a little curiosity about her. "So, what do you intend to do in Pine Bluff on your vacation while you're regrouping?"

She was ready for his question, having thought up a cover story before starting out in case someone she met would ask. "I'm working on some new designs and I think better away from my studio. I like to be outdoors, to take my sketchbook and go walking, then sit quietly and let the ideas flow." She tucked her hair behind one ear and sent him a half smile. "Probably sounds silly and boring to you."

Actually, it sounded more odd than silly to J.D. "You don't have anyplace around Tucson where you could do the same thing?" he asked, watching her face.

Liza busied herself getting a tissue from her purse so she wouldn't have to look at him. Fabricating a plausible reason for her visit, and then being believed, wasn't as easy as she'd thought it would be. Especially with those steady brown eyes studying her. "Oh, you know how it is when you're home—phone always ringing, people dropping in, the office needing some decision or another. I thought spending time in a small town would be more restful." Maybe she could switch the focus. "Is that motel back there the only place to stay near Pine Bluff?"

She seemed a little too breezy in her explanation, and a little nervous at having to explain. J.D.'s suspicious nature had him wondering if there wasn't something that

Liza Parker was unwilling to reveal. "There're no hotels for miles around, but we do have a nice bed-and-breakfast. The owner's a terrific cook. Ethel Bisbee."

Liza tried not to react, but her head shot up before she could stop herself. She prayed he hadn't recognized her quick interest. "Sounds perfect," she told him, masking her response with a nervous smile.

It had been fleeting, J.D. thought, that flicker of recognition in her wide blue eyes. Fleeting but unmistakable. What possible interest could this young woman from Tucson have in a little widow running a bed-and-breakfast in Pine Bluff? he wondered. It was just possible there was more to Liza Parker than met the eye.

"I've been wondering," he said, leaning forward. "What made you challenge me like that back at the light? If I had been a criminal, I could have tossed you out of your car and driven off. Or done worse. Standing up to me was pretty gutsy."

"My father used to say that when I made up my mind about something, I hung on like a dog with his favorite bone." Her smile at the memory was tinged with sadness. "Besides, you made me angry. You seemed to expect instant obedience from a perfect stranger."

"Yeah, well, I never met a woman yet who could handle obedience."

Her eyes stayed on his. "If you want unconditional obedience, you really should get a dog. Personally, I don't like to be told what to do."

He'd already discovered that. A movement outside the window caught J.D.'s attention. He glanced over and saw that his deputy had arrived to pick up Gonzo. It gave him the diversion he needed since he wasn't altogether sure how to respond to her last remark. "If you're finished, we should probably get going," he said as he tossed a generous tip on the table.

"Do you think my car's drivable?"

J.D. slid out of the booth and stood. "I'm pretty sure it is. The fender's dented and the grille will have to be replaced. We've got a good mechanic in town. Jed Freeman's Auto Shop. He'll order the parts and fix you up like new in no time."

Liza picked up her bag and rose. "If you'll tell me where his place is located, I'll head there first."

"I'll drive you to Jed's, then take you to Bisbee's. Jed will lend me his truck." He waved his thanks to Ernie, then, with his hand at her back, he walked with Liza outside.

"But I thought you were on your way to that ranch."

"I can go another day. Besides, I have to get Jed to pull my van out of that ditch back there or I won't have wheels. After causing you this delay, the least I can do is see that you're settled." And perhaps learn a bit more about her while he was at it, J.D. thought.

Bisbee's Bed & Breakfast was in an old neighborhood with lots of cottonwood trees shedding their brown pods onto the wide, winding street. It was a three-story building made of white clapboard with a cozy front porch where several cushioned rattan chairs and a bright red glider waited invitingly. Pink bougainvillea vines grew along the front and twined up onto the half wall of the porch, then trailed down the wooden railing. Liza liked the place on sight.

A fat gray cat opened one yellow eye and lazily checked them out as J.D. and Liza stepped onto the porch, then went back to sleep. "Jasper's a stray who hangs around the neighborhood. He's about fifteen years old, I understand," J.D. told her. "He's a little arthritic now, but I hear he's caught his share of mice." J.D. pressed the doorbell.

"Mice? This place has mice?" She wasn't particularly afraid of mice. Just didn't want to share a room with one.

"Field mice," J.D. explained as a small woman no more than five feet tall swung open the screen door.

"Why, hello, Sheriff," Ethel Bisbee said, wiping her hands on a dish towel. "Did you smell my blackberry pies baking and decide to come by?"

He smiled down at her. "I sure wouldn't turn down a piece, Ethel." He stepped aside and drew Liza forward. "But actually, I brought you a new guest. Liza's from Tucson and she's visiting Pine Bluff for a while."

From behind her tortoiseshell glasses, Ethel's eyes checked out the newcomer before smiling broadly. "How nice. Come in, come in." She led the way through a long hallway toward the rear kitchen.

Liza glanced into a large dining room through an archway off to the left and an old-fashioned living room on the right where two older women sat doing needlepoint in front of a modern television set that looked somewhat out of place. The kitchen had obviously been done over recently. It was huge, with red Mexican tiles on the floor, copper pots hanging above an island sink and stained walnut cupboards surrounding a restaurant-style stove and refrigerator.

"I love to cook," Ethel said, indicating the two pies cooling on the Formica countertop and the two she'd just finished putting together. "We sometimes have a dozen or more to dinner on an evening. Some are weekly guests since meals are included in my rate, and some neighbors. I know it says Breakfast Only on the sign, but I added dinner years ago. You'll find we're real friendly around here." She shoved her glasses higher on her small nose, bent to put the last two pies into the oven, then turned to take a closer look at the newcomer as she poked at a lock of gray hair at her nape with flour-dusted hands. "So you're from Tucson, eh?"

"Yes," Liza answered, not wanting to divulge too much. Her hands were a bit clammy with nerves now that she was here, so close to the woman who apparently had known her as a baby. She judged Ethel to be somewhere in her mid-sixties. She could see no family resemblance, but couldn't help wondering if they were somehow related. "You have a lovely place here."

Ethel nodded in agreement. "Folks seem to think so. Are you a friend of the sheriff's?" she asked, glancing up at him.

"We just met," J.D. answered. "Kind of a long story, Ethel. Liza's car's at Jed's being fixed. If you've got a room available, I'll go get her bags."

Ethel smiled at Liza. "Certainly. I've got a lovely sunny room on the third floor. You go get her things and I'll take her on up." She moved through the archway and motioned Liza to follow. "We can take the back stairs." Holding on to the railing, she huffed her way up. "I've got two older ladies staying with me right now. Their sister, Thelma, is in the hospital and they want to be nearby till she gets better."

"I believe I saw them in the living room."

"That would be Margaret and Maude. Then there's Mr. Grovener in the front room on the second floor. He's a widower, pays by the month. Been with me for years." She glanced back at Liza as she continued on to the third floor. "We're more like a boardinghouse these days, I guess."

"It sounds like it. Have you been open long?"

At the top landing, Ethel stopped to catch her breath. "Oh, my, yes. Nearly forty years, ever since my Herman died." A shaft of sunlight drifted through the gauzy white curtains on the hallway window, falling on Liza's head. The older woman stared a long moment. "You certainly have lovely hair. I always wished I had some red in mine."

"Thank you." Liza watched Ethel open the first door, hoping she could slip in another couple of questions without arousing the woman's suspicions. "It must be a lot of work, running a bed-and-breakfast that's more like a boardinghouse. Do you have family to help you?"

Ethel stood by the open door leading into a large corner room overlooking the shady front yard. "No. I lost my husband before we had any little ones." She sighed heavily as she gazed around the immaculate room, her experienced gaze checking every detail. The young woman's clothes were expensive, she could tell, and she appeared to be educated. She imagined that her newest guest was used to better. "I hope this will do."

Liza glanced inside, pleased with the white eyelet spread on the four-poster bed, the maple dresser and nightstand, the colorful braided rug. "It's lovely."

"Both rooms up here have a private connecting bath and you'll find plenty of clean towels. There's a phone in each room, as well, or I can take messages on my line if you're not in. The only other guest currently up here is Gloria Madison in the room down the hall. She's gone most of the time. Just opened a shop in that new shopping mall west of town."

"I think we passed it on our way in."

"Most likely. I serve breakfast at eight and dinner at six. Lunch is on your own and if you won't be here for meals, I'd appreciate your letting me know in advance."

Ethel turned, needing to get back. "Anything I can get you before I go down to start dinner?"

"No, thank you. I'm sure I'll be very comfortable here."

"Good." Ethel moved to the stairs, then swung around. "I don't believe I caught your last name."

"Parker," Liza said, watching the woman's face.

"Liza Parker. Yes, I'll remember." She took two steps down, then stopped suddenly, grabbing the handrail as she sucked in a deep breath. Quickly she turned back to Liza still standing in the doorway watching her. Ethel's eyes narrowed, studying the younger face, the thick auburn hair, the outstanding blue eyes. A vague memory teased at her. "Parker," she said slowly. "You wouldn't be from Phoenix originally, would you?"

Here it comes, Liza thought. No turning back. "Yes, as a matter of fact. My parents, Blair and Ralph Parker, lived in Phoenix. They're both dead now."

"How . . . how old would you be, then?"

"I'm twenty-eight."

She watched the blood drain from Ethel's face, turning it impossibly white.

"Oh my God," Ethel muttered as her hand flew to her chest. Feeling shaky, she turned back, needing some time to adjust.

And found herself staring into the questioning eyes of a frowning J. D. Kincaid.

Chapter Three

The older-model Ford Escort didn't have a lot of oomph left in it, but J.D. didn't think Liza would mind. He'd finagled the car from Jed for her to use until the parts for her Mazda came in and the repairs were completed. He flipped on the turn signal and went around the corner, heading for Bisbee's Bed & Breakfast.

Ordinarily, he'd have asked one of his deputies to deliver the car for him. But after that odd scene on Ethel's stairs yesterday afternoon, he had to admit that he wanted to see Liza Parker again in person.

Stopping at a light on Main Street, J.D. let his mind roam back to when he'd carried Liza's bag up and found Ethel looking pale and shocked. When he'd asked her if anything was wrong, she'd merely shaken her head and rushed down past him.

Liza hadn't offered much explanation, either, when he'd set her bag inside her room. In answer to his questions, she claimed she'd never met Ethel Bisbee before, nor had she set foot in Pine Bluff. Yet the older woman had looked as if she'd suddenly seen a ghost and Liza had quickly turned to her unpacking, not meeting his eyes. Something there, J.D. decided as the light changed and he eased the Escort forward.

He hadn't been sure he could get a loaner for her, but he'd asked Liza to sit tight this morning until he either called or came by. His curiosity was in high gear, wondering how dinner at Bisbee's had been last night considering the odd strain between Ethel and Liza. Had the other roomers and guests noticed, or had the two women gotten past the incident? He'd always known Ethel to be solid and steady, a person people went to with their problems, knowing she'd listen calmly and offer sound advice. What was there about this newcomer that had upset her so?

J.D. had done some quiet checking from his office after leaving Bisbee's yesterday. He hadn't been able to catch Liza in a lie. She really did live in Tucson in an apartment building in a nice section of town. Her Papagayo, Inc. had its office housed in a high rise right downtown and she had graduated from University of Arizona six years ago as she'd told him. He'd also inquired into the death of Ralph Parker and she'd told the truth there, too. Her father had died of a heart attack last week and been buried two days before Liza had set out for Pine Bluff.

But the question that nagged at him was why she'd come to this particular place. J.D. was very fond of Pine Bluff, but he realized that most outsiders regarded the town as nothing more than a wide spot in the road. Though locals weren't thrilled at the fact, more visitors were arriving each year, drawn by the spectacular red-rock mountain hiking trails and the clear streams that offered some fine fishing. Liza Parker didn't strike him as someone looking for a good fishing hole. She was probably more interested in shopping.

There again, she'd likely be disappointed in Pine Bluff's stores. Main Street was home to a variety of shops: dry goods, a grain-and-feed shop, a book mart next to the library and a drug emporium. There was also a decent-size courthouse since Pine Bluff was the county seat. His own sheriff's office was adjacent to the jail and there was a medical building next to the hospital. She might fare better at the west end of town where a strip mall had recently gone up offering fancier stores such as designer outlets and boutiques, frequented mostly by travelers and tourists.

Pine Bluff itself had ordinary businesses to serve ordinary citizens. The main industry, if you could call it that, was Fleming Construction. Lester Fleming, who was now in his seventies, had started his business some forty years ago and built it into one of the most lucrative firms in upper Arizona. Fleming Construction contracted to build individual homes within a hundred-mile radius of Pine Bluff, as well as shopping malls, the new aluminum barns becoming more popular every year, and even churches and restaurants. Old Lester was a shrewd businessman, but a gruff, short-tempered individual not terribly well liked. However, since he employed half the town and owned several of the independent stores, as well, few openly criticized him.

But J.D. knew that Liza hadn't come looking for work and most probably wasn't looking for a building site.

Certainly J.D. was aware that sometimes people needed to get away after a shattering experience such as a death in the family. But he'd touched foot in nearly every corner of the state of Arizona and knew of several spots in and around Tucson that would have offered the peace and quiet Liza seemed to be seeking in his town. Had it been a random choice as she'd indicated? Perhaps. Then again, maybe not.

He had a naturally suspicious mind and instincts that alerted him frequently when things seemed amiss. They'd saved his hide more than once. However, he had to admit that the questions surrounding Liza Parker's arrival weren't the only reason he was making a special trip to see her again.

She attracted him. J.D. wasn't a man used to lying to himself, so he faced the truth of it. He liked the way she was put together, the deep blue of her eyes and her smile. She also smelled as sweet as sin. It wasn't just that he'd been putting in long hours on the job and finishing his house in his off-hours, either. He always had plenty of opportunities for female companionship if he wanted some. He hadn't, for some time.

Until yesterday when he'd all but crashed into Liza's life.

He remembered the quick sympathy in her eyes when he'd told her about his father deserting his little family and then his mother dying. And by contrast, her feisty stand against him when he'd wanted to appropriate her car. Though he'd been annoyed at the time, he liked a woman with a mind of her own.

If only he didn't have this gut feeling that she was hiding a dark secret or two.

Yesterday, at Ernie's, when he'd mentioned Bisbee's Bed & Breakfast to Liza, she'd revealed an interest she hadn't been quick enough to hide from him. What was there about the innocuous, small-town boardinghouse or Ethel herself that had drawn this well-dressed, sophisticated, educated woman here? A desire to walk in the woods and sketch or go horseback riding didn't seem to cut it. Or was she perhaps interested in someone who was staying at Bisbee's? Somehow he couldn't believe that, for Ethel's current guests seemed a harmless enough group.

Or was he just making a mountain out of a molehill and was she nothing more than exactly what she seemed, a young woman taking a few days off after a traumatic time in her life? J.D. straightened his hat, irritated at his own probing, questioning nature. Why couldn't he take people at face value? he wondered as he pulled up in front of Ethel's place.

Gloria Madison was sitting on the front porch in the glider, pushing herself gently with one bare foot as she filed her nails. J.D. paused on the steps, easing his gray Stetson back a notch. "Good morning."

"Morning, Sheriff," Gloria replied in her honeyed voice, turning on her bright smile. "What brings you out and about so early?"

It was nearly eleven, not at all early, but then, the little he'd seen of Gloria since she'd arrived in town from south Texas last June, he thought she had a habit of rearranging facts to suit herself. She'd told everyone who'd listen that she'd been a model in her teens, spent three years on the rodeo circuit in her twenties, just shed husband number two and was "looking." J.D. hoped she'd look the other way.

He supposed she was attractive, in an obvious, lush sort of way, with plenty of curves needlessly emphasized by the short skirts and tight tops she usually wore. Somewhere in her mid-thirties, she looked a little shopworn with her long blond hair and heavy eye makeup, he thought. Still, he'd seen more than one ranch hand at

Sal's Bar & Barbecue where she often stopped for lunch sidle alongside and strike up a conversation.

Friendly as Gloria was, J.D. knew she wasn't for him.

"I'm looking for Liza Parker, the young lady who arrived yesterday." He indicated the gray Escort at the curb. "I brought her a loaner while her car's being fixed."

Gloria's long-lashed eyes widened. "My, my. Such service. Almost worth driving your car into a tree for." She stretched her legs out, her eyes on the pink toenails she'd just polished. "Too bad you missed her. She left about an hour ago."

J.D. frowned. "Left, as in moved out?" Had Ethel upset Liza so much, she'd gone home, leaving her car behind?

"No," Gloria drawled, dragging the word out. "Left as in a walk into town." She raised a curious penciled brow. "You know Liza from somewhere, Sheriff?"

"I only met her yesterday." But even on short acquaintance, he wasn't surprised that she'd ignored his request to stay put and decided to strike out on her own. Liza Parker wasn't good at following orders. "Is Ethel around?"

"Nope, not her, either. It's her morning to play canasta with her little card-playing buddies. They're over at Priscilla's, I believe Ethel said. Rest of the tenants are out, too." She drew her legs up onto the swing and smiled at him, her teeth very white against her red lips. "Guess you'll have to settle for li'l ole me." She patted the space next to her. "Come sit a spell, Sheriff. You look as if you could use a little R and R."

That was about the last thing he wanted to do. "Thanks, but I think I'll drive on into town. Liza might need her car later."

"She seems perfectly capable of getting along on her own."

Maybe he could get a little information from the talkative woman. "Were you here for dinner last night?"

"Sure was. Some pipes broke in my building and flooded the place. I can't open my shop again until the carpeting dries. They're working on it even as we speak."

He'd wondered why she was hanging around in midday. "Was everything all right? I mean, with a new person joining you, and all." He was saying this badly, but maybe Gloria would tell him anyhow.

"I'm not sure what you mean, Sheriff," Gloria said, wrinkling her brow. "Ethel made her usually fine dinner and everyone chatted around the table. Pretty much like always. Henry Grovener talked nonstop about the new species he'd spotted on his daily bird-watching jaunt. Margaret and Maude were moaning about their sister taking her own sweet time in getting well and they were probably going to miss the fall festival in Prescott this year. Fascinating stuff. Liza didn't have much to say, but then, who can get a word in edgewise with those three old-timers chirping constantly?"

"And Ethel was her usual pleasant self?"

"I didn't see Ethel, actually. Her day helper, Marie, served dinner. Ethel went to bed with a migraine, I was told."

So the older woman *had* been upset. Maybe he could learn why from Liza. He could see the curiosity in Gloria's eyes and decided to leave. "Okay, talk with you later." Settling his hat on his head, he stepped down.

"J.D.," she called after him, "you sure you don't want to join me? I could get us a nice glass of lemonade."

He glanced back at her, seeing that hopeful look in her eyes. He wished Gloria luck in her search for Mr. Right,

but he wasn't in the running. "Maybe some other time."
J.D. walked to the Escort and folded his long frame inside.

Starting out, he decided to drive around town. It
shouldn't be too hard to spot a long-legged redhead in
designer clothes strolling the streets of Pine Bluff.

Liza skipped down the steps of the county courthouse
and glanced up at the sun high in the sky. It was warmer
in Pine Bluff in mid-September than she'd imagined,
considering it was quite a bit north of Tucson. Summer
was lingering overly long this year.

Settling the strap of her shoulder bag more comfortably, she gazed back at the two-story building she'd just
left. She'd just faced her first disappointment, discover-
ing that there was no record of a baby girl being born on
her birth date in Pine Bluff. She'd known the search
wouldn't be easy, but that fact didn't keep her from feeling discouraged.

However, perhaps folks in small towns weren't quite as
fastidious about recording births and deaths as they were
in big cities. She wasn't one to give up easily—certainly
not this early in the game, anyway. Setting off, she
headed for the Pine Bluff Hospital at the far end of Main
Street.

She passed a beige stucco building with two wide windows and a door bearing a sign: Sheriff J. D. Kincaid.
She wondered if he'd gotten his van out of that ditch. She
couldn't see it in the side parking lot. Attached to his office was a larger building labeled Pine Bluff Jail. There
were no windows in front so she couldn't tell if the fellow from the red Toyota was in one of the cells. It seemed
odd to have a jail right here on a main thoroughfare.
Then again, perhaps there was so little crime in Pine Bluff

that the jail's proximity to downtown businesses wasn't a threat.

Her thoughts shifted to that wild ride with J.D. yesterday, and she felt a rush of heat skitter up her spine that had nothing to do with the warmth of the morning. Liza led a relatively unexciting life in Tucson, working mostly with women, shopping with Dawn, dining with friends, evenings with Tony. None of that had ever given her that razor-sharp awareness that she'd felt in just being with J.D.

There was an earthiness about him that she found surprisingly appealing. Tony smelled like expensive aftershave, and she'd always liked that. But J.D. smelled like the outdoors—pine and leather and heat. She'd been annoyed with the way he'd taken over, yet awed by his strength, by his sheer masculine energy. By comparison, he made her feel delicate when she knew she wasn't. Walking beside the tall length of him had made her feel very feminine, almost fragile.

She wasn't given to fanciful thoughts as a rule, yet she could picture him astride a horse—a huge black stallion, most likely—those hard thighs encased in well-worn jeans, his shirtsleeves rolled up, a white hat on his dark hair, riding against the wind, at one with the powerful animal. He was a throwback to the golden days of the wild West when cowboys roamed the land and lived by their wits and by the way they handled a gun.

Liza shook her head, entirely too attracted to the image she'd conjured up. Perhaps she'd been out in the sun too long.

Strolling past his office, she wondered if J.D. was inside, perhaps doing paperwork on the criminal he'd captured yesterday. He appeared to be a thorough man, one who neglected no details. And that worried her.

J.D. saw more than most and missed not a word. His seemingly lazy glances took in everything. He'd certainly immediately picked up on the tension between Ethel and her yesterday. She hadn't revealed anything to him, though she'd seen the questions in his eyes, but she wasn't sure how long she could keep silent. Duplicity wasn't something she was experienced in or comfortable with. The sheriff didn't appear to be a man who'd walk away from a puzzle easily. Avoiding him in this small town wouldn't be a simple matter, either. Maybe his job would keep him busy until she'd completed her mission.

Arriving in front of the three-story hospital with its sign indicating that the emergency entrance was around back, Liza paused. Had she been born here? she wondered. Would the personnel inside be helpful, as the young records clerk at the courthouse had been? The key to cooperation, she decided, was to ask someone youthful, someone who hadn't been around when she'd been born and had no reason to protect anyone who might not want her snooping around.

Taking a deep breath, Liza walked through the sliding doors.

She followed the signs to Medical Records and was dismayed to see that the woman at the desk looked grandmotherly. Sitting down, Liza made her request and hoped for the best. The woman was pleasant enough and asked her to wait while she checked.

Ten minutes later, Liza left the office, struggling with the disappointment of another dead end. No baby girl born at this hospital on her birth date twenty-eight years ago.

There are other ways, she reminded herself. The library undoubtedly had newspapers from the year of her birth on microfiche, which might give her a lead. She could talk with some of the older citizens who could have a wealth of knowledge they'd be willing to share, if she approached them in a friendly way. And she could corner Ethel Bisbee and question her. The moment the older woman had learned that Liza's name was Parker and that she was twenty-eight, she'd reacted as someone in shock. Ethel undoubtedly knew something and she couldn't avoid Liza forever.

Leaving Medical Records, Liza walked down the hallway and paused at the glassed-in nursery. Two small bassinets each held a sleeping baby, one wearing a blue knit cap and the other a pink one. A nurse sat at a desk working on a chart. Had one of those tiny beds housed her years ago? Had her mother stood here at the glass, looking at the child she was giving up, choking back tears?

Liza cleared her throat, wishing these emotional moments would lessen. Since arriving in Pine Bluff, she imagined herself as a child in every setting, trying to recognize a relative in every face she passed. She'd have to get a grip before people started running from her.

Continuing down the hall, she was very aware of the sound of her own footsteps on the polished floor. An orderly pushing a gurney that held a white-faced little boy with his eyes closed passed on her right. A phone was ringing up ahead and a Dr. Clark was being paged. Just before the nurses' station, she reached a wide doorway on the left and heard the sound of a woman's gentle voice. Intrigued, Liza stopped, peering inside the room.

A slender woman with short dark hair was seated on a rocker with several children gathered around her. Two were sitting cross-legged on the floor while two others were in wheelchairs. A fifth lay in the bed near the rocker and still another leaned on crutches beside a uniformed nurse. All were intently listening to the woman read a story.

Something about the scene kept Liza rooted to the spot: the children's rapt attention, the lilting tones of the woman's voice, the smiles when the story ended. As the nurse thanked the storyteller and helped the children back to their rooms, Liza stood aside, still watching. The woman hugged each child in turn, then walked out with a promise to return next week.

Her huge gray eyes settled on Liza and the woman smiled. "Hello. Are you one of the parents?"

Liza shook her head, but before she could speak, the woman went on with another guess.

"Are you interested in our volunteer program, then, perhaps?" she asked. "I assure you it's very rewarding."

"It certainly looks as if it would be. Actually, I was just on my way out when I stopped to listen. They were hanging on your every word." Despite the warmth of her smile, there was a haunting sadness in the woman's eyes.

"Yes, it's so boring, being in a hospital. Especially for a child." She held out her hand. "I'm Roseanne Mitchell and you must be new in town."

"Liza Parker," Liza said, watching the woman's face for a reaction. She could see none. "I'm only here for a few days, staying at Bisbee's."

Roseanne nodded as they started down the hall toward the elevators. "Ethel's a lovely person." As Liza stopped at the bank of elevators, Roseanne turned to face her. "Well, if you change your mind, we could use another volunteer, even for a short time."

"Thanks, I'll keep that in mind."

"Enjoy your stay." Roseanne walked away, her back straight, her stride unhurried.

The elevator arrived and Liza stepped in, her mind still on the woman. Liza guessed Roseanne Mitchell to be in her early forties with no sign of gray in her dark hair, and her oval face remarkably unlined. She wore very little makeup and there'd been no rings on her slim fingers. Such a lovely, gentle person. She'd have to ask at Bisbee's if anyone knew her.

Liza walked out into the noonday sun and paused at the foot of the steps, wondering where to go next. The library was down and across the street. Maybe she should stop to have lunch first since she'd had only a cup of coffee this morning. Ethel had been nowhere in sight again. Her assistant had explained she'd gone to the market, but Liza wondered if the woman was trying to avoid her. She'd have to—

"There you are," said a deep voice directly behind her.

Liza jolted, her hand flying to her throat as she swiveled around and found herself looking up into the dark eyes of the sheriff. "Good Lord, you scared me half to death."

"Sorry. I didn't know you were so jumpy."

She took a step back. He was wearing the tan slacks and shirt that apparently passed for the sheriff's uniform in Pine Bluff, his badge prominently displayed on his shirt pocket this time. His gun belt hung low on his narrow hips and his black boots were polished to a spit shine. The Stetson on his dark head was gray, not the white she'd imagined earlier. "I'm not usually jumpy. But then, I'm not used to people creeping up behind me on little cat feet."

Smiling, J.D. raised his booted foot. "Size twelve. Hardly little. And I wasn't creeping. You were lost in thought." He glanced up at the hospital doors he'd seen her come through. "You're not feeling well?"

She wasn't about to explain why she'd been inside. "I feel just fine."

There was that look, that hint of defiant evasiveness. Patience, J.D. reminded himself. "I went over to Bisbee's looking for you. I thought I'd told you I'd be there this morning or call."

Liza shoved her hands into the pockets of her yellow jumpsuit and glanced up at the cloudless blue sky. "I believe I mentioned before that I'm not real crazy about following orders. Besides, it was too nice a morning to sit around waiting. What is it you want, Sheriff?"

She'd caught her dark red hair at her nape with a heavy gold clip, but a few wispy strands had escaped and brushed her cheeks in a light breeze. Standing close to her in the sunshine, he caught the unadulterated scent of woman, and swallowed. Her tongue swept over her full lips in what might be a hint of nerves, yet her blue eyes challenged him. Her question hung between them. *What is it you want, Sheriff?* You, he almost said aloud, then frowned as the word echoed through his mind. The one he was obviously losing.

J.D. pushed back his hat an inch, then pointed across the street. "I brought you a loaner to use until your car's fixed."

Her gaze followed his hand. The little gray car wasn't much, but it would get her around. She felt chagrined for being short with him when he'd only been trying to be helpful. What was there about this man that got her back up so quickly? she wondered. "Thank you. That's awfully nice of you."

She wouldn't think so if she knew what he'd been thinking just moments ago. An older man wearing a bolo tie strolled past and greeted him. J.D. nodded to the rancher, then held out his hand to Liza. ''Here are the keys.''

''Great.'' She took them, then looked back up at him. ''Now you have no wheels. Can I drop you somewhere?''

He motioned to the left with his head. ''My van's parked behind my office just down the street.'' His gaze drifted over her and he saw that she carried only a large leather bag hanging on her shoulder. ''You haven't got your sketchbook.'' Or did she even have one? What business would she have had in their small hospital? He was getting more and more skeptical about her motives.

''I'm not sketching today. Just familiarizing myself with Pine Bluff. Nice little town you have here.''

''Yes.'' And he'd like to keep it that way. He acknowledged the druggist who rushed past on his way to lunch. ''Can I show you around?''

She sent him an apologetic smile. ''Oh, thanks, but I think I'll just wander about on my own.''

''You sure? I know just about every man, woman and child in town, and I'm familiar with most of the shops and businesses.'' He touched her shoulders and turned her around. ''For instance, over there's one of our newest places, the Blaine Art Gallery. Lots of nice watercolors, some Indian art, scenes of the red-rock country. You might like to browse in there.''

''I might take a look later.'' She stepped away from the touch of his hands and the heat she felt from his fingers through the thin cotton of her clothes. Realizing she'd have to put off going to the library since he apparently was intent on keeping his eyes on her, she dangled the car keys. ''For now, I think I'll go exploring. Thanks, again.''

If he pressed now, he'd make her suspicious, J.D. decided. There'd be time enough. She wouldn't shake him loose so easily, he thought as he walked toward his office.

Inside the Escort, Liza watched him stroll off. He looks like an ad for the Marlboro man, she thought, her heartbeat turning slightly erratic. As her friend, Dawn, often said, there's something about a cowboy that gives a woman pause.

She started the engine and was about to pull out into light traffic when a big white Cadillac turned onto Main Street and parked somewhat crookedly in front of the hospital alongside a No Parking sign. An older man with white hair and a long cigar clamped between his lips got out, hurried up the steps and through the double doors. Puzzled, Liza wondered who could so flagrantly park in a restricted area, disregarding the law. She glanced down the street, but could see no sign of Sheriff Kincaid.

That's the law for you, she thought, swinging out into the lane. Never around when you need them, always around when you don't.

"I see the sheriff found you," Gloria drawled as Liza climbed the steps to Bisbee's porch after parking the Escort out front. She set aside the paperback she'd been reading and patted the space next to her on the glider. "Come sit down, honey. You look beat."

She was tired, Liza realized, as she glanced at the yellow Lincoln in the side drive. From sleeping restlessly in an unfamiliar bed last night and walking around in the sunshine, she supposed. And fencing with J.D. Setting down her bag, she dropped to the swing and sighed. "It's hot today."

"Sure is." Gloria reached to the end table and poured another glass of lemonade from the thermal pitcher. "Here, try this."

"Thanks." It did taste good. She leaned back, stretching out her legs, closing her eyes for a moment.

"He's some hunk, isn't he?" Gloria asked, envying the younger woman's slender form.

Liza's head popped up. "Who?"

Gloria's red mouth widened. "Why, J. D. Kincaid, honey. He sure seemed anxious to find you."

Whatever had he told this woman? She pointed to the car. "To give me that loaner. He feels responsible for my car getting smashed, I guess."

"Really?" Gloria turned toward her. "What happened?"

Liza gave her a capsule version as Gloria listened with avid interest.

"Nothing as romantic as that ever happens to me," the blonde complained.

"Romantic? It was hardly romantic. He could have gotten us both killed. Even when he's not chasing criminals, he drives like a wild man, like he was late for some appointment. I thought small-town folks were supposed to be laid-back."

"Did you? Ain't nothing laid-back about J.D., honey. I wouldn't mind going for a wild ride with him any day of the week."

Liza finished her lemonade and stood. "You're welcome to him. Thanks for the drink. See you later."

Entering the house and walking down the cool hallway, she saw that both the living and dining rooms were empty. She was nearly to the back stairs when she heard low voices coming from the kitchen. Maybe she could catch Ethel on an off moment and get some answers as to why learning her name had upset her so. She swung open the door.

Ethel was seated at the maple drop leaf table in the alcove across from a woman with tightly permed white hair who looked to be about her age. A plate of cookies and two glasses of ice tea were in front of them. The two glanced up as she entered, both looking more than a little startled. Liza pretended not to notice. "Hello," she said, trying for a cheery note. "I've just come back from a walk. Such a nice little town."

"Yes, isn't it?" Ethel twisted her napkin in shaky hands. "You . . . you've never been here before?"

"No." Liza walked closer, smiling to put them at ease. She'd never learn a thing if she didn't win this woman over. "I've lived in Tucson for over ten years, but, as I mentioned, I was raised in Phoenix. Have you ever been there?"

"Once or twice. It's too big for me." Ethel seemed to belatedly remember her manners. "This is my friend, Priscilla Sparks. Liza's the new guest I was telling you about. Liza Parker." She emphasized the name.

So they had been talking about her. Liza had guessed as much. But she'd learn more by playing along. "It's nice to meet you, Priscilla. Have you lived in Pine Bluff long?"

"All my life," Priscilla answered, rubbing her knuckles swollen by arthritis.

"That's nice." Liza brushed back a strand of hair that kept escaping her clip. "I've always wanted to live in a small town."

Ethel looked up, her expression strained. "You're not thinking of moving here, are you? Because there's not much to do in Pine Bluff for young people. Not much work, either. You're better off in Tucson. Right, Priscilla?"

Priscilla adjusted her rimless glasses and sent her friend a reproachful look. "Ethel, I'm sure Miss Parker has no plans to move here." Studying Liza, she gave her a warm smile. "She's right, though. This is a lazy little town with not much doing."

That certainly was not true. New businesses were moving in, as she'd seen in her stroll around town, and there was a goodly amount of building going on. Why were these two so intent on discouraging new residents? Or was it just her? "I like lazy towns, the peacefulness, the mountains, that wonderful stream I walked along today. And I love horses." She tucked the strap of her purse firmly onto her shoulder and sent her landlady a dazzling smile. "Ethel, you may have given me a really fine idea. See you later, ladies." She left the room, swinging the door behind her.

Liza wasn't one to eavesdrop, but this time, she simply couldn't resist. Pausing, she leaned close to the door.

"Now look what I've done," Ethel moaned. "She simply can't move here, Priscilla. It…it would upset too many lives if…if…"

"There, there, Ethel." Priscilla's voice was calmer. "Don't get yourself all worked up. She's only been here twenty-four hours. She could very well hate it in a week or so. Let's just wait and see what happens."

"Do you see the resemblance I told you about?" Ethel asked.

"Unmistakable," Priscilla answered with conviction.

"Do you think anyone else will notice?"

"Doubtful. No one else knows the whole story." A chair scraped back on the tiled floor. "I've got to be going. Now, don't you worry. Things will work out."

"I just don't want anyone to get hurt," Ethel said.

Liza heard their footsteps approaching. Hurriedly, she turned and quietly made her way upstairs to her room. Leaning against her closed door, she let out a sigh.

No one else knows the whole story. No one but those two little ladies. And a story they'd kept quiet about for twenty-eight long years.

But why did they have to? Liza could come up with only a couple of plausible guesses. The woman who'd given birth to her might have been married to someone other than her father. Or perhaps her father was someone prominent, married to another woman, so that an illegitimate child would have embarrassed him. Might still embarrass him. Or her.

Too bad. Whoever they were, she would discover their identities. Not to embarrass either one, but because she had to know. She could learn to live with it if they still didn't want her in their lives. But she couldn't rest until she knew who had given her life.

Priscilla Sparks and Ethel Bisbee were the key. But they were skittish as two newborn fillies. She'd have to go easy, prod them here and there and get them to open up on their own. She wouldn't let them hug tight their little secrets, for they were the only possible leads she had, as of now.

Tossing down her bag and slipping off her shoes, she lay down on the bed. Tomorrow. She'd start out again tomorrow.

Chapter Four

Pine Bluff's library wasn't very large, but it was quite modern, with three computers for book searches, an extensive reference department and a section that housed yearbooks from the local high school since it opened its doors thirty-two years ago. That's where Liza headed late the next afternoon after looking around the quiet, inviting room.

It was her contention that most likely her mother had been quite young when she'd become pregnant with Liza. An unwed teenager seemed the most likely candidate. Choosing senior yearbooks that would have put the woman from sixteen to eighteen in the year of her birth, she gathered up the armload and carried the leather-bound volumes to a deserted corner table. Taking her time, she began to leaf through each one.

They were small editions, since Pine Bluff's graduating classes were less than a hundred back in those days.

She'd learned that several bordering towns had no schools, so that those teenagers also were bused or driven to Pine Bluff High. Slowly Liza examined the young, eager faces, searching for that spark of resemblance that surely she'd notice. She hadn't looked like either of her adoptive parents, of course. Now she was counting on finding that she was at least similar in coloring or build to one of her birth parents.

After all, she'd overheard Ethel and Priscilla say that they'd noticed the resemblance. To whom? was the question. If those two had lived here all their lives, the person Liza resembled must also live in Pine Bluff. She noticed that her palms were damp in anticipation.

It was in the third book that she found something that had her peering more closely at the picture of a laughing senior. The photo wasn't in color, but the girl had wide-set eyes and the same oval shape to her face as Liza had. Her hair was long and thick, and appeared to be light brown or possibly even dark blond. The name under the picture was Roseanne Fleming.

Could Roseanne Mitchell, the woman she'd met yesterday at the hospital, be Roseanne Fleming? Her physical characteristics resembled hers and her hair could have darkened since her teens. This carefree teenager could be the forerunner of the classically lovely woman who'd been quietly friendly. She'd worn no rings, but that didn't necessarily mean she wasn't married to someone named Mitchell. In her stroll down Main Street, Liza had noticed Fleming Dry Goods and Fleming Grain & Feed Store as well as Fleming Drugs. Whoever the Flemings were, they apparently owned several businesses. If, in fact, Roseanne was a member of that Fleming family.

The year on the book would have put Roseanne Fleming at seventeen or eighteen in the year of Liza's birth.

Could that sweet, soft-spoken woman be a relative? Liza wondered, trying to push back her rising excitement. Perhaps even her mother? Some similarities were evident, but there wasn't a startling resemblance. Of course, if Ethel and Priscilla had known the young Roseanne, perhaps they saw more.

Still, if Roseanne had given birth to Liza, why was it that *she* hadn't noticed a resemblance yesterday when they'd been face-to-face, or reacted to her name as strongly as Ethel had? If, for reasons unknown, she'd been forced to give up a baby girl, wouldn't she constantly be wondering if every new female of the approximate age whom she ran across might be her daughter? Liza had seen no undue interest in Roseanne's eyes, nor had she quizzed her about her origins. The Phoenix attorney's secretary Liza had talked with had said that her mother undoubtedly had signed the original Consent to Adopt form. Surely, a woman never forgot giving away her child.

Determined to stay calm, Liza finished looking through the other yearbooks, but couldn't find anyone else who resembled her quite so strongly as Roseanne Fleming. Nor a young man, either. She forced herself to go on.

In the library's microfiche section, she located newspapers dating back to several years before she'd been born and began scrolling them, hoping for something to jump out at her. Some twenty minutes into her viewing, she ran across a picture of Roseanne Fleming, daughter of prominent builder Lester Fleming, pictured at her Sweet Sixteen party given on a spacious lawn surrounded by a sea of smiling guests. The resemblance to Liza at sixteen in snapshots in her father's photo album were even more jarring than the yearbook photo.

Could she have found a connection to her birth mother this quickly?

Continuing through the following years, it was another ten minutes before Liza located the wedding picture of Roseanne Fleming and a tall, bookish-looking attorney wearing glasses, his name Reid Mitchell. The bride looked thinner and wasn't smiling. The date would have put Roseanne's age at nineteen, a year and a half after Liza was born.

So much for that. Probably another dead end. After all, there had to be any number of dark-haired, blue-eyed slender young women living in Arizona when she'd been born. Then again, Roseanne could have gotten pregnant as an unmarried teenager by someone other than Reid Mitchell and given up the child, perhaps to prevent a scandal in the Fleming family.

But then, why hadn't Roseanne recognized their resemblance?

Fighting discouragement, Liza continued to scroll through copies of the weekly *Pine Bluff Gazette,* hoping for something else. Anything else.

In an issue dated five years after the wedding, she found a brief announcement that Roseanne and Reid Mitchell had divorced. That explained why Roseanne wore no rings. Moving on, she learned that Reid Mitchell had remarried six months after his divorce from Roseanne. Liza couldn't help wondering if Roseanne's marriage had been troubled, considering how quickly her ex-husband had found someone else.

Feeling disappointed and a shade weary, Liza shut off the viewing machine and returned the newspaper films. Sitting down at the table again, she wondered where to look next. After a few minutes, she rose, gathering up her leather bag. People. If there were no more records she could check, she'd have to talk with people who were living in the area back then.

Ethel seemed unwilling to open up, having done everything she could last evening at dinner and again this morning around the breakfast table to avoid being alone with Liza. She probably wouldn't get much out of Priscilla, either, since the two older women were such good friends. But there were others in town.

The librarian who'd been away from her desk when Liza had entered was just finishing a call as Liza approached her. The wooden nameplate read Mrs. Helene Dixon. She looked to be in her sixties, with thinning hair and thick glasses framed in red. Liza gave her a friendly smile as the woman turned to her.

"Did you find what you were looking for?" Mrs. Dixon asked.

"Not really." Liza chose her words carefully. "My father died recently in Phoenix and I learned from his papers that we had some relatives who lived in Pine Bluff some thirty years ago. I was looking through old newspapers and yearbooks, trying to locate them. Not much luck."

"Perhaps I can help. What are their names?"

"That's just it. I don't know." Inventing on the spot, Liza went on. "I ran across some old letters that mentioned cousins up this way. One of them referred to a baby girl born in Pine Bluff twenty-eight years ago last April 15. She might have been adopted out. Were you living here back then?"

"Yes, since my wedding thirty-two years ago. My husband had just been taken on as an electrician at Fleming Construction. He retires in two more years." The woman looked skeptical. "If that's all the information you have, it isn't much to go on."

"I know it's a long shot, but I've checked the county records and even the hospital. No baby girl born that date recorded in Pine Bluff." Her expression turned sad. "It's just that I don't have any other living relatives and it would be so nice to locate one or two." Which certainly was the truth.

The woman's pale blue eyes softened. "Of course it would, dear. I wish I could help, but with so little information, I don't know where to begin."

Liza decided to give it one more shot. "Are you sure you don't remember a young woman twenty-nine or thirty years ago—she'd have been in her late teens or early twenties then—with a slender build and sort of tall?"

Mrs. Dixon wrinkled her forehead. "No, not specifically. I was the librarian in the high school then. There were so many young girls through the years."

"This one would have had auburn hair, like mine, or maybe lighter brown, and probably blue eyes. Family traits, you know." Liza was conjecturing now, going by instinct. "She might have had a particular boyfriend she spent a lot of time with. She was someone who might have had a child around that time, perhaps out of wedlock? Perhaps she disappeared for a while, then came back to town, kind of hush-hush, maybe?"

Mrs. Dixon began to shake her head, then jolted as if startled, her eyes registering a memory that her lips immediately denied. "No, no one. I don't know anyone who fit that description, then or now." Quickly she lifted a stack of several books and stepped away from her desk. "If you'll excuse me, I have work to do."

Liza stood watching the woman walk to the back and busy herself stocking the shelves. How very strange. She was certain the librarian had remembered something.

But what? And why was she unwilling to share that with Liza?

J.D. was seated on the Bisbee front porch on the glider, his gray Stetson beside him, both his arms stretched across the back, pushing the swing in a gentle rocking motion with one booted foot. Walking up the steps, Liza wondered if Gloria had taken her literally when she'd told her last night that she was welcome to J. D. Kincaid. Was the lawman now waiting for the sultry blonde to finish dressing for their date? "Hello, Sheriff," she said, stopping to lean against one of the wooden support pillars. "What brings you to this neck of the woods? Another criminal you're chasing?"

She looked pale and oddly defeated, J.D. thought, and wondered where she'd been all day. He'd called a couple of times and finally decided to come by and wait for her, enduring Ethel's curious look when he'd explained that he'd wait awhile on her front porch. He told himself that Liza Parker was an unsolved mystery and that was the reason he was here. He didn't want to examine his motives any further than that right now.

"Nobody on the loose that I know of," he said slowly, watching her. "And what have you been up to today?"

She tossed her hair back and shrugged. "Nothing much. Just sight-seeing."

"No sketch pad, I see. Did you discover one of our ranches and go horseback riding?"

Just filled with questions, wasn't he? She frowned as she shook her head. "No, just wandering around." She pushed back from the post. "I imagine you're waiting for someone, so I'll see you later." She opened the screen door.

"Yes, I am. You."

Liza let the screen close. "Me? Why?"

J.D. picked up his hat and set it on his head. "I thought you might like a change of pace from Ethel's cooking. I know a nice little Greek restaurant out aways. The food's wonderful and Ari imports his own ouzo from his hometown."

Hand on the doorknob, she studied him several seconds. "Are you asking me out, Sheriff?"

He propped one ankle on the opposite knee and gave her a lazy smile. "Yeah, I guess I am. Provided you could drop the sheriff and call me J.D."

"Doesn't anyone call you Jonathan David?"

"My mother used to. Everyone else knows better."

Her lips twitched as she struggled with a smile. "My, my. Touchy." Actually, it might do her good to get away from Bisbee's tonight. Though J.D. made her very aware and a little nervous, at least he wasn't turning from her for reasons unknown. "I'll just go tell Ethel I won't be staying for dinner." Not that the tense little woman would mind, she was certain.

J.D. stood while he waited, wondering what there was about Liza Parker that tugged at his interest. It wasn't only the vague mystery surrounding her arrival. Something about her had gotten under his skin from their very first minutes together. He wasn't sure if he was glad or if he wished she'd never happened along.

Maybe a little more time in her company would help him decide. And net him a few answers, as well.

She'd changed into kelly green slacks and a matching top with a scooped neck. Small yellow embroidered parrots trailed up one fitted sleeve and down the other. Her hair was loose and shiny, falling to her shoulders. He helped her up onto the high seat of his silver van, wishing she didn't smell so damn female.

They were on the highway in short order, whirling along toward a setting sun. Liza fastened her seat belt and braced herself on the door handle. "Where did you learn to drive? I've never before ridden with anyone who drives like he's trying out for the Indy."

He slowed fractionally. "Sorry. I learned on the ranch where I grew up. Dirt roads, trails, scrub grass. No traffic signs, no speed limits. Hard habit to break."

Liza's fingers wrapped around her seat belt. "It's a good thing you're the law or some cop would be writing you up regularly."

He let up on the pedal a bit more. "Relax. I've never had an accident. Not once."

"That's a comfort. I think." She remembered the van slamming into the ditch. "Apparently your vehicle came out of that skirmish without a scratch. Have you got that fellow from the red Toyota locked up in your jail on Main Street?"

"Sure do, but he leaves tomorrow. Sheriff up in Flagstaff's coming for him. Gonzo's got a long rap sheet in Arizona."

She angled to look at him more closely. He was out of uniform again, wearing jeans and a striped shirt. Apparently, he was a nonconformist. "So what exactly is it you do as sheriff other than go after petty crooks like Gonzo?"

J.D. whipped around a van with tinted windows before answering. "Keep the peace. Go out on domestic calls, cooperate with neighboring law enforcement, make court appearances. Pine Bluff's expanding, though most of its older residents aren't happy about it. Teenage gangs are prevalent in many big cities with their guns and drive-by shootings. Innocent citizens are getting hurt, so more folks are moving up this way where they think it's safer.

But it won't be for long." He gestured toward the west. "Couple of shopping malls going up out that way to join the one already there. With the influx of more stores and new homes being built, the tourists have found us and crime is on the increase. Sad but true."

Liza hadn't considered that, had always thought of small towns as peaceful. "How many deputies do you have?"

"Two now, but I'm hoping to get authorization for another. We've also been training half a dozen men— Pine Bluff and area residents—as posse members to help us out."

"A posse, like in the old West?"

"Sort of, only they're in all-terrain vehicles instead of on horseback. At first, I plan to use them to patrol the malls and downtown areas. That's where most of our break-ins have occurred so far, and where shoppers occasionally get mugged. Seeing trained men monitoring the area often is a crime deterrent in itself."

"And you do the training?"

J.D. switched on his right-turn signal as he sent her a quick grin. "It's a dirty job but someone has to teach the locals how to handle a gun, how to disarm a suspect, how to tell the white hats from the black." He angled the van into a corner parking space in front of a low-slung stucco building and turned off the engine. "Here we are. The Apollo." He opened his door. "Stay put and I'll help you down. It's a high step."

Chivalry, alive and well in Pine Bluff, Arizona, Liza thought as she did as he requested. But instead of offering her his hand, J.D. waited until she'd swung her knees toward the open passenger door, then circled her waist with his big hands and eased her out. Her feet touched the ground as her body came up close against his. She felt her breath catch in her throat as she looked up into dark eyes hot and challenging.

J.D. held her there for the space of three long heartbeats, then stepped back and led her inside. His pulse had scrambled at her nearness, and he knew she was far from unaffected. Wondering just why he'd done that, he waved to Ari who came over and escorted them to J.D.'s favorite table in a back corner.

The place wasn't large, no more than twenty tables, and only half of them occupied on this weeknight. Scenes of Athens decorated the walls in large hand-painted murals, the lighting was subdued, with candles on each of the tables draped in white linen with bold red napkins and chunky wineglasses. Foot-stomping Greek music drifted from two recessed speakers, the volume blessedly low. Liza noticed that all the waiters were mustachioed men, including the owner who sported a full handlebar. Liza liked the place immediately.

"Long time no see, Sheriff," Ari said in his thick accent. He cocked his head, looking J.D. over from head to toe. "You get skinny without my cooking."

"Hardly that, Ari." J.D. introduced Liza, and the restaurateur greeted her warmly.

"You trust me to order for you, like always?" he asked, looking from one to the other.

"Are you feeling adventurous?" J.D. asked Liza.

"Absolutely."

"Bring it on, Ari. Along with some of your best ouzo."

"For sure." He shuffled off, heading for the kitchen.

J.D. broke off a piece of unleavened bread from the basket that magically appeared, and leaned back in his chair, his gaze on the woman across from him. "All right, I'm ready to listen."

Liza felt a muscle twitch beneath one eye. Had he brought her here to question her? "Listen to what?"

"Your life story. Isn't that what people do on a first date?"

She relaxed, even let herself smile. "Is that what we're having here, a date?"

"Damn straight. I already told you about my inauspicious beginnings in the back of a truck. Your turn."

"Nothing nearly that exciting in my background. My parents were both teachers. My mother died when I was four and my father raised me. We lived in a small house six blocks from the school. Very quiet upbringing, predictable, uneventful."

"So you settled in Tucson after college. Why Tucson? You can design clothes anywhere."

A tall waiter arrived with the ouzo, poured some for each in smoky, fluted glasses and left them alone.

Liza took a sip and found that the sweet, clear liquid packed a punch. She took a moment before answering his questions. "Tucson is cozier, homier somehow. Phoenix is too busy, too much traffic, too noisy."

"Or is it more than that, like maybe a man who keeps you there?" He hadn't intended to blurt that out quite so bluntly, but he wanted to know.

Her eyes met his. "I have both men and women friends."

His hands toyed with his glass, but his eyes never left hers. "No one special man?"

He wasn't going to let it be, and Liza wondered why she was being evasive. A special man. Tony was a good friend, one who'd hinted at marriage. She knew her feelings for him didn't include wedding bells, yet she felt odd labeling him just another friend. Still, in her mind, that's just what he was. "There's a doctor I see, but we're not exactly picking out china patterns." Was it her imagination or did he suddenly appear less tense?

Ari appeared with two plates of appetizers—feta cheese and dark olives, marinated octopus and red caviar on crusty bread chunks. He lingered long enough to bask in their praise after the first taste, then quietly withdrew.

Choosing an olive, Liza glanced up. "All right, back to you." Since he was nosy, she would be, too. "Is there someone special in your life?" She watched his full lips part in a smile, as if he'd known she'd ask that.

"I'm married to the law. No time for women."

"Why is it I don't believe that?" Because he was too damn attractive, a fact that couldn't have escaped any female over the age of ten. She remembered Gloria's assessment: "a hunk." That he was, and more. Then again, she'd noticed a hint of arrogance in his manner, though he tried to camouflage it.

As usual, J.D. ate heartily, but he was far from finished with his questions. "Are you catching up on your reading?"

Liza frowned. "What do you mean?"

"One of my men saw you coming out of the library today." Only she hadn't been carrying any books.

Slowly Liza put down her fork. "Are you having me followed?"

He put on his most trustworthy expression. "Why would I? Richie just happened to be passing by and mentioned he'd seen the new woman in town leaving the library, that's all."

The new woman in town. Like the new plague in town. Had J.D. stopped in to talk with the librarian, the reticent Mrs. Dixon, and discovered that she'd frightened the poor woman half to death? Still annoyed, she sent him a cool look. "Perhaps I could save you a lot of trouble and submit a daily itinerary each morning so you could free your deputies for more important work?''

Cleaning up his plate, J.D. wiped his mouth and decided on the direct approach.

"Isn't it time we stopped fencing, Liza? I know you're not just a typical tourist visiting Pine Bluff. I know you've visited the county courthouse, the hospital and the library. Not usual for someone on vacation. Now, I'm certainly not accusing you of anything, but I admit to a healthy curiosity. Why are you really here?''

The strain of pretending she had no hidden agenda for her visit was making her jumpy. Besides which, as a basically honest person, she hated the evasiveness, the half truths. Perhaps it was time she took someone into her confidence.

But was the local sheriff the right someone?

"Are you asking officially, or off the record?''

"Unofficially, as a friend, not as a lawman." Unspoken was the fact that if she was involved in something illegal, his interest would turn official in a hurry.

Ari came over with dinner just then, serving them large helpings of a pungent moussaka, lamb-stuffed grape leaves and souvlaki over rice. After pouring more ouzo, he left them.

Liza drew in a breath at the mouth-watering spread. "This isn't what I'd expected in a small-town restaurant."

"A lot of traffic comes by here. Ari picked a good spot."

"And so much food. Does he really expect us to eat all this?''

J.D. was already finishing a steaming taste of moussaka. "What we don't finish, I usually have wrapped up for Zeke, my deputy's black Labrador."

"A dog that eats rich food? You're killing him with calories and cholesterol, I hope you realize."

J.D. laughed. "Listen, Zeke's fourteen, been fixed since he was a young pup, lost the hearing in one ear in a fight with a cougar a while back and has arthritis in his back legs. You think he doesn't deserve a treat now and then?"

"I suppose." She tasted the souvlaki and nearly purred as the flavors burst on her tongue. "This is wonderful." Suddenly she looked up sharply. "You have cougars roaming around here?"

"Not roaming, actually, but I've spotted a few from my upstairs windows. I had to put barbed wire atop my stone fence just in case."

Liza shuddered. "You must live out a ways from town."

"Yeah, just northeast." He broke off another piece of the thin bread. "Are you, by any chance, trying to change the subject?"

"No, just delaying." She took another couple of bites, thoughtfully chewing. "It's nothing illegal, if that's what you're thinking. My parents, the ones I mentioned earlier, adopted me, and I'm here trying to find my biological parents." As he listened intently and ate hungrily, Liza told J.D. the rest, about the packet she'd received from Abby Thatcher the day after her father's funeral, about the information it contained and about her father's letter. For reasons she couldn't explain, she didn't mention the black lacquered box that she'd taken to carrying around with her in her large leather purse.

"Dad was rather timid, so I wasn't surprised that he never returned after that first harrowing trip to Pine Bluff. What puzzles me is why several residents felt the need to be so rude to him. And why Ethel is acting so peculiar even now." She finished by telling him of her encounter with Ethel and Priscilla Sparks in the Bisbee kitchen.

J.D. shoved aside his plate, his appetite satisfied, his curiosity still aroused. He'd known by instinct that there was more to Liza than met the eye. "I can't understand Ethel's behavior, either. I've never known her to be unkind or mysterious. She's like a rock, the kind of motherly woman who should have had lots of children, a person who sympathizes with other people's problems."

Unable to eat any more, Liza picked up her glass and studied its contents. "If that's so, then perhaps the woman who gave birth to me went to Ethel as a pregnant teenager, and Ethel helped her with her problem by seeing to it that I was adopted."

"Only Ethel knows if that's so. I didn't live here twenty-eight years ago, and since I was only six at the time, I probably wouldn't have noticed anyway. You didn't learn anything at the courthouse?"

She shook her head, then told him in detail of her search through the county records, the hospital files, the yearbooks and old newspapers in the library. So involved in her story was she that she didn't hear someone approaching until the man was alongside their table.

The recognition was immediate. He had a full head of white hair and piercing blue eyes. He had on what appeared to her practiced eye to be a custom-made Western suit in coffee brown worn with hand-tooled leather boots. He was the man she'd seen illegally park his Cadillac in front of the hospital and hurry inside.

J.D. looked up, then stood, offering his hand. "Good evening, Lester. I see you're fond of Ari's cooking, too."

"Good seeing you, J.D." The voice was gravelly, perhaps from smoking too many of the cigars lined up in his breast pocket. "Heard you nabbed that Gonzo fellow. Nice work."

"Thanks." He turned to indicate Liza. "I'd like you to meet Liza Parker. She's visiting Pine Bluff for a while. Liza, this is Lester Fleming."

The older man looked her over thoroughly, his blue eyes suddenly turning as cold as a winter sky. "Parker. Where'd you say you're from?"

Liza put on a smile though she couldn't help wondering why this man was so cool to someone he'd never met. "From Tucson. I design clothes. That's a wonderful suit you're wearing."

Lester ignored her compliment. "No place in our town for a fancy designer. I expect you'd be happier going back to Tucson." With a brisk nod to J.D., the man strode to the door and outside.

Looking after him, J.D. was at a loss to explain Lester's chilly response to a stranger. Sitting down, he sent Liza an apologetic look. "I don't know what got into Fleming tonight. He's not a very pleasant man under the best of circumstances, but I've never seen him be quite that rude. I'm sorry."

Liza turned from watching Fleming's departure. "Don't be. It isn't your fault." She was quiet while Ari brought over the dessert tray, refusing to sample anything, accepting thick, dark coffee instead. After they were served, she decided to speak her thoughts aloud. "Do you suppose Mr. Fleming's reaction to me has something to do with my search? It's exactly the cold treatment my father received here years ago. And the librarian, Mrs. Dixon, I could swear she remembered something, but she suddenly turned from me as if I had some contagious disease. She told me her husband works for Fleming Construction. Maybe she called Lester and he followed us here."

"Now, that's bordering on paranoia. Lester's a cranky old bird, all right, but I doubt that he'd follow us out here. Besides, what would be his motive?"

Liza tapped a nail on the rim of her glass. "Exactly what I'd like to know. Maybe I'm asking too many questions around town and making some people nervous. Maybe Lester Fleming's one of them." She leaned forward intently. "Tell me about the Flemings. I already know they own several companies and are probably quite wealthy. I met Roseanne Mitchell at the hospital and learned later that she's Lester's daughter. She seemed nice, a very gentle lady. Hard to imagine she and Lester are related."

"They're nothing alike, that's for sure. I've lived in Pine Bluff only ten years, so most of what I know, I learned from others. It seems that Lester's wife died when Roseanne was only a baby, his only child. He doted on her even though she was kind of wild as a teenager. He had trouble keeping her in line, I heard."

Liza frowned. "She's certainly anything but that now."

"I agree." J.D. swallowed some coffee. "The story is that Roseanne was all set to go to college the fall after high school graduation when she suddenly came down with some mysterious ailment. Lester had doctors coming and going, but Roseanne never left the house. People caught glimpses of her sitting in the garden just staring at the flowers, all bundled up in shawls and robes, looking pale and sickly."

"How long did that last?"

He shrugged. "A year or so, was what I was told. She was seen going to town again after that, mostly with

Lester, but she'd changed. She wasn't the happy-go-lucky girl she'd been, but rather someone who looked like they'd just gotten over a very serious illness. Which I guess she had."

Or a very serious hush-hush pregnancy. "Did anyone pinpoint what this mysterious illness was?"

"No one I talked to seemed to know. People around these parts don't question much of what Lester does, and he wasn't talking. More than half the residents rely on one of the Fleming companies for their paycheck, so folks are careful not to offend Lester. Anyhow, soon afterward, Roseanne married Reid Mitchell."

"I saw their wedding picture in an old newspaper article in the library. Roseanne looked thin and not terribly happy."

"She probably wasn't. They divorced a couple of years later. I've had some dealings with Reid. He's a nice enough guy, an attorney like his father, but he's very serious and sort of humorless. His father is Lester's best friend."

"And Roseanne never remarried?"

"No. She still lives in the house her father built for her and Reid, about a block from his place. She does a lot of volunteer work, things like that. But she keeps to herself." J.D. shoved aside his empty coffee cup and narrowed his eyes. "Why all this interest in the Flemings?"

"Just curious." She watched as Ari brought over the check. J.D. thanked him as he put several bills on the little tray. Ari left after effusively inviting them to come back soon. Liza's thoughts were still on their conversation. "I wonder why Reid divorced Roseanne."

J.D. stood, taking her arm. "Rumor has it that Roseanne couldn't have children and Reid wanted a family.

He remarried soon after they divorced and quickly had two sons.''

Couldn't have children. Well, that took care of that. She walked alongside him to the van. ''That's true love for you, divorcing her because of something that surely wasn't her fault.''

''Yeah, well, I don't imagine it was the love match of the century. But then, how many marriages are?'' He opened the door for her and helped her up.

Liza chose to ignore his last comment, her curiosity still unsatisfied. ''Did that gruff old man raise Roseanne all by himself from when she was a baby?''

''Nah. He had help. A housekeeper who lived in.'' He shut her door, walked around to the driver's side and climbed behind the wheel.

''Do you happen to know the housekeeper's name?''

''Sure. She retired a couple of years ago. Priscilla Sparks.''

Chapter Five

The silver van hurtled along the highway, but for once, Liza's mind was too preoccupied to comment on J.D.'s driving. The moon was high overhead and the air streaming in through his open window was much cooler since the sun had disappeared, reminding them that fall was rapidly approaching. Yet Liza wasn't thinking about the weather, either.

Fragments of the conversation she'd overheard in Ethel's kitchen came drifting back to her. *Do you see the resemblance I told you about?* Ethel had asked Priscilla. *Unmistakable,* Priscilla had answered. *Do you think anyone else will notice?* Ethel had wanted to know. *Doubtful. No one else knows the whole story.*

The key to her birth parents apparently rested with those two women. Somehow, they'd been involved. Now that J.D. had told her that Priscilla Sparks had raised Roseanne Fleming, the trail seemed to lead back to that slender woman she'd met at the hospital. The direct approach—going to Roseanne and asking outright—seemed out of the question until she knew more. But how was she going to get the two older women to explain the connection?

J.D.'s hand suddenly touched her arm and Liza looked at him, her eyes reflecting confusion.

"Penny for your thoughts? By the look on your face, they aren't happy ones." He'd been glancing over at her since they'd left the restaurant and seen her lost in her musings.

"I was just wondering what Ethel and Priscilla might know about my birth."

His eyes on the road, J.D. was quiet a long moment. "Tell me, did you love your adoptive parents? Were they good to you?"

"I can't remember much about my mother, but Dad was the best. It wasn't until a few years ago that I realized how difficult it must have been for him, losing his wife and having to cope with a small girl. But he was always there, taking me camping, horseback riding, shopping. He even learned to braid my hair." She swallowed hard around a lump in her throat, the reality of her loss revisiting her.

"If that's the case, then why are you putting yourself through this? Why do you want to find people who obviously gave you up? You might be setting yourself up for a big disappointment."

Liza had considered that. "That's certainly possible. I've read about adopted children who sought out their birth parents, only to be rejected again. I'm willing to take that chance. I just have this burning need to meet the two people who gave me life." She turned to him with a puzzled frown. "Don't you ever feel the need to find your father?"

J.D. flipped on his turn signal before easing onto the road leading to Pine Bluff. "No. I don't want anything to do with a man who walked out on his family. My mother had to work hard all her life because of him. I *never* want to see him." The thought of Roscoe Kincaid was enough to make him ball his fists. He'd received occasional notes from his father over the years, the last as recently as two months ago. As with the others, he'd thrown it away. "There's a hell of a lot more to parenting than biology."

Liza sighed, wondering if perhaps J.D. was right and she should drop the whole thing. Was she just leaving herself open for heartbreak?

"Take my friend, Gray Eubanks, for instance," J.D. went on, hoping to convince her. "He grew up pretty much like I did, only he was abandoned by both his parents. Ranch hands raised him, taught him how to get along in a tough world. As a teenager, he drifted from one ranch to another, worked the rodeo some, did anything and everything to get along. Then he was lucky enough to stumble onto Mac Duffy."

Interested despite her skepticism, Liza studied his strong profile as he told his story.

"Mac owned this big old ranch in Palo Verde not far from here. Horses mostly, some cattle. He'd just started this sideline, Jeep tours and hiking expeditions, so he hired Gray to run that for him while he worked the ranch. Mac was a widower with no kids of his own, and luckily, the two of them hit it off."

"Is that the ranch you were going to visit the other day, the Flying D?"

"That's the one. Mac died when I was about twelve, and left everything to Gray. No blood ties, but he looked on Gray like a son. And here I was with no real male role model, so Gray took me under his wing. For the first time ever, I had a father figure who cared about me." Cutting the engine, J.D. let the van cruise to a stop in front of Bisbee's, then turned to Liza. "I could have gone either way in my teens, been a wild kid or focused on a future. Gray made the difference. He's only fourteen years older than me, but he's like the father I never had. And again, no blood ties."

Unbuckling her seat belt, Liza nodded. "I understand what you're saying. Men like Mac and Gray are rare, taking on other people's children to guide. But there's a difference here, J.D. You knew your father was a heavy drinker and a drifter years ago because he'd left you and your mother. I don't know if my biological parents left me because they *wanted* to or because they *had* to."

She was nothing if not stubborn. "If they'd have wanted you, they'd have found a way. The trouble is that far too many people marry when they shouldn't and have children they don't want."

She understood how his own situation had caused him to be bitter. But hers wasn't quite the same. "While that may be true, what about a teenage girl who falls in love, gets pregnant and somehow the two lovers get separated? She has no money and a family who can't face having an unwed daughter give birth. And suppose the boy, also a teenager at the time, wasn't even aware he'd fathered a child? These things happen, and nearly thirty years ago families felt the shame of unwanted pregnancies more profoundly than today, I think."

J.D. slipped out of his seat belt. The night air was fragrant with pine, and crickets in the bushes along Ethel's porch were serenading with their monotonous tune. But the beauty of the evening was lost on him because of their serious conversation. He couldn't have said why exactly, but he felt a need to dissuade her from her mission, to keep her from being disappointed.

"And you think these two people, now in their mid-forties, will be tickled to death to learn about you? What if they're both married now—which they easily could be—to people who know nothing about a child they'd once had? What about the effect this will have on their marriages, on other children they may have had?"

Feeling suddenly deflated, Liza leaned her head on the seat back. "Maybe you're right." Inhaling the sweet night air, she closed her eyes. She didn't want him to be right, but what if he was?

He hadn't expected her to acquiesce so readily, and he felt a little guilty for destroying her hopes. Reaching across the console, he took her hand in his and studied the fine bones in a sprinkling of moonlight. Her skin was soft, her fingers almost delicate. She looked small and vulnerable tonight, and troubled. He stretched his arm along the seat back and lightly touched her hair, finding it silky and fragrant. "It's just that I'd hate to see you get hurt."

She opened her eyes but the smile that had formed over his last remark slipped from her. He was much closer than she'd realized and his hand that had been playing with her hair now caressed her shoulder. In his dark eyes she saw not only concern but a deep awareness. "I should go in," she said quickly. Too quickly, for his hand tightened on her, holding her in place.

"It's not that late." He drew her closer so that she was facing him as his hand slipped down to curve around her waist. "Even Cinderella had until midnight."

The warning bells she relied on in situations like this had come too late. She was mesmerized by the dark purpose she recognized in his intense gaze. Her hand fluttered to his chest, a feeble gesture that wouldn't have held back a much smaller man. "I'm not looking for this," she heard herself say in a voice that sounded oddly foreign to her ears.

His other hand moved up to thread through her thick hair, his blunt fingers touching her scalp, and he felt a shiver take her. "Sometimes when we go looking for one thing, we find another." He lowered his head, his mouth gently sampling the corner of hers.

Liza's pulse was pounding, the blood suddenly rushing through her veins. This fiery attraction was the last thing she'd thought to find on her trip here, but only a fool would deny J.D.'s effect on her system. Tony's most sensual kisses hadn't excited her half as much as the one fleeting taste J.D. had teased her with. And she wanted more.

From under lowered lids, she saw his tongue skim along her bottom lip, then complete the journey. On a throaty moan, she felt the world around her tilt. She must have reached for him for the next thing she knew, his mouth was crushing hers.

She'd never known anyone who kissed so...so thoroughly. He used everything at his command, lips and teeth and tongue, to taste and nip and plunder. Here was that sizzle, that undeniable sexual pull. One of his hands fisted in her hair while the other roamed her back, easing her ever nearer until her breasts yielded against his hard chest.

She felt what little breath she had slip from her as he shifted angles and deepened the kiss. His mouth was impatient and greedy, sapping her strength, destroying her will. If she'd wanted to resist him, she had no energy left to draw on. Even as the thought flittered through her mind, she knew she much preferred this sensual surrender.

He hadn't intended to take it this far, J.D. acknowledged to himself as her tongue mated with his in a soul-splintering dance. He'd thought her cool and unapproachable at first meeting, a sophisticated city girl slumming in the country. But as they'd spent time together, he'd seen her mellowing, softening, looking attainable. Tonight she appeared to be confused by the events and a shade defenseless. He was a man who thoroughly enjoyed sex but one who would never take advantage or push the point if the lady felt skittish.

She was far from skittish. She was as avid as he, her mouth seeking his as fervently, her eyes reflecting the dark desire in his own. Her scent wrapped itself around him, her breathy moan set him to quivering and her surprisingly wild taste had him wishing he had her in a much more private place where he could sample all her hot flavors.

Liza hadn't thought she had a passionate nature, hadn't dreamed she did. No one had released the tight rein she'd held herself in thus far, no one had made her want to lose herself thoroughly in another. Not until now, not until J.D. His lips trailed along her throat and she found herself wanting to press herself shamelessly to the lean, hard length of him. Frustrated by the console separating them, she became annoyed at the confines of the front seat of the van.

The front seat of the van. The thought registered finally, the implications slamming into her consciousness. She was grappling with a man she scarcely knew in the

front seat of his van, like some teenager parked on a back
street. It was that thought that had her pushing back
from him, her hand firm on his chest now, trying desperately to slow her pounding heart.

"I . . . I don't think we should get carried away," Liza
finally managed, moving back onto her side.

Reluctantly, J.D. straightened, noticing with irritation
that his hands were damp. No woman had ever made him
sweat and he wasn't pleased that this one had managed
the unthinkable. Raising his head, he saw that she wasn't
embarrassed, or even angry, but rather still as aroused as
he and fighting it in the only way she knew how: by re-
treating.

"I guess this isn't the right time or place," he said,
struggling with the frustration that had his mind loose
and his jeans far too tight.

She didn't like his assumption that, if they'd been
elsewhere, say at his house, she'd have fallen into his bed
the very next moment. The fact that she wanted to do
exactly that put a sharpness in her voice. "There will be
no right time and place for us. I'm here for a purpose, as
I explained to you tonight. I didn't come to Pine Bluff for
fun and games." She reached for the door handle.

He grabbed her arm, yanked her back. "Did you think
we were playing games just now? I admit that I wanted
to kiss you ever since I looked into your Mazda and saw
you sitting there with those big blue eyes defying me. So
I finally kissed you, only it wasn't like I'd planned." He
held out his hand to demonstrate. "Minutes later and I'm
still shaking." To prove his point, he pressed his fingers
to the blouse that covered her thundering heart. In her
eyes, he saw that he had her. "I don't know about you,
but this sort of thing isn't usual for me."

It was far from usual for Liza, too, yet she didn't want to admit it. The problem was that her traitorous body was revealing everything she was feeling. Silently she sat watching her hands grip one another in her lap, unable to think of a single good comeback line.

Calmer now, J.D. touched her chin and tilted it upward toward him. "If it's any consolation, I'm as surprised at this as you are." Still, she didn't speak, only stared at him. "Are you going to say anything, one way or the other?"

"I don't know what you want me to say."

He didn't know, either. He did know he didn't need someone in his life who made him weak in the knees and soft in the head. Maybe if he got her out of his system, he could think clearly once more. He bent his head, moving toward her again, but she placed a solid hand on his chest, stopping him. He struggled with a rush of annoyance. "Why the brakes now? It was just going to be a little kiss."

"That wasn't just a little kiss we shared. I've been kissed before. That . . . that was an explosion." And if he kissed her again, her overheated system would surely burst. Because giving in would be so easy and she'd never trusted too easy. Because she desperately needed to be in control of some aspect of her life since the day the attorney's packet had tilted her world. "This is all happening too fast for me. My father's heart attack, the confusion and frustration of searching for my birth parents, and now this . . . this thing with you. I'm a risk taker, but I don't completely ignore danger signs. Coming to Pine Bluff was the most adventurous thing I've done in quite a while. I'm usually thoughtful and introspective and . . ."

"And beautiful." He hadn't meant to reach out, yet suddenly his hand was in her hair, the silky texture wrapping around his fingers. "Very beautiful."

She hadn't thought a hard-driving cowboy turned sheriff would try sweet talk. She found herself softening again and knew she had to put some space between them. "I have to go in."

Without another word, he got out and helped her down, then walked her up onto Bisbee's porch. Through the small window in the closed door, she could see a hall light on, but the big house was otherwise dark. It wasn't that late, at least not by her standards, but it seemed that people in small towns went to bed early in order to be up with the sun. The air was cool and she shivered as she turned to face J.D.

He put his arms around her as naturally as if he'd been doing it for years. She allowed the light embrace, then stepped back, finding herself hard up against the door. "Thank you for a lovely evening." Lame words for the tumultuous emotions raging through her, but the best she could manage.

"What are your plans for tomorrow?" J.D. asked, resting his hands on her forearms.

"I'm not sure. Maybe I can get Ethel to talk to me."

Crazily, he wanted to keep her talking, unwilling to let her go. The memory of how she tasted, of her reaction in his arms, had him searching for a reason to see her again and soon. Though it didn't please him, it was still so. "Since you're obviously intent on continuing your search, why don't you let me help you?"

"I don't know." Had she made a mistake in confiding in him, especially since he didn't approve of her mission? "I'd rather you didn't mention the reason for my trip to anyone. I think I can get further if no one else knows, for now."

"No problem. I'll call you."

She saw his head lowering, had guessed his intent when he'd moved closer. "J.D., I don't think..."

"Good plan. Don't think." His hands encircled and his mouth devoured.

She'd known what to expect after the session in the van, yet the effect was no less devastating. Her senses began to swim the second his lips took hers. She hadn't known, couldn't have guessed, that a mere kiss could blot out the world and narrow it down to this place and this man. How could she have lived twenty-eight years and never sampled such an overwhelming sensual flare-up?

Her back was to the door, and there was no way she could move farther away, so instead, as his mouth began to wander, she turned her head. He got the message and didn't press. She saw him thrust a hand through his hair and noticed the trembling. Impossible, that she could shake this big man to his shoes.

"Good night, Liza," he said quietly. "Sleep well."

"You, too," she whispered, then moved inside and closed the door. She leaned back against it for a moment, drawing in a deep breath, hoping no one was awake. She was certain every unsettling emotion she felt would be obvious to anyone she'd bump into.

Propped against the shaded lamp on the hall table was a folded note with her name on it. She opened the sheet and read the message that Tony had called and would try to reach her again tomorrow.

Climbing the stairs quietly, Liza was glad he hadn't asked her to call him back tonight. Their last conversation had been stilted and unsatisfying. She was not in the best frame of mind to talk with him right now. Her thoughts were too jumbled, her feelings too tangled.

Inside her own room, she ran her tongue along her lips and could taste J.D. He'd attracted her from that first morning, but not until this evening had she realized that he could made her feel so needy. Lying down on the bed, she wrapped her arms around herself as a wave of desire had her churning.

She'd come looking for her birth parents and had instead found more than she'd bargained for.

"I can manage quite well without help, thank you," Ethel Bisbee said as she carried a heavy tray laden with dirty dishes from the dining room to the kitchen.

"You've already worked too hard preparing breakfast without Marie's help," Liza said, following behind with the large coffee urn. Ethel's assistant wasn't feeling well and hadn't shown up this morning, giving Liza the opportunity to seize the moment for some conversation after the rest of the boarders had scattered. "I really admire the way you run this place. I don't believe I've ever stayed anywhere more comfortable."

Despite her obvious misgivings at being trapped alone with the one guest she apparently most wanted to avoid, Ethel seemed to warm at the flattery. "That's nice of you to say. I do my best. Little homey touches, I feel, make a big difference." She began rinsing the plates and stacking them in the dishwasher.

At the sink, Liza emptied the coffee urn. "They surely do. I have a friend who took a long driving trip on the eastern seaboard and stayed only at bed-and-breakfasts along the way. But her descriptions didn't match your place. For instance, your linens are so soft and even your towels. How do you do that?" Liza truly felt that Bisbee's was special, but she was also aware that buttering up Ethel might cause the older woman to drop her guard and answer the other questions she had.

Ethel smiled, as if about to reveal an important secret. "Fabric softener in the rinse water *and* in the dryer. Also all my sheets are percale, not that cheaper stiff cotton that can rub at your skin."

"Ah. I'll remember that." She busied herself washing the urn for a moment. "I can see by the number of area residents who come for your evening meals that Pine Bluff locals know good food." Here goes nothing, Liza thought. "Does Lester Fleming ever come to one of your wonderful dinners?"

Ethel straightened so quickly, she nearly hit her head on an open cupboard door. "Occasionally. What makes you ask about Lester?"

"He came over to our table last evening while J.D. and I were having dinner at the Apollo. He seems like a cranky sort and I wonder why since he's the richest man in town, isn't he?" Reaching for the towel, she kept her eyes on Ethel, gauging her reaction.

"Perhaps he was having an off day," Ethel ventured, seemingly anxious to excuse one of Pine Bluff's finest citizens. "Lester has done more for our town than any other living soul. He provides jobs for so many people, he donates thousands to the hospital and he put up most of the money for the library some years back. He has his grumpy ways, but he's a wonderful man, loyal and giving."

Sounds like a living saint, Liza thought, having trouble reconciling her brief brush with the somewhat rude man with this woman's almost beatific description of him. "Perhaps he simply doesn't like newcomers."

Ethel went back to work. "We're all kind of set in our ways here. We don't take quickly to strangers."

That was an understatement, but Liza chose to ignore her implications. She also decided not to remind Ethel that on the day she'd moved in, Ethel had told Liza that Pine Bluff residents were a friendly bunch. "His daughter's certainly nothing like Lester, is she?"

Again, Ethel whirled about. "You've met Roseanne?"

"Yes, at the hospital. She volunteers there and asked if I'd want to join the program."

"You're not going to, are you? I mean, that would mean you'd be staying, and you said you were only on a short visit." Nervously, Ethel pushed her glasses more snugly onto her nose.

Actually, she hadn't ever mentioned how long she'd be staying. Nothing like making a person feel welcome, Liza thought. "I really don't know what my plans are right now," she said, deliberately vague. "But I really enjoyed talking with Roseanne. She's one of the few people in town who's genuinely friendly."

The comment sailed over Ethel's head, but her frown deepened. "Roseanne is a dear, always so polite and kind. But she keeps to herself, you know. She's not inclined to take up with strangers. She spends a lot of time in her garden and, of course, there's her art."

Liza's ears perked up. "She's an artist?"

This topic seemed safe enough to Ethel as she dropped silverware into the basket of the dishwasher. "Oh, my, yes. She paints the most beautiful, restful watercolor scenes. They're mostly views from her own extensive garden. Roseanne's very artistic, even in the way she arranges flowers."

Artistic, as she herself was. Liza's excitement grew, despite the fact that she'd given up on Roseanne as a possible parent just yesterday. "Do you have one of her paintings?"

"I'm afraid not. But Priscilla has two. And, of course, there are several hanging in the Blaine Art Gallery in town."

Liza had been wondering where to look next. Perhaps the art gallery would be a good place to start. But she wasn't finished with Ethel yet. "You mentioned Priscilla. I understand she used to be the Flemings' housekeeper. So she must be the woman who helped raise Roseanne after her mother died."

Ethel dropped a glass onto the open door of the dishwasher. It didn't break, but the clunk froze them both for a heartbeat. Then the older woman turned to Liza, her expression anxious. "Who told you that?"

"J.D. Why, is it a secret?"

"Of course not. I just wonder why you, a stranger, would come here and start asking so many questions about the Flemings. They're salt-of-the-earth kind of people, I tell you. And now, you're curious about my friend Priscilla. I thought you were on vacation, getting over the death of your father, Liza."

She could see she'd upset Ethel, which would get her no further information. "I am. But I've always had an insatiable curiosity. I certainly didn't mean to offend you. I was merely making conversation."

"You might want to remember that curiosity harms even cats." Ethel took the towel out of Liza's hands. "I've got too much to do to stand here gabbing. You run along and sightsee or whatever, so I can get on with my work."

"All right, Ethel." She had very little choice in the matter, so she'd let it be, for now. After one last question. Pausing at the doorway, she swung back to face the little woman. "By the way, have we ever met before? I have this eerie feeling we have, perhaps years ago?"

The color drained from Ethel's face as she twisted the dish towel between her hands. "If we have, I must have forgotten." Quickly she turned to the sink and began running the water.

She remembers it exactly, Liza thought as she grabbed her leather bag, slung the strap over her shoulder and left Bisbee's Bed & Breakfast.

Brendan Blaine was a robust-faced Irishman with carrot red hair and thick arms covered with freckles. He'd opened his gallery on Pine Bluff's Main Street twenty years ago, having moved to Arizona that same year from Dublin to control a severe asthmatic condition. He looked nothing like anyone's mental picture of an artist, but he knew paintings as he lengthily explained to Liza while showing her around his deserted gallery.

"Up north of us in Sedona, they're up to their armpits in artists, don't you know?" he said, his lilting voice carrying just a hint of disdain. "That's all well and good, but how many paintings of red rocks does any one person wish to hang in his home? I prefer to present a more eclectic offering for my clients." He waved a pudgy finger toward the archway as he led her into the next room. "Now here we have Impressionistic works, wonderful portraits of Indian elders and some soothing watercolors. Variety is the spice of life, don't you know?"

"I agree." Liza strolled closer to a large watercolor done in shades of green with touches of yellow. She didn't recognize the name scrawled in the right corner. "Are these mostly the work of local artists?"

"Yes, from Pine Bluff and several bordering cities. Mine is the only gallery between here and Sedona. I believe in giving a hand to beginning artists by displaying their work." He reached to straighten a painting that needed no adjustment, fussing like an old woman.

Liza crossed the room when another scene caught her eye. Flowers in muted shades seemingly shimmering in an unseen breeze as they lifted to the sun alongside a gently rolling stream done in a dazzling blue. She bent to examine the signature and found what she'd been seeking. The signature read simply Roseanne.

"Is this by a local artist?" she asked.

Brendan bustled over, nodding. "Yes, Roseanne Fleming. Well, Mitchell's her married name, but most folks around here refer to her as Lester Fleming's daughter. A lovely woman."

"I believe I've seen her. Do you have others she's done?"

Brendan frowned as he indicated the back wall. "A couple that she did during her dark period, as I call it. They're not nearly as peaceful as this one. Quite the opposite, actually. I'm sorry I don't have but one of her watercolors at the moment. She sells well. I'll be getting more soon if this isn't to your liking."

But Liza was walking back to check out the other paintings. The contrast was startling. The first was done in shades of brown with dark green, the scene depicting trees twisting in a fierce wind in a barren woods, the sky a murky gray. The second rendered a lone bent pine with a shadowy figure weeping on the ground beneath it, all in shades of black and stark white except for the forest green tree.

"You see what I mean?" Brendan asked from behind her.

"I wonder what she was trying to convey."

"Hard to say. Artistic people are often moody and difficult for the average person to understand. These have hung here for years, but no one's shown even minor interest in them. I should probably ask Roseanne to take them back. I doubt anyone will ever purchase one."

Liza studied them both with a critical eye. "I believe I'll take this one," she said, pointing to the painting detailing the figure in obvious pain. There was something about the scene that tore at her heart, upsetting though it was. Yet she wanted to have it. Her taste in art ran the gamut, her apartment reflecting her ever-changing moods. This would be a fine addition.

Surprised, the rotund man quickly changed his sales pitch. "Well, how nice to find someone who truly understands art in all its many forms." Removing the painting, he walked to the front to package it.

After Liza paid for her purchase, she decided to ask one last question. "Does Roseanne live nearby?"

"As a matter of fact, she does. Laurel Lane is just the next corner. Her house is at the south end, backing up to a woods. Lester's big place is only a block away. Roseanne's rather reclusive, but I'm sure she'd like to speak to someone who's interested in her paintings."

Picking up the painting, Liza smiled at him. "Thank you so much." Not today, but perhaps another time she'd go visit Roseanne. Nothing ventured, nothing gained, she decided as she went to her car.

The moment she walked into her room, Liza knew something was amiss. A creature of habit and a neatnik to boot, she always left things a certain way. She could sense more than actually tell that someone had been in since she'd left.

Carefully setting down the painting to lean against one wall, she tossed her bag onto the bed and looked around. It hadn't been Marie in changing the linens, for Ethel's assistant was still ill. Ethel had announced that she'd leave clean sheets and towels on the downstairs hall table so people could help themselves while she was short-handed. No one had seemed to mind and Liza had changed her bed and towels before she'd left to visit the art gallery.

By rights, no one should have had a reason to be in her room. Her suitcase, which she'd shoved under the bed the first night, stuck out at one corner, disturbing the bed-spread. She pushed it back under, not bothering to look inside since she knew she'd left it empty. She began by opening the dresser drawers and saw that her clothing had been disturbed, the piles rearranged. The clothes in her closet had been shifted on the rod. Even the shoes weren't quite the way she'd lined them up.

Growing more annoyed by the minute, she went into the connecting bath and found that the two shelves where she'd placed her cosmetics were arranged differently. Her robe that she'd left hanging neatly on the hook of the bathroom door was crumpled in a heap in a corner, as if tossed aside.

Back in her room, hands on her hips, she gazed around wearing an angry frown. Even the curtains at the win-dow were askew. Who would have done this and why? Small wonder her father had fled this town.

What had they thought to find? There was nothing in the room that would reveal anything she didn't want known. Fortunately, she carried with her any papers she'd brought along plus the black lacquered box. What threat did she represent to someone? And who was that someone? Did this have anything to do with her abortive conversation with Ethel this morning?

She had to know. Leaving her room, her footsteps heavy, Liza marched downstairs to find the energetic little woman.

It was dark out when Liza returned to her room. The confrontation with Ethel hadn't gone well. The innkeeper had denied any knowledge of intruders and had grown huffy and irate at the suggestion. Those things didn't happen in peaceful Pine Bluff, and certainly not in her charming little bed-and-breakfast. She'd been on the premises every minute and not a soul she didn't know had entered.

Which led Liza to the obvious conclusion: the trespasser had been someone Ethel knew. Because there definitely had been a trespasser. Whether the person had searched the room with or without Ethel's full knowledge, Liza didn't know. But short of accusing the older woman without tangible proof, she could do nothing but accept her weak explanation.

Having lost her appetite, she'd skipped dinner and gone for a long walk, winding up at Laurel Lane facing the woods that ran along the back of Roseanne's impressive home. Lights were on in several rooms, but Liza hadn't rung the bell. In the dim light of dusk, she'd noticed the large flower garden off to one side and several white wrought-iron benches, as well as an elaborate birdbath and a number of bird feeders. Apparently Roseanne was a lover of nature.

As Liza herself was, often going on extended hikes into the countryside near her home. So many things pointed to a connection between Roseanne and herself. Yet she couldn't march up to the woman and ask if she'd once given birth to a daughter she'd given up. And she couldn't quite zero in on the truth that the entire town seemed to be conspiring to keep from her.

But she would get to the truth in time.

Closing the door to her room, she turned the lock. It appeared to be the only way she'd feel safe. The two elderly sisters had been in the living room watching television when she'd walked in, but she hadn't seen anyone else moving about. Which was just as well as she didn't feel particularly chatty.

Suddenly she thought of Ralph Parker, of his strength, his love for her. *Oh, Dad, what have I gotten myself into?*

In the bathroom, she undressed, cleaned her face and slipped into her nightshirt. She'd walked off her anger, but not her annoyance. Why was someone doing this to her? Who was made so uneasy by her presence? Lester Fleming? Ethel Bisbee? Priscilla Sparks? Try as she would, Liza couldn't picture any one of the three skulking about her room and going through her things, not even the rude Mr. Fleming.

Liza lay down on her bed, her mind unable to rest. What were they looking for? Whatever it was, they hadn't found it, for nothing was missing. Still...

The shrill ringing of the bedside phone had her jumping. Most likely Tony. She should be pleased to talk with someone sane, but Tony would probably sense there was something wrong and she didn't feel like going into it all with him just now. Reluctantly she picked it up on the second ring.

The voice was definitely masculine but not long-distance. "I was hoping you'd be in," J.D. said.

Unbidden, a smile formed on her lips and her heart rate picked up. "Were you now? Well, here I am."

"Have you had a good day?"

She couldn't remember the last time anyone had asked her that and made it sound as if he really wanted to know. "Not particularly. How about you?"

"A rotten day, as well. Do you think it's the full of the moon?"

She glanced out her window. "That might be it."

"Learn anything more?"

She debated telling him about her room being searched. But she felt oddly hesitant to say much, wondering if her uninvited visitor had bugged her room. Or was she really getting paranoid as J.D. had suggested? "Not much. Lock up any bad guys today?"

"Nope. Picked up a flasher at the mall. Turned out he'd escaped from a work patrol up north last week. I had to drive him back nearly to the Canyon."

She'd wondered where he'd been all day. She'd told herself she welcomed some time alone after their unsettling evening together. But the truth was she was more pleased to hear from him than she cared to admit. "Just get back?"

"Minutes ago." He'd pulled in the drive and walked right to the phone, having spent most of the day and a good part of the night thinking about her. "I'm taking tomorrow afternoon off. How would you like to go horseback riding?"

That's what she needed, some exercise and time away from this house. How quickly she was ready to abandon her need for a little time and space from him. "That sounds wonderful."

"Pick you up about one?"

"I'll be ready."

"Great." Walking with his portable phone, J.D. gazed out his back window and saw a bright moon shining down on his pool and sloping lawn. He wished she were here with him, that they could have a swim and broil a steak, then sit and talk under the stars. Why the hell was he so anxious to dip his hand into this particular flame?

"Liza?"

"Yes?"

"I really enjoyed last night." His voice was deep, intimate.

"I did, too."

"I'll see you tomorrow. Sleep well."

She hung up the phone, feeling better than she had all day.

Chapter Six

It felt good to have her car back, Liza thought as she buckled her seat belt. Jed Freeman had called this morning to say he'd finished working on the Mazda. Right after breakfast, she'd returned the Escort and had been handed her keys. True to his word, J.D. had arranged payment, courtesy of the sheriff's office.

"You have any trouble with her, bring her back to me and I'll fix you right up," Jed said, wiping his stained hands on a rag as he squinted into the morning sun. "J.D. said to take real good care of you."

"I'm sure it'll be fine," Liza assured him. "There is one thing you can do for me. Would you happen to know where Priscilla Sparks lives?" She'd thought things over and decided to pay a visit to Ethel's friend. But she'd known better than to ask Ethel for the address.

"Sure thing. Go east about half a mile, then turn south on Marshall Street. Keep going half a dozen blocks.

Number's two-ten on the right-hand side, beige stucco with red bougainvillea growing along the fence. You can't miss it."

"Thanks again, Jed." Liza pulled out of his station and onto Main Street, searching for Marshall Street.

It didn't take her long to find it. Turning, she tried to think of a good approach to the grandmotherly-looking woman. The one time she'd met her, Priscilla had seemed less excitable and more sensible than Ethel. But then, perhaps she had less interest in Liza's visit than the inn-keeper.

Cruising slowly down the street, she eyed the numbers on the mailboxes. The homes here were all beautifully kept, quite large and obviously fairly expensive. She had no idea that housekeeping paid so well, or was it that the Flemings' live-in nanny had been extremely frugal all her life?

Just as she spotted two-ten, she noticed Priscilla backing out of her driveway in a new-model pale yellow Lincoln. Her home was beige stucco as Jed had said, a sprawling ranch with spacious grounds and several healthy flower beds all in bloom. The woman squinted through her rimless glasses, recognition registering as Liza stopped alongside her. Priscilla hadn't recognized the blue Mazda since she'd only seen her driving the loaner. Facing in opposite directions, they were only a few feet apart, with both driver's-side windows rolled down.

"Hello, Ms. Sparks," Liza said with a warm smile. "I was just coming to see you."

The pale forehead wrinkled and Priscilla didn't return her smile. "Really? Is there something I can do for you?"

Probably a great deal, Liza thought. Aloud, she said, "I was just in the neighborhood and thought I'd stop in for a visit. I don't know too many people in town and, since we've met, I thought we could talk."

Priscilla seemed taken aback, her expression revealing that she hadn't much to say to Liza Parker. Still, her good manners wouldn't permit her to be outright rude. "That would have been nice, dear. But, as you can see, I'm leaving just now." She dabbed at her moist upper lip with a dainty white handkerchief. "You're certain there isn't something specific you wish to discuss?"

Liza gave her another smile, wanting to appear friendly and without a hidden agenda, leaving the door open to another visit. "Something specific? I don't see how, since we've never met. Or have we?"

"No, no, of course not."

Her answer had come too quickly, too defensively. Along with Ethel's peculiar behavior, this more than anything convinced Liza that these two women had known her as a baby here in this town. They probably also knew who her birth parents were. But they weren't about to reveal anything for fear of harming someone. Or perhaps angering someone.

"I'll let you be on your way, Ms. Sparks," Liza said. "I'll drop by again another time. Have a good day."

Liza drove off, noting Priscilla's puzzled expression in her rearview mirror. She almost chuckled out loud. She wasn't learning much from these two little old ladies, but she was surely setting them to buzzing about the motivation for her visit. She wouldn't be at all surprised if Priscilla's itinerary for the day would include a stop at Ethel's to discuss and ponder their conversation and its possible ramifications.

Turning the corner, she sighed, the sunny morning suddenly turning a bit glum for her. Getting to the bottom of things was taking far too long, yet she hadn't a thought as to how to hurry the process. Ask too many pointed questions of anyone she'd met so far and they'd clam up tighter than a sealed coffin. Confront someone skittish, touch on a nerve and she might never get another chance.

Yet she couldn't leave without getting better answers, without someone breaking down and telling her the truth about her past. This morning, Liza had caught Dawn as she was coming off a night shift at the hospital, calling from a pay phone at the drugstore, still not trusting her room phone. She'd poured out her frustration to her friend and had felt better. For a few moments.

Then she'd phoned Tony since she kept missing his calls. The hospital had paged him and he'd finally picked it up, sounding rushed and impatient as most doctors always are. He'd dispensed with the small talk and asked outright when she was going to end this wild-goose chase and return home. When she hadn't been able to give him a definite answer, the annoyance he rarely showed her surfaced. Tony liked things to go his way.

He'd reminded her that they had tickets to a play next weekend at the Little Theater in Tucson, a production in which his twin brother had a major role. Of course, she'd totally forgotten, a fact that didn't sit well with Tony. They'd hung up, both feeling a little wounded and confused.

She hadn't set out to deliberately hurt Tony. Time and again since they'd begun dating, she'd told him she wasn't in the market for a serious relationship. Which hadn't been exactly true. Perhaps she was, but not with him. She liked Tony and enjoyed being with him. Yet not in the all-encompassing, breathless, passionate way she'd suspected was possible.

Not like the way she felt about J.D.

She'd known J.D. less than a week, yet the mere thought of him could make her blood heat. Was it simply physical? She had no way of knowing at this stage. She needed more time to decide if these feelings developing between them were real, time to get to know him and determine if what she felt might last.

She'd also phoned her studio and talked with both her assistant and her part-time helper. Marianne had said things were going well and Liza had answered a couple of troubling questions for her. Luckily, Tina was able to work full-time during her absence, so no major crises loomed on the foreseeable horizon. Liza felt good that at least her business was going well even though her personal life seemed to be in shambles.

Turning onto Grant Avenue, she saw that J.D.'s silver van was parked in front of Bisbee's. Parking behind it, she had to smile as she noticed Priscilla's yellow Lincoln in Ethel's driveway. Just as she'd suspected, the two little ladies were probably huddled over ice tea and cookies in the kitchen discussing what to make of Liza.

Climbing out, Liza strolled up the walk toward J.D., who was standing on the porch talking with Gloria who was curled up on the glider. The blonde was wearing hot pink today, a scooped-neck cotton T-shirt that displayed a great deal of her assets, and skintight knit slacks. Her hair hung to her shoulders and her full lips were a slash of matching pink. Liza couldn't help feeling a bit like a small brown wren alongside a colorful peacock.

But as she stopped at the bottom of the steps, J.D. turned to her, his dark eyes warming as they traveled the length of her and back up, his slow smile telegraphing his approval, and she forgot about Gloria.

"Hi," J.D. said, stepping down to meet her. "I'm early. I hope you don't mind."

She was more than ready to leave this town behind for a couple of hours. "Not at all." She glanced down at her denim shirt with a discreet red parrot on the pocket, her favorite jeans and brown leather boots. "Am I dressed all right for this outing?"

She'd tied her hair back with a piece of red yarn, making her look younger. J.D. knew that men should never compare two women, but alongside Gloria, Liza looked fresh-faced and utterly appealing. "Perfect," he said, noticing the way the soft material of her jeans clung to her gentle curves.

"I've got my car back. Thanks for taking care of everything."

"My pleasure. I wouldn't want someone new in town to think that the law around here didn't do right by its visitors."

Mindful of her three-inch heels, Gloria started down the steps. "Where are you two off to, if you don't mind my asking?" Liza supposed that Gloria was wondering how Liza had been able to interest J. D. Kincaid more in a few days than she herself had in several weeks.

J.D.'s arm slipped around Liza's waist. "I'm taking Liza to the Flying D for some horseback riding." He looked down into eyes so blue, he felt as if he could drown in them. "Ready to go?"

"Anytime you are."

Gloria appeared resigned. "Have fun, you hear?" Gloria called after them as they gave her a wave and climbed into the van. Her steps slow and a little hesitant, Gloria wandered back to the porch swing.

"I feel kind of sorry for her," Liza said as they pulled away from in front of Bisbee's, her eyes on Gloria. "She seems lonely somehow."

"I doubt that she will be for long," J.D. answered. "Every single man in town has taken her out, and a few of the married ones, I'd be willing to bet. If Gloria wants company, all she has to do is walk into Sal's Bar. Guys will be fighting to buy her drinks or dinner in minutes."

"Maybe so, but she wants more than drinks and dinner. She wants someone permanent in her life. She told me that the first day we met."

J.D. downshifted as he swung out onto the highway. "Same thing she tells anyone who'll listen. Apparently she feels that the best way to find a husband is to tell the world she's in the market."

Liza's lips twitched. "She also told me she thinks you're a hunk."

He rolled his eyes. "Just what I always wanted, to be the third husband of a woman who's always on the prowl." He glanced down to where Liza's hand rested in her lap, picked it up and placed it on his thigh, threading his fingers through hers. "I missed seeing you yesterday."

She'd missed seeing him, too, yet she was hesitant to tell him so. "I wouldn't have been very good company last evening." She told him that she was certain someone had searched her room.

J.D. listened intently, wondering if perhaps her suspicions about someone wanting her out of town had been correct all along. He would do some quiet checking without her knowledge, because if he appeared worried, she'd pick up on it. "Are you sure? Maybe Ethel went in to straighten your room after all, part of the housekeeping service in Marie's absence. Or maybe you thought you'd put something one place and had, in fact, put it elsewhere." There was always room for doubt.

She knew he was a hard sell, but she also was positive of her facts. "I'm almost maddeningly methodical. Dawn, my old roommate, used to swear I aligned the magazines on the tabletop and the pencils on the desk just so, and would notice if one was out of sync. Besides, what business would Ethel have going into the dresser drawers and rearranging my clothes, unless she was looking for something?"

He turned left onto the road leading to Palo Verde. "You have a point there. Did you ask her if she'd seen any strangers around?"

"Yes, and she said no one she didn't personally know had set foot inside Bisbee's. She was quite upset that I'd even suggest such a thing."

"Well, she's built that place up from nothing into a thriving business, so it's understandable she'd be defensive. What I can't figure is what connection Ethel would have to your birth, if we're going by the assumption that you were born in Pine Bluff, and why she wouldn't want to talk about it so many years later. Then again, maybe she knows nothing."

"She knows something, I'm certain." Liza reached into her leather bag and removed the sheet of yellow legal paper that had been in the packet she'd received from the attorney's office. "I know you can't read this while you're driving. It's something I'm sure I wasn't intended to receive." She told him the circumstances of how she'd come to sign for the information. "Right here at the bottom is a notation that the child, who was me, was brought in by an Ethel Bisbee of Pine Bluff, Arizona, at one o'clock on Tuesday, and the date. That woman has to be my landlady."

J.D. took a quick look, then dragged his gaze back to the light traffic. "If that's so, then why don't you just show that paper to Ethel Bisbee, confront her with the evidence?''

Liza shook her head. ''Because she's already hostile toward me. She'd simply deny it and how could I prove anything? The Consent to Adopt form is unavailable to me without a court order. The attorney who handled the adoption is dead, as are my parents. I have no proof other than a letter from my father about his upsetting visit to Pine Bluff, a few items he left me in a black lacquered box that apparently had come with me, along with the few clothes I was wearing and a pink blanket, all listed on this yellow sheet.''

J.D. could tell she was getting worked up emotionally, so he kept talking, hoping to defuse her anxiety. ''What was in the lacquered box?''

Liza stuffed the letter back into her shoulder bag. ''A child-size chain with a tiny gold heart, a green leather diary containing a dried rose, and a ring that appears to have been carved from an acorn. At least, it looks like an acorn to me.''

J.D.'s interest was aroused. As they stopped for a light, he turned to her. ''Where is the carved ring?''

''Right here.'' Again she reached into her purse, fished around and came up with the ring, holding it up for him to see.

He turned it around, checking the inside for initials or some identifying marks. ''Interesting. You should show it to Gray. He does a lot of carving. Mostly animals, but he's real good. Maybe he can tell you something about where it might have come from.''

''It's worth a try,'' Liza said, putting the ring away again.

J.D. checked his watch. "We'll be on time for a change. I'm usually late, but the kids are so good about it. They call me the late J.D."

"What kids?"

"Oh, I guess I didn't tell you. Gray's got this program going at his ranch for handicapped children. He's got us all involved in it. His foreman, Henry, teaches the kids to swim, the cook lets them help out in the kitchen and I got elected to teach them to ride horses."

She wasn't all that surprised, for she was quickly learning that J.D. had a lot of irons in the fire. "That sounds wonderful."

"Yeah, it's pretty special. The rehab center buses them in from Phoenix once a week to spend the day. Usually we have a cookout and eat around the campfire or in the mess hall, which they love. Sometimes the kids help make cookies or pies. Other weeks, Gray sends one of the guys into town for fast food."

"Sounds like you really enjoy being with the kids."

"I hope you will, too." Swinging the wheel right, he drove under a large arched sign that proclaimed the area they were entering as the Flying D Ranch. "I'm anxious for you to meet Gray. He's a terrific guy."

Gray Eubanks sat atop the sorrel stallion looking as if he'd been born in the saddle. The big animal swished his white tail and shuffled his feet impatiently as J.D. introduced Liza to his mentor.

Gray leaned down to shake her hand, his teeth very white in his tan face, his eyes a vivid blue. "J.D.'s told me about you. Welcome to the Flying D."

"It's good of you to have me," she said, liking his slow, easy manner. She watched him remove his hat, revealing black hair with just a touch of white on his sideburns. A very attractive man, she found herself thinking.

"You were right, J.D.," Gray commented. "She's prettier than anyone around these parts."

Liza smiled at the compliment as a gust of wind ruffled her hair. Instead of fighting the persistent breezes, she pulled off the yarn and shook out her hair.

Gray pulled his stallion up short, his eyes narrowing as he studied the young woman standing next to J.D. Caught in the grip of déjà vu, he could do nothing but stare for a long moment. The resemblance was startling, uncanny, even.

Noticing his sudden stillness, Liza looked from Gray to J.D. and back. "Is something the matter?"

Shaking his head, Gray gripped the reins tightly and regained his control. "For a moment there, you reminded me a great deal of someone I'd once known." He smiled, breaking the tension. "Probably because I don't meet that many lovely women anymore." He glanced toward the barn. "The kids are waiting over by the barn in the next corral, J.D. They've been chomping at the bit for the last half an hour."

"And I'm not even late this time," J.D. said with a grin. He took Liza's hand in his. "Come on. You've got to meet these kids. They've got more guts than most combat soldiers." He looked up at Gray still astride his skittery stallion. "We'll see you inside later for dinner?"

"Right," Gray said, replacing his hat, his gaze on Liza as she fell in step with J.D. Even the walk was similar, he thought. But, of course, there couldn't be a connection.

"Nice meeting you," Liza called over her shoulder as J.D. hurried her along.

Gray tipped two fingers to the brim of his hat in acknowledgment. The similarities were so close that Liza

Parker could have passed for her sister. But he knew there were no sisters, despite the resemblance. Except for the eyes. They were very different. Liza's were blue whereas deep-set gray eyes haunted his dreams.

With a melancholy sigh, he reined the stallion around and aimed him for the open corral gate. Perhaps a hard ride would erase the memories and the pain of what could never be.

The nine-year-old towhead handled the rake like a pro despite the brace on his left leg. "J.D. says you got to take good care of your horse and your horse will always take good care of you," Matt told Liza as she watched him from outside the stall.

"So he not only teaches you to ride the horses, but to care for them, is that it?" Liza asked.

"Yeah. I know how to groom, too. And where the tack goes and stuff like that." He nodded toward a stall across the concrete walkway. "That's Bessie, the horse I get to ride. Arnie likes to go fast so he rides Dusty, the gray one down there. Arnie's twelve. J.D. says when I get bigger, I'll probably like to go fast, too." Finished arranging the fresh straw, he looked up at Liza. "Do you like to go fast?"

"Sometimes. Other times, I like to go slower and enjoy the scenery."

"You mean you like to canter instead of gallop. J.D.'s teaching me the right words." He left the stall, his limp barely noticeable as he walked alongside Liza.

"I guess you like J.D. a lot."

"Everyone does. He's a regular guy."

Exactly. What's not to like? she thought. Earlier she'd watched J.D. patiently take first one child then another, help each one mount, then climb on his own horse and ride alongside them in the open area beyond the corrals. There was Gracie who was learning disabled and hyperactive, and Peter who was blind, and Emma, the six-year-old who'd come from an abused home and had only thirty percent hearing, a souvenir from her alcoholic father.

He talked to each one, making them feel special, letting them build their skills slowly so they'd feel confident. They trusted him, Liza could see. J.D. interacting with the children was something to see.

Outside the barn, she sat down with Matt on a wooden bench where twelve-year-old Danny was carefully working on a piece of wood. She could just make out the vague outline of a sleeping dog. "Hey, that's good. Who taught you to carve?"

"Gray. He's the best. He's got this horse that's reared up on its hind legs that's so cool." Danny tossed his head, his silken hair rearranging with the gesture. "He gave it to me to take home," he told her with pride. "He only gives his carvings to a couple of people."

"He must think you're special," she told him, her heart going out to the young boy who'd barely survived an automobile accident in which both his parents had died. His right ankle was still in a cast and he'd had skin grafts on one arm from a bad burn. J.D. had been right. These children were exceptionally brave. She hadn't heard one complain.

Her admiration for Gray and J.D. grew with each passing minute. She'd never have dreamed that a man who drove maniacally and captured criminals for a living could be so sensitive with defenseless children who had special needs.

Liza looked up and saw him walking toward her, carrying Gracie. He was facing her so she could read his lips as they spoke. Four hours later and he looked less tired than when they'd arrived, energized by the kids and the affection they lavished on him.

"Anyone hungry?" J.D. called out as he set Gracie down and spotted Henry coming toward them from the direction of the mess hall. "It's pizza night." The announcement was met with great hoots of delight as the kids gathered around. After saying their goodbyes, liberally sprinkled with hugs, they went with Henry.

J.D. turned to Liza. "I hope you weren't too bored."

"I haven't spent such a nice afternoon in years," she told him honestly. "If I'm still around next week on their day, can I come back?"

"It's a date." The sun was low in the sky, reflecting on her auburn hair, turning it fiery. He slipped his arms around her, studying her upturned face. "You're glad you came, then?"

They stood under the overhang where the scent of hay and leather and musk drifted, and the whinnying of horses broke the late-afternoon quiet. Liza's hands settled on the broad expanse of his back, her heart already cartwheeling around in her chest at his nearness. "Mmm, very," she answered.

He watched her eyes as he drew her body closer to his, saw them widen and grow heated as she became aware of how quickly he'd become aroused at her nearness. "I want you," he whispered, his voice low and husky. "I want to take you to my house where we can be alone, where no one will interrupt us for hours and hours. I want to slowly explore every inch of you."

Senses swimming, Liza wasn't sure she could speak. Or walk, if it came to that. "I know what you want. I'm not saying I don't want that, too. But I don't trust anything that happens fast. I ..."

"Need time. I know. I'm not happy about it, but I'll give you time. Just don't take too long." He took her mouth then, and took himself on that incredible journey into newly discovered passion.

She'd said she needed time, but she held nothing back in her kiss, J.D. thought. She opened to him and he drank from her. Her heated response as her arms wound around him had him again struggling for the control he rarely relinquished.

Liza felt as if she'd just leapt onto a hurtling train. The rush, the power, the beauty of the race tugged at her senses. Needs she couldn't put a name to made themselves known. Desires she'd relegated to the back burner surfaced and clamored to be recognized. Awash in pleasure, she let him take her where he would.

In his chair by the dining room window of his rambling ranch house, Gray Eubanks witnessed Liza and J.D.'s embrace and felt no small amount of envy. He'd never seen J.D. this taken with a woman and it had all happened so quickly.

As it once had to him.

She'd been every bit as beautiful as Liza Parker, though much younger then. He'd kissed her with that same fervor, wanted with that same hint of impatience and loved with all his heart. Only, he'd lost her. Lost her forever, first because of youth and stupidity and lastly because of circumstances beyond his control.

Gray let the curtain drop and moved his chair to the head of the table, unable to watch the young lovers a moment longer. He wished them well, but it hurt too much to remember. He silently prayed that those two would never know the pain he'd lived with for so long.

A tall, powerfully built man entered the dining room as Gray looked up. Rudy had been with him for twenty years now, a companion, a friend, a cook and a man he couldn't do without. His formidable strength belied his gentle, caring nature. "Rudy, is dinner nearly ready?"

"Yes. The soup is chilled, the fish ready to be broiled."

"Good." Gray indicated the table set with red cloth, white dinnerware and black wrought iron candle holders. "Nice job. Mary taught you well." J.D.'s mother had been special. He still missed her gentle ways.

Rudy smiled, but shook his head. "Anyone can set a table, but no one can cook as good as Mary did."

Gray heard a burst of laughter come from the vicinity of the front door. "Looks like J.D.'s arrived with his guest. Make a pitcher of margaritas, will you, please, Rudy?"

"Coming right up."

Smoothing back his thick hair, Gray waited for them to join him.

Liza stabbed a piece of tender baby asparagus as she looked at Gray seated at the head of the table. "I couldn't help noticing the beautiful carvings on your mantel when J.D. showed me around. You're very talented."

He shrugged off the compliment. "I've been doing it for years. It's something to keep my hands busy while I'm thinking."

They were everywhere throughout the house, some as bookends on shelves, other pieces on tables, still more in clusters. "Do you ever offer them for sale, say on consignment at a local store?"

He'd been asked often, yet he preferred not to. "No, but I give some away. Did you find one you like particularly?"

She didn't feel she could accept one of his carvings on such short acquaintance. "They're all lovely."

J.D. finished the last of his fish, wiped his mouth and sat back. "Liza's got a ring that someone carved a long time ago that she'd like you to see. She thinks it's made from an acorn and wonders if you can tell."

Gray set down his wineglass. "I'd be glad to take a look. When I was young, knocking around from ranch to ranch, a lot of guys did whittling and carving, which is how I learned. Out of boredom, sometimes they'd have contests to see who could make the smallest, most difficult carving, and acorns were often used."

Liza handed him the ring she'd retrieved from her bag. "I could be wrong, but this looks like it could have been made from an acorn."

Gray turned the small ring in his big hands. "I'd say it definitely is. I've carved several myself just like this." One in particular that he'd given to a special someone along with his heart. But she'd left him, taking both, and he hadn't been the same since.

He handed back the ring. "Does this belong to someone you know, or did you find it?"

Liza glanced over at J.D. and saw his encouraging nod. On the way in, she'd mentioned that she'd like to tell Gray about her quest. Though she was aware he seldom went into Pine Bluff, Gray had lived in the area for over two decades and J.D. said he knew people for miles around. Liza was willing to disclose her situation in the hope that he might shed some light.

"I'm not sure who it belongs to," Liza said with a sigh, gazing at the ring, wishing it could talk. So, as Rudy cleared the table and poured coffee all around, she told Gray about her adoption, the attorney's packet and the other details involving her search for her birth parents, including Ethel Bisbee's odd behavior. "I have this strong feeling that Ethel knows a great deal more than she's saying."

Gray was thoughtful as he considered all that she'd told him. He could tell by the intent way J.D. watched Liza that her problems had become important to him, though they hadn't known each other long. Sometimes, falling in love takes but moments. It had for him. For that alone, he wanted to help. "And this acorn ring was apparently handed over to the attorney by Ethel Bisbee when she took you to him as an infant for adoption?"

"That's what I think." From her purse, she removed the folded yellow sheet and handed it to him. "There's an inventory written of the items that accompanied me."

Reading the notation, Gray frowned thoughtfully. "Do you have all these items?"

"Yes." Carefully she removed the black lacquered box. "For some reason, I decided to carry these things with me each time I left Bisbee's. My intuition was certainly on target."

"Liza's room was thoroughly searched yesterday while she was out," J.D. went on to explain, "yet nothing was missing."

"How would anyone know these things existed, if that's even what they were after?" Gray asked.

Liza felt a rush of warmth that J.D. really seemed to believe that an intruder had visited her room, though he'd appeared dubious in the van. "I don't know exactly. But someone had to send the box with me." She handed it to him. "There's nothing of value in there. However, if the person was trying to keep me from learning who my birth parents are, perhaps the contents somehow reveal their identity to someone who knows."

Gray lifted out the small gold chain and heart, looking it over before setting it aside. Next he examined the diary, carefully handling the dried rose that fell out, then finding the lone entry and studying the message written on June 8. Keeping his expression unchanged, he finally looked up. "I take it you don't recognize the handwriting?"

She shook her head. "I was hoping you might."

"I'm afraid not." Again, he fingered the acorn ring. "Once, years ago, I gave a ring like this to a girl." His vision blurred as memories moved in on him. "She was beautiful with long strawberry blond hair. Full of life, with a laugh like music."

Liza, watching him closely, realized that he was talking about someone he'd once loved deeply. Odd that J.D. had not mentioned a woman in Gray's life. "Where is she now?"

Gray blinked, shaking off his musings. "She left me." He held up the ring one last time. "But I wasn't the only ranch hand who carved rings for girls as a young man." Slowly he put everything back in the box, replaced the lid and handed the box to Liza. "I'm sorry I can't help you."

"Thanks for trying." He looked so sad that Liza felt he appeared more in need of help than she. "Do you know Ethel Bisbee?"

"Only by reputation. I hear she's honest and runs a good house."

"How about Priscilla Sparks?" Quickly she told him about the conversation she'd overheard in Ethel's kitchen.

Gray's frown returned. "No one else knows the whole story," he said, repeating the words Liza attributed to Priscilla. "Have you confronted either of these ladies?"

Liza sighed wearily. She felt as if she were a dog chasing its own tail in circles. "Not an outright confrontation, but I've said a few leading things, and they both clammed up immediately."

"You're aware that Priscilla was Lester Fleming's housekeeper for years?" He saw her nod. "A very circumspect woman, from what I know. Never married nor had children of her own. I can't imagine someone like that involved in a clandestine adoption. Nor Ethel, either, for that matter."

"Lester stopped by our table at the Apollo the other evening," J.D. added. "He was outright rude to Liza, all but telling her not to linger in his town. These same people had treated her adopted father badly years ago when he'd tried to find Liza's real parents. I don't know what to make of it."

Gray rubbed his chin thoughtfully. "Someone apparently has something to hide. Of course, I know Lester. He builds all over and he's been here to the Flying D on several occasions. I'm not surprised he was rude because I've seen him in action before. He's got a bad temper and a lousy disposition."

"Some people are just nasty by nature," J.D. commented, having run across more than his share in his work.

"Do you know Roseanne Fleming?" Liza asked, looking at Gray. "I guess her married name is Roseanne Mitchell." Did his blue eyes darken at the mention of Roseanne, or had she imagined his response? Liza wondered.

"You've been busy," Gray said quietly. "You've met Roseanne?"

"Yes, at the hospital where I was trying to look up old records. She volunteers there. She's so nice that I have trouble believing she's that grumpy old man's daughter. I bought one of her paintings at the art gallery.''

Gray thought of the watercolor hanging in his bedroom and of the lovely woman whose talent had put it on canvas. With no small effort, he kept his features even. "I understand she's nothing like Lester." Hands not quite steady, he gripped the arms of his chair and looked over at Rudy who was hovering nearby. "I think I'll retire now, Rudy. I'm a little tired." He managed a smile that included both J.D. and Liza. "You two stay as long as you like. I hope you'll come again, Liza."

"Thank you." As Rudy moved to Gray's side, she decided to ask something that she hoped Gray wouldn't find offensive. "Can I ask you about the woman you'd carved the ring for, the one who left you? Forgive my curiosity, but I'm a romantic at heart. Did you ever go after her?"

A muscle in Gray's cheek tightened. "No, I didn't. At the time, I had nothing to offer her."

She felt a wave of sadness for his obvious distress even at the memory. "And later?" Obviously he had much to offer a woman now, both as a man and as a provider.

"My circumstances improved," he answered, his voice soft, "but sometimes life brings about changes you can't overcome."

As Liza pondered that, Rudy released the brake and pulled back on Gray's wheelchair, turned it and headed for the archway leading to the hall. She knew her face registered shock as she swung her eyes to J.D.

He waited until Rudy and Gray had disappeared down the hallway. "A riding accident," J.D. explained. "It happened about twenty years ago. A horse he was breaking in threw him and the stallion's front hooves came down hard on Gray's back before he could roll out of the way. He hasn't walked since.''

She understood now why Gray Eubanks opened his ranch to handicapped children. And why he felt he couldn't go after the woman he still obviously loved deeply.

Chapter Seven

Clouds whipped about in a gray afternoon sky the following day as Liza turned her Mazda onto Laurel Lane. Her frustrations over coming up empty-handed for days now had made her decide to drop in on the one person she'd begun to feel might have some answers: Roseanne Fleming Mitchell.

Earlier that morning, she'd gone back to the library to take another look at the pictures of Roseanne in the yearbooks, sailing past the frowning librarian with merely a nod. She'd wanted to examine the photos more closely and she had. The resemblance was definitely there, in the shape of the face and the thick hair, even though the color was lighter. If Roseanne was indeed the woman who'd given birth to her, Liza intended to get her to admit it one way or the other today.

The day they'd met at the hospital, Roseanne hadn't shown any untoward interest in her, not a sign that Liza's face reminded her of herself in her youth. Yet the way Lester Fleming had acted when he'd run into her at the Apollo, the whispered conversation between Ethel and Priscilla in the kitchen and even Gray's altered expression yesterday when she'd mentioned Roseanne's name all seemed to indicate she was on the right track.

The puzzling factor was why Roseanne herself seemed unaware of the situation, for surely she'd heard around town that Liza had been questioning everyone. Roseanne's father certainly had or he never would have been so abrupt with Liza. But the big question was, so many years later and with no husband to shield from a youthful indiscretion, would Roseanne deny her daughter if she showed up on her doorstep?

She was about to find out. Liza pulled up in front of Roseanne's home and turned off the motor. She was in luck, for she could see Roseanne in the back section of the side garden, seated on a chair in front of an easel. Taking a deep breath, Liza got out and strolled over, hoping she hadn't misjudged the woman in their brief meeting, only to learn today that she was more like Lester after all.

Walking between the rows of carefully tended perennials, Liza took her time, studying Roseanne while she was engrossed in her work and before she was aware she had company. Even with a lack of sun, Liza could see that the woman's brown hair had a lot of reddish highlights. Or was she simply determined to find similarities? She was small boned and willowy, as Liza herself was. Her fingers were slender and tapered, her feet long and narrow, another likeness. And she didn't appear to be plagued with freckles as were so many redheads, a fate Liza had also escaped.

Coming up behind her, she noticed that Roseanne was painting in background, shrubs and trees and the like, with nothing else yet on the canvas.

The woman glanced up and gave Liza a soft smile, seemingly not a bit surprised someone she'd met only once was here in her garden. "How nice that you stopped over, Liza. That's a lovely color on you," she said, indicating the turquoise top Liza had on with white slacks.

Roseanne, she noticed, was wearing slim slacks and a multicolored loose tunic top that somehow suited her. "Thank you. I hope you don't mind my just dropping by like this. I bought one of your paintings the other day and the gallery owner told me where you lived."

"Not at all. I so seldom get company." She pointed to a wrought iron chair painted white. "Please, have a seat."

Liza sat, placing her bag alongside her as she glanced up at clouds. "Not the best day to catch good light."

Roseanne followed her gaze. "I suppose not. But sometimes shadowy subjects are more intriguing, don't you think? Things can't always be sunny and bright."

"That's true." She saw that Roseanne had stopped painting and had plunged her brush in a jar filled with liquid. "Please, don't let me interrupt your work."

"It's time I finished for the day. Which of my paintings did you choose?" Carefully she closed up her paints.

Liza wondered how best to describe the disturbing scene propped now across from her bed at Bisbee's. "It's set in a woods and there's a single forest green pine and what appears to be a figure weeping beneath."

Methodically, Roseanne wiped her hands on a cloth already paint spattered. "I know the one. Brendan calls it from *my dark period*." She laughed softly. "I don't recall having a dark period, actually, but I suppose everyone has mood fluctuations.''

Had that dark period been when she'd been pregnant and upset? "You're very talented. Have you been painting long?"

"Yes, quite a while. Do you paint?"

"No, I'm a fashion designer. I suppose some call that an artistic endeavor. And I love to sketch."

"I sometimes design my own clothes, mostly because I can't find what I want in the stores, and I love to sew. I do sketches, too, of outdoor scenes and children in the park. Art is so soothing. You can get lost in it, in any form of art, and not think about your everyday problems. It helps you get through the days."

Liza had never used her art for that purpose, but she supposed that Roseanne was right. She glanced over her shoulder at the thick growth of evergreens and cottonwoods behind Roseanne's home where lengthening shadows gave the trees an eerie appearance. "Did you do that painting somewhere in those woods?"

Roseanne paused, wrinkling her forehead as if trying to remember. "I'm not sure. It's one of my earlier ones. Actually, I believe that bent tree is closer to my father's place down the block a ways." She covered the canvas and slipped it into a leather carrying case, then broke down the easel.

"Do you walk in the woods a lot?" Liza was curious as to how this serene woman would have come to paint such a disturbing scene, and curious about her dark period.

"I used to, when I was much younger. I had a dog, just a little white mutt who'd wandered into the yard one day as a stray. I called him Scrappy because he was such a fighter for a little guy." She smiled at her own youthful whimsy. "Scrappy used to love to run into the woods and I'd go in and chase him. It was a game we both enjoyed." Her features rearranged and she looked sad. "But I never go in those woods anymore. I don't know what ever happened to Scrappy. One day I woke up and he was nowhere to be found. Gone, just like that."

The lovely face looked so sad, even haunted suddenly, as if she'd seen her share of troubles. Who hasn't? Liza wondered. She turned on the chair, looking pointedly at Roseanne's big home. "That's a lot of house for one person," she commented.

Roseanne nodded. "Yes, it is. I'm fairly used to living alone, but every so often, I wish I'd had children." She looked back to Liza, checking out her ring finger. "You're not married?"

"No, but I share your love of children. One of these days I hope to have some."

"Don't wait too long. Things happen and you can never turn back the clock. Perhaps if I'd been able to have a child, Reid wouldn't have been so disappointed in me." She'd been speaking almost as if to herself, then waved a dismissive hand. "Ah, but you don't want to hear all that." She put on a smile. "Are you enjoying your stay? Pine Bluff's such a nice little town."

Liza felt a rush of sympathy for Roseanne who apparently blamed herself for not being able to give her ex-husband a family. But had she always been infertile, say before her marriage? "Yes, I am. I've met some lovely people. Priscilla Sparks, for one. I understand she used to work for your father."

"Priscilla raised me, actually. My mother died when I was very young." Her smile returned, warm and sincere. "She's a wonderful woman. She'd do anything for me or my father. She still comes to visit, though her arthritis bothers her a lot. She's lonely, too, I think, with no family of her own."

"At least she has a lovely home. I've driven by it. And a brand-new car."

"My father pays the people who work for him very well. That's why they're all so loyal."

Yes, loyal to a fault. Was loyalty to Lester the reason she couldn't get anyone in this town to open up to her? But what was it that they might reveal that Lester would consider disloyal? She had to try another angle. "I've also met J. D. Kincaid, your sheriff."

"Ah, yes, J.D." Roseanne's smile was womanly. "He's so nice and very attractive, don't you think?" She crossed her long legs, leaning back.

"Yes, he is very attractive. I've never known anyone quite like him. Yet it's so hard to know if what you feel for someone new is attraction or something more. Did you ever feel that way?"

Roseanne wrinkled her forehead as if trying to capture an elusive memory. "Not really. I dated a lot when I was young. All my friends did. We'd all grown up together and had known each other forever. We went out in groups mostly and we were kind of reckless in those days, drinking too much, staying out till all hours. But I settled down and married the man Dad picked out for me. Reid was good to me, but honestly, I don't believe there was this burning attraction between us like you probably mean." She met Liza's eyes, her expression serious. "Are you in love with J.D.?"

It was surprising to Liza that she was having such a personal conversation with someone she scarcely knew. Perhaps it was because she felt very comfortable with Roseanne, as if she'd known her a long while. "I'm attracted," she answered. "I'm not sure how being in love feels."

"Mmm, it feels wonderful." Roseanne closed her eyes briefly, her smile secretive. "You want to shout it to the world, yet you want to clutch it to your heart. You want to be with him every second, afraid he'll leave if he's out of your sight a minute. You want to touch him, to hold him to you and keep him yours alone the rest of your days."

Liza had trouble keeping her surprise from showing. The woman was a dichotomy. "Is that how you felt about Reid Mitchell?" Hadn't she just said she hadn't felt that deeply for her ex-husband?

Roseanne seemed to come back to herself, then shook her head. "No, not Reid. We were more like friends than two people married to one another."

Her heart in her throat, Liza had to ask. "Then who? Who did you feel that wonderful rush of feeling for?"

Roseanne stared at her for a moment, then squinted up at the darkening sky. "You know, I believe it's going to rain." Rising, she folded her canvas chair, picked up her box of paints and carrying case, then grabbed her easel.

"Can I help you with that?" Liza asked, getting to her feet, for apparently their visit had just ended.

"I can manage, thank you. I've so enjoyed talking with you, Liza. I hope you'll come back soon." Without another word, Roseanne walked along the garden path toward her side door.

Watching her go, Liza stood there, frowning. Roseanne was a lovely puzzle who'd revealed just enough to cause more questions to pop into her mind. As vague as she appeared at times, she'd remembered her name after only one meeting. Had she decided to go in because she didn't want to discuss a painful memory, or were her remembrances as fragile as she herself seemed?

Raindrops splashing on her broke into her thoughts and she glanced up at heavy clouds shifting and churning in a dull sky. Sighing with frustration, Liza walked to her car. It was a light rainfall so far. Maybe she could continue her questing another little while before a real storm developed.

Turning the Mazda around, she decided to drive farther down the road and have a look at Lester Fleming's place. In minutes, she was in front of the imposing two-story structure and cruised to a stop. Drapes were closed on all the windows facing the street, as if Lester wanted to block out the world. With no housekeeper to help out, she wondered what the inside looked like. She couldn't picture that crusty old man dusting and vacuuming, cooking and washing. How did he manage after years of Priscilla running his house for him? Or had he replaced her?

The door to the attached garage was closed and she could see no sign of Lester's Cadillac. Quite likely, with so many businesses to run, he wasn't home at this hour of the afternoon. She checked the sky again and decided it probably wouldn't pour for another little while. Hesitantly, she got out and walked toward the back woods, keeping a watchful eye on the Fleming house for signs of life.

She wasn't really an adventurous sort, Liza reminded herself. All she wanted to do was to walk through those trees bordering the back and see if she could find that pine tree Roseanne had depicted in that troubling painting. She wasn't sure why, but she just wanted to see it. As she arrived at the tree line, she glanced back at the imposing house. All was quiet and she was relieved, for she hadn't thought what she'd say if someone rushed out and accused her of trespassing.

Was the wooded section a part of Lester's property, or was it for anyone to enjoy? She didn't have the time to check. Why would he mind, Liza thought as she walked around clusters of tall evergreens, even if it was his? She meant no harm. He seemed like such a grouch that he might not like her anywhere near his place on general principles, though.

She'd been walking only a few minutes, peering through the density of the thick, old trees, when she heard an ominous rumbling of thunder. The rain had picked up only slightly, but it did seem as though it might turn nasty. She shivered as a cooling breeze caressed her. Narrowing her eyes, Liza tried to spot that bent pine, yet she could see nothing that resembled it. Perhaps another day, she thought as she turned and headed back to her car.

She rounded the bend on the far side of the house and was startled to see a white pickup idling close to her Mazda, and a man wearing a dark hat was huddled over the driver's door, as if trying to break in. She'd left her purse on the passenger seat, but had locked the car and taken the keys. "Hey!" she yelled.

The man's head popped up momentarily, then he went back to work. There was nothing of great value inside. What could he be after? Her wallet? Liza broke into a run. She reached his side and grabbed his arm, noticing that he had some sort of tool inserted in the door lock. "What are you doing? That's my car."

"You're trespassing, missy" came the raspy growl as he pulled away from her clutching fingers.

"Get away from my car," she said, her anger overtaking her good sense. He had a slight build and was wearing soiled jeans and a dirty blue shirt. His black hat was pulled down low over his face so all she could see was a grubby chin with a smattering of white whiskers.

Angrily he retrieved his tool and turned to her. "You don't belong here. Go back where you came from before you get hurt." Walking around her, he shuffled away, his gait indicating that he wasn't a young man.

"Wait a minute," Liza said, grabbing his arm again. "Who are you and why were you trying to break into my car?"

Quicker than she'd have thought possible, the man turned and backhanded her across the face, the blow landing hard and catching her off guard. Liza staggered backward, banging her hip against the Mazda's rear fender line. She blinked, trying to focus on his face. She saw him lift his hand to strike her again. Bracing herself, she turned her head and closed her eyes against the expected blow.

It came, harder than the first. She cried out, the pain bouncing from her cheek to the back of her head as it slammed into the Mazda. As she slipped to the ground, she thought she heard a car's engine in the distance before the blackness claimed her.

She heard a voice, echoing as if coming from down a long tunnel. Someone saying her name. Her eyes felt heavy; she struggled to open them, but couldn't quite manage it. There was a feeling of slick dampness, of discomfort. She moved and became aware of pain centered at the back of her head. Her face felt as if it were on fire. A strong hand gripped hers, offering comfort, encouragement.

Liza forced her lids open and saw angry, worried eyes watching her. J.D. was frowning down at her, his features grim. "Where am I?" she asked, sounding like a television show cliché even to her own ears. Her gaze moved past his bent head and she saw a ceiling close above her and felt soft leather beneath her. A car.

"You're in my van," he said, verifying her guess. "I found you lying on the ground by your car." He banked the rage he felt, but just barely. "Someone did a real number on you. Who was it?" he asked, the cop in him needing to know almost as much as the man.

She tried to sit up, but her head throbbed. "I wish I knew." She reached a hand to her stinging cheeks, touching gingerly. "Oh, that hurts."

J.D. guessed that the guy had slapped her, not lightly but hard enough to leave angry red marks on both her cheeks. Apparently she'd fallen against the Mazda, bumped her head and passed out. "I saw a truck race off as I drove up, but he was already too far away for me to see his plates. Did you get the number, by any chance?"

"No. It was a white pickup, engine running, facing my car with no license plates in front." Liza finally managed to shift to a sitting position, and reached shaky fingers to explore the bump on her head. It wasn't too bad, but her hair was wet and gritty from where she'd fallen.

He straightened, allowing her more room. He'd picked her up and put her in the van, out of the rain. She'd scared the hell out of him. He'd have gone after the guy who did this to her, and probably would have had him by now, but he couldn't leave her lying in the rain and dirt. "How about the man? Did you get a good look at him?" If he hit her in the face, she must have seen him.

Liza was adjusting her turquoise blouse, noticing that it was wet and streaked with dirt. Her slacks were a muddy mess, too. "Not really. He wore a black hat pulled down on his face."

Now that he was sure she'd be all right, he had questions, unanswered questions, lots of them. "Your car is locked. I'm trying to figure out what you were doing here and why this guy attacked you."

She brushed her hair back off her face, the movement costing her. "I was looking for something in the woods." She caught the disapproving look on his face. "I know, it was probably stupid. Anyhow, I'd locked my car and walked along the narrow path back there." Through the window, she could see the rain falling hard now, and she felt chilled. "It was only drizzling then and I was gone but a few minutes. When I came back, this man was trying to jimmy my car door. I grabbed him and told him to get lost."

There it was again, that feistiness that he'd recognized the day he'd met her. "One of these days, you're going to get seriously hurt. Don't you know better than to challenge a hood trying to break into your car?"

"He wasn't a hood who just happened along. He seemed to know who I was. He told me I didn't belong here and to go back where I came from."

"Did you recognize him?"

"No. He seemed older, with gray stubble, and he didn't walk like a young man. I'm sure I've never seen him before."

Her description of the man and his own glimpse of the white truck, vague though they both were, made J.D. think the man sounded like Clarence Hobbs, a man who'd worked for Lester for years. He'd go have a talk with Clarence, J.D. decided, though he had a feeling that the crafty old man would have half a dozen witnesses swearing he'd been miles from here all day. As angry as he was, perhaps he could get Clarence to open up.

Years ago, there'd been some talk about unions trying to organize Fleming Construction workers, and Lester had hired Clarence and a couple of other shady characters to discourage his men from joining. Their tactics hadn't followed the letter of the law by a long shot, but they'd worked. Lester had kept the unions out and kept Clarence on his payroll all this time, using him for occasional persuasion when someone was a little too slow in paying, and the like. J.D. was aware of their connection, but could never prove anything. Witnesses against Lester were few and far between, because of the power he held in Pine Bluff.

But why would Lester have put Clarence on Liza's tail? he wondered. The man had been rude that night at the Apollo, but J.D. had dismissed his behavior as a general crabbiness. Perhaps there was more here than he'd suspected.

He heard Liza's suppressed groan and shifted his attention back to her. "I think I should take you to the hospital and have that bump looked at." He'd examined it before she'd awakened and it hadn't seemed all that bad, but she could have a concussion.

"No, I'm all right. Really." Or she would be if only she could stop shaking. Damn, but she hated J.D. to see her like this.

Like hell she was all right. "Why don't you just lie back and I'll take you to my place?" he asked, needing to keep an eye on her, knowing she would fight him all the way.

"I'll be fine. I want to get back to my room to clean up." She reached for the door handle, but quickly closed her eyes on a sharp stab of pain.

"I don't think you should go to Bisbee's just now." He'd been more than a little skeptical about all she'd been telling him regarding her search. But this attack changed his opinion. Despite the fact that he was in his fifties, Clarence Hobbs was a barely disguised hired hood. Liza had apparently ruffled someone's feathers or he wouldn't have been told to go after her. "It's getting late and it's pouring down rain. You can clean up at my place. I'm taking you home with me and that's it."

Despite her injuries, her temper flared. "There you go again, bossing me around."

It galled him, but he rephrased his order into a request. "*Please* come home with me and let me take care of you."

"Well, since you asked so nicely." She waved a trembling hand toward her Mazda, still parked where she'd left it. "My car. I can't leave it here." Not in front of Lester Fleming's house. She had this odd feeling that that unfriendly man had something to do with her attack.

"I'll radio my deputy to come get it and drive it to my place." He'd already contacted his other deputy, Eddie Reynolds, before she'd awakened, telling him to keep his eyes peeled for a white pickup, though he hadn't had much to go on. The way the truck had hightailed it down the road when he'd caught sight of J.D.'s van told him that the driver had been up to no good. Of course, J.D. knew that Clarence had probably hurried to the location of his alibi, even if Eddie had gotten lucky and come across the old geezer.

Liza let out a ragged sigh, her head hurting too much to comment. "Would you get my purse from the front seat please?" She dug in her pocket for her keys and handed them to him. Besides, the last thing she wanted to do was drive feeling as she did, and then walk into Bisbee's looking as if she'd been run over by a bus. She could just hear Ethel telling her she'd better go on home where she'd be safer.

Why were so many people so anxious to get her out of Pine Bluff?

She lay huddled in the back seat as the vehicle raced along in the rain at J.D.'s usual breakneck speed, bouncing and bumping, the seat belt keeping her from rolling to the floor. It had hit her moments after he'd started up, the fear that she should have felt earlier. Someone had actually hit her, not once but twice. Lord only knew what he'd have done, this total stranger, if J.D. hadn't happened along.

She couldn't control the shudders that had her body trembling so hard she had to press a fist to her mouth to keep him from hearing the sobs threatening to break free. Why, for God's sake, she wanted to know, was someone trying to harm her? What had she done but ask a few questions? Who in this crazy town was so afraid of what she'd learn that they'd hire someone to slap her around?

Liza had never been exposed to physical violence on a personal level. She'd never even been spanked as a child. The remembered helplessness she'd just experienced flooded her, and she cringed, hating the feeling. She should have asked J.D. to take her back to Bisbee's to the privacy of her room where she could work her way through this humiliation alone. But privacy in a small town, she was beginning to learn, was a precious commodity.

Closing her eyes, Liza prayed they'd reach J.D.'s house soon and that he'd leave her alone until she had herself under control.

In the rearview mirror, J.D. saw her trembling, cowering, pulling into herself, and knew she was reliving the attack. He'd seen it before, many times—delayed reaction. Swearing under his breath, he pressed down on the accelerator, and the van raced along the wet, nearly deserted road leading to his home.

First he had to take care of her. She needed him now, especially since she had no other friend in town. Then, while she was resting, he'd get on the phone and track down the coward who'd hit her, then had run away like the rat he was. J.D.'s hands curled around the steering wheel as his eyes blazed. Right now he'd like five minutes alone with that rat Clarence, if in fact he had been the attacker. Either way, he'd find the man and make him pay.

He pulled the van up alongside the steps leading to his front stoop. The rain had turned into a downpour, but he scarcely noticed. He got out, hurried around and opened the back door as she struggled to sit up. "Can you walk?" Maybe he should just carry her and ask questions later.

"Yes," she answered, determined to make it on her own. She couldn't give in to the weakness. She took hold of his hands, though, and stepped out, leaning on him only a little as they moved to the door. Once inside, her knees threatened to buckle and she reached out for him.

J.D. caught her up in his arms and carried her to his long leather couch facing a bank of windows. That's when he noticed that the moisture on her face was from tears, not rain as he'd been thinking. He pushed back the white-hot fury that gripped him as he sat down and gathered her to him.

"I'll...I'll mess up your couch," she muttered through half sobs. "I'm all dirty and wet and..."

"Will you just be still and let me hold you?" he said, his voice low and soft, trying for reassurance. He knew what shock could do to someone and he badly wanted to ease hers.

He was being so damn nice and she was such a mess. She didn't want him to see her fall apart, but there seemed no way out. "Oh, God, J.D.," she said, her breath shuddering out. "He wanted to hurt me. He..."

"Shh, now. Don't think about it." Carefully he angled her head so it rested against his chest, his hands caressing her back. He felt her hot tears through his shirt and gentled his touch. He didn't know what to say, so he kept still, just holding her, letting her cry it out. He waited until the tremors had quieted, until the hiccuping sobs had ceased.

At last, the worst of it was over and Liza pulled back, swiping at her flaming cheeks. "I'm sorry. I didn't mean to—"

He stopped her with a kiss, a light touching of lips, wanting to show her it was okay. When he looked at her, he saw she seemed startled.

"How could you want to kiss me? I must look a sight with my hair all dirty and my face..." She touched her cheeks, then dropped her hands. "Is it really terrible?"

He smiled then, realizing she was better if her looks were capturing her attention. "No, not terrible. Just a little red, but that will fade." He raised a hand to gently push back a fall of hair. "And, for your information, every time I look at you, I want to kiss you."

She frowned in disbelief. "Even now when..."

He nodded emphatically. "Even now." To prove his point, he kissed her again.

Her head still ached, but she felt better, despite having sobbed all over him. Straightening, she set her feet on the floor and looked at her clothes. "I need to clean up."

J.D. stood. "Come on. I'll show you to the bath. Think you can manage to shower alone?"

She shot him a look, despite her wobbly walk. "Definitely." If she had to hold on to the walls, she'd manage alone.

He left her in his bathroom with clean towels and his terry-cloth robe, the only thing he could think of to give her to wear. "Just yell if you need me," he said, then grinned when she sent him another cool look.

She managed to shower and carefully wash her hair, standing under the water a long while. But after drying off and wrapping herself in J.D.'s robe, she'd totally depleted her energy. As she walked through his adjoining bedroom, she stopped to study his huge bed covered in a thick navy quilt. It looked too inviting to resist.

Just for a minute or two, she thought, lying down. Inhaling the scent of his after-shave clinging to his robe, she fell immediately asleep.

It was dim in the room when she awoke and she felt disoriented. Not frightened, just uncertain for a moment where she was. Someone had placed a plaid blanket over her. Looking around, she recognized the room she'd seen only briefly on her way through to shower.

It was nice. Upstairs, the floor-to-ceiling windows would offer a wonderful view in the daytime, she was sure. Planked flooring covered by a large area rug in shades of blue and beige. Heavy dark furniture, a corduroy easy chair and ottoman, a whimsical mobile with dangling Holstein cows. There was an adobe fireplace in one corner flanked by recessed bookcases, each shelf brimming over, paperback and hardcover volumes tucked among carved wooden figures. J.D. was apparently a reader and a collector of Gray's work.

Slowly she got to her feet, pleased that the headache was gone. In the bathroom mirror, she saw that her cheeks had lost most of their redness, and she paused to brush out her hair. Looking about, she couldn't see her clothes anywhere. Picking up her purse, she left the room, making her way down the winding stairway.

She found him reading the newspaper on the couch in the big room with a wall of windows, a fire blazing in the grate in the far corner lending a nice glow. He'd changed into clean jeans and a white T-shirt, and kept his feet bare. He must have heard her, for he turned, tossed aside the paper and smiled up at her. "Feeling better?"

He saw that her face had lost that battered redness, and her eyes were bright once more.

"Much." She walked to the opposite corner of the couch, sitting down and pulling up her legs, all but lost in the folds of his navy robe. "Sorry I passed out on you."

"You needed the rest. I threw your clothes in the washer. They'll be dry soon. Are you hungry? I'm a fair cook."

She shook her head. "I wouldn't mind a cup of tea, though."

"Coming right up."

She gazed about while he went to fix her tea, pleased with the warmth, the hominess of his house. The masculine cut of the furniture, the sturdy fabrics he'd chosen, suited him. He'd turned on a yard light in the back and she saw that it was still raining, big drops splashing into a pool she could see off to one side and onto the sloping lawn that flowed into a thick copse of trees. She heard the clock chime seven and was surprised she'd slept nearly two hours.

"Try this," J.D. said, setting down a cup of steaming brew on the end table nearest her. He sat down again, a bit closer this time.

She looked so small, huddled in his big robe, so vulnerable with her face washed clean and her hair smelling of his shampoo. "You scared me, lady."

Her eyes met his and stayed. "Thank you for coming along when you did. How did you happen to be there?"

"I was looking for you." He stretched out his legs to the coffee table and took her hand, wrapping it in his. "I was finished for the day and called you. Ethel said you'd been gone for some time, but she didn't know where. So I started driving around. I don't know what made me drive down Laurel Lane."

She squeezed his hand. "Whatever it was, I'm glad you did. I apologize, though, for weeping all over you and then falling asleep on your bed." She picked up the cup and took a sip.

"No need."

He'd laced the tea with whiskey, using a heavy hand. It warmed a path all the way down. "I see you've slipped in a surprise. Trying to ply me with alcohol, Sheriff?"

He smiled. "Whatever works." His thumb rubbed along the tender skin of her wrist and he felt her pulse skitter. "What exactly were you doing taking a walk in those woods, Liza?" The question had been bothering him all the while she'd slept.

She set down her cup, knowing he'd probably find out if she didn't tell him. He seemed to know what everyone in town was doing at any given moment. So she told him of her visit to Roseanne Mitchell and their odd conversation, and of her decision to find the bent pine from the painting she'd bought.

"Aren't you carrying this sleuthing a little far? You could have gotten seriously hurt, or been hauled in on trespassing charges. That was Lester Fleming's house you were in front of and—"

"I know. Roseanne told me the tree was behind his home." She ran a hand through her hair, pushing it back. "In retrospect, it was a dumb move, I guess. But Roseanne puzzles me. I think she was madly in love once, and I don't think it was with her ex-husband."

"And you think you were the result of her mad love affair?" J.D. had trouble keeping his expression free of reproach. "You're such a romantic."

"Maybe I am, but you have to admit, it's possible." She told him again about revisiting the library and the early pictures of Roseanne that resembled her own youthful snapshots.

"There were probably half a dozen other young girls in that book who resembled you, if you took the time to look closely."

She wasn't going to convince him, so she decided to shift the focus. "Tell me more about Gray Eubanks. He mentioned that he worked at several ranches in the area as a young man. Did he ever speak to you about someone he cared for back then?"

Knowing her to be a dyed-in-the-wool sentimentalist, he might have realized she'd have picked up on some of the things Gray had said that evening, rearranging them into her own romantic scenario. "You mean the strawberry blonde he mentioned? He's mentioned her occasionally through the years, even getting quite melancholy after a couple of glasses of wine. I know he met her on a dude ranch where he worked one summer, in Wickenburg, I believe."

"What happened to break them up?"

"As Gray told you, she left abruptly, in the middle of the night. The next day, one of the other hands gave him a message from her, telling him she had to leave and that he mustn't try to find her."

"I can't believe he didn't go looking for her. He appears to be still very much in love with her."

"I understand why. Like Gray said, he didn't have much to offer her. I gather she came from money. A man with nothing in his pockets would have a hard time going after a rich girl."

"Perhaps, but what about later? He's well-off now and..."

"And he can't walk. He's been in a wheelchair for twenty years. I can also understand why he wouldn't seek out a woman, feeling as he does about his limitations."

"That's ridiculous," Liza stated firmly. "A woman doesn't fall in love with a man for his two good legs. What makes him think that that young woman, older now, isn't also sitting around wishing he were with her? The only things in life that we truly regret are the risks we don't take. Ask any old person."

Studying her, J.D. nodded knowingly. "I see where you're going with this. You think Gray met Roseanne Fleming years ago, that she's the one he still cares for. And you also think that they might be your biological parents. Am I right?"

Liza crossed her arms over her chest, feeling defensive, certain he was going to blow her theory out of the water. "I say that it's certainly possible."

"Ridiculous." J.D. got to his feet, moving to stir up the fire. "I know Gray very well. He never would have lived thirty miles from the woman he loves and not gone to see her, handicap or not. He's a risk taker, a man who puts his money where his mouth is. If she'd have turned from him, he'd have handled it.''

"You said a moment ago that you understood why a man wouldn't seek out an old love if he feels he's impaired.''

J.D. jabbed at the logs with the poker, then tossed on another before turning back to her. "That was in theory. In fact, Gray would.'' He walked closer to her, stood looking down into her large blue eyes, wishing they'd never gotten started on this. "I think you badly want to find *someone* you can call a parent and you're grabbing at straws. Roseanne Fleming can't have children. If Gray knew the woman he cared about was nearby, he'd have gone to her. You've picked on the wrong pair.''

"I don't think so.'' Stubbornly she held on to her theory.

J.D. held on to his temper, just barely. "Listen, I think you better drop this whole parent search before you wind up with more than a couple of slaps and a bump on the head. The man who hit you was trying to get into your car. Have you asked yourself what he was after? I doubt that he was a random thief. Could it be that he was after something in your purse, something he didn't find when he searched your room? Maybe that little black box and your adoption papers?''

Her eyes had grown wide, frightened. "There's nothing revealing in the papers, and why would anyone want an old diary, a child's chain and an acorn ring?''

"If we knew that, we'd probably know who that bum is working for. However, since they don't know what you have in your purse, they may just be fishing.'' He had his suspicions about all this, but couldn't come up with a solid motive. However, he was certain of one thing: the man who'd biffed her around hadn't been fooling.

J.D. sat down beside her, taking her hand again. "I think this has gone on long enough. I think you should end this search. Surely finding your birth parents isn't worth your life?"

"You can't honestly think my life is in danger, can you?"

The loud ringing of the doorbell had them both swiveling.

Chapter Eight

Shaking the rain from his hat, Deputy Eddie Reynolds stood on J.D.'s stoop holding out the keys to Liza's car. "I parked the Mazda in the carport, J.D."

A thought occurred to J.D., something that might settle the discussion he and Liza seemed to be on opposite sides of. "Come in a minute, Eddie," he invited.

The deputy glanced out toward his tan Blazer pulled up behind the van, engine running. "Richie's waiting. I had him follow me so I'd have a ride back."

"This won't take long." He drew the older man inside, walking him over to where Liza sat looking at them over the back of the couch. Eddie was in his late fifties, a widower and a lifelong resident of Pine Bluff who knew the history of most all its residents.

Quickly J.D. introduced the two of them. "Eddie, you know the Flemings fairly well, don't you?" he asked.

"Hell, J.D., everyone for miles around knows old Lester."

"How about Roseanne?"

Eddie twirled his damp hat in strong, wiry fingers. "Her, too. Mighty fine woman. Nice to everyone." He squinted at J.D. "Why the questions? You know them same as me."

"But not as long as you. Did you ever hear of Roseanne, back when she was a teenager, let's say, running around with some young fellow she was real crazy about?" He noticed that Liza had angled around and was watching Eddie closely.

Eddie ran a hand over his curly gray hair. "No one special, that I recollect. She was on the wild side back then, her and the kids she ran with. I remember Lester really had his hands full with her. She never seemed to cozy up to no local boy I know of."

Liza propped an elbow on the couch back. "Would you know if she ever went away to a dude ranch, maybe one in Wickenburg?" she asked.

Eddie brightened, pleased to be finally able to come up with a positive answer. "She sure did, worked there two summers in a row. Can't remember the name of it offhand, but Lester was pals with the owner. They'd known each other for years and he made sure the guy kept close tabs on his daughter."

Liza felt elated, her eyes locking with J.D.'s. "I rest my case."

Confused, Eddie looked from one to the other. "Is something wrong with Roseanne?"

"No," J.D. assured him. "We were just having a discussion." He wasn't happy about what he'd just learned, but he was beginning to think Liza might have stumbled onto something. If she was right, Lester wasn't going to be easy to handle. "I heard that she got real sick one year, didn't even go on to college. Did you ever learn what ailed her?"

Eddie shook his head. "Ain't nobody who knows. Lots of guesses, some talk. But you know most folks clam up when something concerns Lester, for fear they'll lose their jobs or whatever. Probably Miz Sparks would know. She took care of Roseanne back then. And Doc Rogers. We used to see him coming and going to the house."

"How long did Roseanne's illness last?" Liza wanted to know.

"'Bout a year, I'd say. Maybe a little longer. She never went nowhere all that time, then suddenly, she was marrying the Mitchell boy. Seemed odd but no one said much about it. Lester has a temper, I can tell you, especially when it comes to his daughter."

A year or more, long enough to have a baby and recover. Liza clamped down on her rising excitement. She had a strong feeling that she was on the right track.

J.D. rubbed the back of his neck. He'd thought he'd shore up his argument by having Eddie knock her theory out of the water. Instead, he'd added fuel to the fire. "Did you get a bead on Clarence Hobbs?"

Eddie replaced his hat. "I couldn't find him nowhere till about half an hour ago. Spotted his white pickup parked behind Sal's Barbecue. Sure enough, he was inside. Him and two other guys swear he's been with them since noon, playing pool. He's a slick one, old Clarence is."

"Okay, Eddie. Thanks a lot for bringing the Mazda back." He walked to the door with his deputy. "And I'd appreciate it if you'd keep this conversation to yourself for now till I get a few things straightened out."

"Sure thing, boss." With a wave to Liza, Eddie left.

Liza waited until he joined her on the couch. "Who's Clarence Hobbs?"

He might as well tell her since she could find out from most anyone in town. "He works for Lester doing odd jobs."

"And he owns a white pickup." She touched his arm. "Do you believe my theory now? Roseanne got pregnant at that dude ranch in Wickenburg that summer, came home and her father had a raging fit. Lester Fleming isn't a man I'd want to confess that sort of problem to. He kept her home during the pregnancy, lied to everyone that she was sick, then gave the baby to Ethel to have adopted out. That baby was me. Lester's probably the one who scared off my father, or hired someone to do it for him. And now he's got his henchman, Clarence Hobbs, trying to scare me off."

J.D. still wasn't altogether convinced. "Certainly seems reasonable, but there's something I can't figure in here. If things did fall like that, maybe Lester didn't want your father poking around because along about the time Ralph Parker visited Pine Bluff, Roseanne was married and maybe he didn't want to upset the apple cart. But why does he want to run you off? Roseanne's single now, even lonely, as you mentioned earlier. You'd be his granddaughter, for heaven's sake. Why wouldn't he want to get to know his own flesh and blood when all he's got left is Roseanne?"

Liza thought that over. "You have a point. I can't imagine why Lester would still be upset over something that happened nearly thirty years ago. Unless he hates the man who fathered me, or has a problem with his family."

J.D. felt as if he were stepping into quicksand with this one. Never in a million years would he believe that Gray would have walked away from a child he'd fathered. Still, both Roseanne and Gray being at the Wickenburg dude ranch that summer seemed too coincidental to ignore. "If your father is Gray, he couldn't have known he'd gotten Roseanne pregnant. And I doubt that Lester knew the father's identity back then. Gray moved around a lot and didn't exactly hobnob in the same circle as the wealthy Flemings until much later. So why is Lester still not able to accept a granddaughter?"

"Maybe Roseanne lied and told him someone else was the father."

"Could be." He moved closer, reaching out to touch her hair, to stroke her cheek with the backs of his fingers. "Are you still sure you want to pursue this? I don't think your troubles are over with the Flemings. If Lester feels his back is to the wall, he'll strike out again and again."

Liza sighed, threading her fingers through his. "I imagine you're right. And I know you don't want me to go on with this. But please understand, J.D., I *have* to do this."

"Even if I ask you not to?"

"Please don't ask me."

"What if you find neither one wants you?"

She studied their hands locked together. "That would be hard." She raised her eyes to his. "Roseanne's a puzzle to me yet, but do you honestly believe that if I could prove to Gray that I'm his daughter, he'd turn me away?" She'd only met him once, but her impression had been that he was a strong, caring man.

J.D. examined his heart. "No, I don't."

She smiled slowly. "Then don't fight me. Help me."

"You're very persuasive." He leaned in, his mouth settling on the pulse point at her throat.

Liza felt heat race up her spine, and it had nothing to do with the blazing fire across the room. "You're not so bad at persuasion yourself." She felt him moving up, nipping at her neck; then his lips took hers. She curled her arms around him.

His hands traveled to thrust into her hair, and he heard her quick intake of breath. He remembered her bruise and groaned out an apology, gentling his touch. Then she molded her body to his as he shifted their positions on the couch, and the breath backed up in his lungs.

Blood pounded in his head and pooled much lower. Amazed at his own fierce need for her, he deepened the kiss. The damn robe was bunched between them, frustrating him. Tunneling a hand in, he loosened the belt while his mouth made love to hers. Then he spread the opening and leaned back. Firelight danced on her skin, turning her golden. Her face was damp from the blaze, her eyes registering the first stages of sensual awakening. He drew in a shaky breath.

Liza raised her hand to pull the robe over her breasts, then stopped as she saw the darkening passion in his eyes as he looked his fill. She felt the warmth of his gaze touch her deep inside, and a melting began, one she'd never experienced quite like this before.

J.D. lifted a hand and curled it around one breast, all the while watching her eyes as if seeking permission. He saw them mist over and heard a soft sigh escape from her parted lips as he caressed her swollen flesh. Then he lowered his head and touched his mouth to her, and she moaned out loud.

Soaring. He had her deliciously soaring as he drew on her. Feelings she'd longed to feel rose to the surface and overflowed. She found her hands in his hair and wondered when they'd moved there as she pressed his head closer, closer. Ah, the sweet joy of it, the almost painful pleasure of it.

Hadn't she guessed, hadn't she somehow known that there was more than she'd so far experienced? She'd found him, found the one who could unleash all the wildness she'd been saving for the right someone. But her life was so disorderly right now, her heritage still unknown, her plans all up in the air.

But tonight, she wouldn't think of all that. She wouldn't think at all, just feel. And, oh, he had her feeling so much as his clever hands roamed her back, his wonderful mouth moved back to hers and his tongue coaxed hers into sharing another dance.

J.D. lifted his head to look at her, saw the stain of arousal pinkening her cheeks. But he'd never liked loose ends and needed to clear up one. "This man, the one in Tucson. Does he see himself somewhere in your future?"

Surprised that he'd thought of that, she would be honest. "Perhaps. But I don't see him there."

He needed to zero in, to hear it all. "Why not?"

"Because since coming here, all I see is you." Her arms around him tightened. "All I want is you."

It was what he needed to hear. He slipped the robe from her shoulders and bared all of her to his hungry eyes.

"Things are a little too one-sided here," she told him as she struggled to pull his shirt off over his head, then tossed it onto the floor. He let her work his belt loose while his work-roughened hands skimmed over her body, leaving her all but whimpering. Her fingers were shaky, clumsy, and the zipper wouldn't budge. "Help me," she all but begged.

"Uh-uh. Anything worth having is worth working for," he said into her neck in a husky whisper.

Two could play that game, she decided, and instead slipped a hand beneath his waistband, into his briefs, and closed around him. She heard the breath huff from him just before he reared back and shoved off the rest of his clothes, all but tearing them free. Returning to her, he trailed openmouthed kisses down her slim, sleek body, then returned to capture her mouth and steal her breath as her fingers frantically kneaded his shoulders.

He'd wanted to make love to her slowly, with soft music playing and clean, cool sheets beneath them while the moon drifted into his bedroom, bathing them in silvery light. He'd imagined the scene, dreamed it even, repeatedly since meeting her. But slow wasn't on the bill tonight and romance would have to wait for another day. They were instead tangled together on the soft leather of his couch, seconds away from exploding. He was too desperate to have her to slow down, too obsessed with her to take the time to carry her upstairs.

Again, he knelt back, drinking in her beauty, the way her tousled hair lay spread out around her lovely face, her blue eyes dark and aware and on him. A log shifted and crackled in the grate, and still she watched, waiting.

His gaze locked with hers, he reached to touch her, and felt her arch toward him. She made a sound deep in her throat as he stroked her, aroused beyond belief at the abandoned way she let the feelings take her. Her search for pleasure was as intense as her quest for her parents, he thought. As the explosion shook her, he bent closer to take her mouth, swallowing her soft sounds of completion.

From the beginning, Liza had suspected what his touch would do to her. What she hadn't suspected was what hers would do to him. Now she felt him tremble as he gazed down at her, the strain of holding back etched on his darkly handsome face. Reaching, she took him inside her, and heard his low groan as he adjusted to her.

Like lovers perfectly attuned from years of practice, they found the rhythm quickly. Outside, the wind whistled and moaned, the rain dashed against the windows and the sky rumbled and flashed. Inside, two lovers were lost together in a storm of their own making.

Liza wasn't a bit sleepy, just drowsy and replete. And her right arm was nearly numb from where it was squished between her body and the couch back. Though she hated to move, she knew it was time. She smoothed back J.D.'s hair from his face and kissed his forehead. "I think we should get up. I can't feel my one arm."

"I can't feel either arm, nor both legs. Did you get the number of that truck?"

She smiled. "Packed a wallop, didn't it?"

"You can say that again." He edged back, then rolled onto the carpeted floor, pulling her down on top of him, listening to her yelp of surprise. "That better?"

"Mmm," she murmured, flexing her right hand.

He tucked her head under his chin. "Why don't we take a little nap?"

She gave an exaggerated sigh. "Just like a man. A little exertion and he's wiped out."

In one swift movement, he rolled her onto her back and shifted their positions, nearly bumping into the long oak coffee table. "I'll show you who's wiped out." He kissed her deeply, thoroughly.

The kiss went on and on, kindling a spark quickly when just moments ago, Liza had thought she'd not be interested again for hours. It went on so long that in no time she felt movement between them, down low. "Now, look what you've done."

"No, look what *you've* done. I was ready to nap." He nibbled on her neck, well aware that sleep came in a distant second compared to making love to Liza. Once was definitely not enough.

"How could I have done that?" she asked, feigning innocence. "I didn't even touch you."

Suddenly he was serious, surprising himself. "You don't have to touch me. You don't even have to look at me, or be with me. Since meeting you, all I have to do is think about you, and I want you."

"I want you, too, J.D.," she told him, matching his mood.

"Don't let it get around, but I'm nuts about you, lady."

"Ditto."

The clock chose that moment to chime the hour. Liza frowned. "It's late. I should go." She stroked back the hair that fell onto his forehead, reluctant to end this evening.

"Stay the night, Liza. I want you to."

"I want to, as well," she said, and realized it was true. "But I can't. Pine Bluff's a small town and my car's right outside. I'm already not well thought of around here. If people started saying that I'm spending nights with their sheriff, it wouldn't help me get any answers. They'd probably run me out of town."

He hated admitting it, but she was probably right. He trailed a hand along her cheek, loving the satin smoothness of her skin. "But don't leave just yet." He pressed into her, letting her know how badly he wanted her again.

She wanted him just as much. What would another hour matter? Picking up his hand, she laced her fingers with his. "Maybe we should try this again, just in case the first time was a fluke."

"Yeah. I love a challenge." He lowered his head to kiss her.

Liza waited two days, but couldn't wait another minute. She simply had to force some action. On a bright, sunny afternoon, she drove down Laurel Lane again, glancing at the cardboard box on the passenger seat. It wiggled and squirmed, and small snuffling sounds came from within. She smiled as she stopped her car in front of Roseanne's house.

As she'd hoped, Roseanne was in her garden again. Quickly Liza got out, walked around and tugged the box out, clutching it to her. Moving carefully, she strolled to where Roseanne sat, painting at her easel, and smiled when the woman looked up at her. "Hi. I've brought you a present."

Roseanne's slow smile lit up her face. "For me? What's the occasion?" She wiped her hands and placed her brush to soak.

"No occasion. Just a thanks because your paintings give me so much pleasure. And because I thought you might like him."

"Him?" Roseanne stood, peering into the box Liza held. "Oh!" she squealed.

Liza set the box on the wrought iron bench and picked up the small white terrier puppy wearing a red plaid collar.

"Oh, he's adorable," Roseanne said, her hands fairly itching to hold the wiggly bundle.

Liza handed him over, glad that she seemed pleased. She'd taken a heck of a chance, not knowing Roseanne all that well. "You'd mentioned the other day that you had a dog once, so I thought I'd replace Scrappy for you." She ruffled the soft fur. "The pet shop owner in Carefree where I went to get him said that his name is Max, but you can change that. He's two months old and *almost* housebroken."

The puppy was madly licking Roseanne's chin as she held him up close to her face. "He's wonderful. Thank you so much, Liza." Roseanne blinked back a sudden rush of tears.

Liza sat down, placing the box on the ground. "I've got a food-and-water dish in here, a leash and a couple of chew toys. And he's had his shots."

Roseanne scarcely heard, she was so busy getting acquainted. Bending down, she let the puppy loose, then laughed as he ran around between the plants and flowering bushes, smelling each, sprinkling a few. But he scampered back to the two women every little while before dashing off again.

Sitting back down, Roseanne kept watching the dog. "What a treat!" She shifted to study Liza. "Why are you so nice to me?"

The question took her aback, so childlike was it. She answered with her first thought. "Because I like you."

Her cheeks flushed, Roseanne reached to touch Liza's hand. "I like you, too. I want to give you something in return. You can choose another of my paintings. I don't have much else to offer."

"I don't want anything from you, Roseanne. Just friendship." Which wasn't exactly so. She also wanted the truth and wondered if she could win the confidence of this soft-spoken woman. "So, does Max remind you of the dog you had years ago?"

"Yes, some." She watched the puppy chase a butter-fly, falling over his own feet, and laughed lightheartedly, a musical sound.

Gray had mentioned that the young woman he'd known had had a wonderful laugh. Could Roseanne be that woman? Could she be Liza's mother? Enchanted with the puppy, the haunted expression seemed to leave Roseanne's face, yet Liza couldn't help wondering what had put it there. "What did you say happened to Scrappy?"

Roseanne frowned. "I'm not sure. He ran into the woods and disappeared."

Liza thought it best to stay clear of a discussion of the woods. She decided to hit to the heart of the matter in-stead. "I understand there are some really nice dude ranches up this way. Could you recommend one?"

Roseanne shook her head. "No, but you mentioned knowing J.D. He gets around a lot. You could ask him."

"Then you've never visited a dude ranch?"

Roseanne's face, when she turned it to Liza, was open and guileless. "Why, no, I haven't. What made you think I had?"

Disappointed and confused, Liza shrugged. "I guess I just thought, living near them, you might have worked there, like one summer in your teens?"

She shook her head. "My father was pretty strict. He didn't let me go too far. A couple of my friends went, but he always made me stay home. We...we fought a lot back then."

Liza could well imagine. Studying Roseanne's face, she came to the conclusion that the woman was being truth-ful. That shot down her theory but good. She hated let-ting go when she'd felt so certain she'd finally figured things out. Perhaps another approach. "J.D. took me riding the other day to the Flying D Ranch in Palo Verde. Do you like horses?''

Roseanne stooped down, rubbing the puppy's tummy as he lay on his back loving the attention. "I do. I used to ride quite a bit, when I was young.''

"Maybe you know Gray Eubanks, the man who owns the Flying D? He's a close friend of J.D.'s.''

Without hesitation, Roseanne shook her head. "I don't believe so. The name's not familiar. Dad probably knows him. Dad knows everyone.''

How very odd, Liza thought. She couldn't be that good an actress and, besides, what reason would she have to lie to Liza? If Roseanne had never worked on a dude ranch and didn't know Gray, she was back to square one. With a discouraged sigh, she rose. "I'd better be going. I hope you enjoy the puppy.''

"Thank you so much for Max.'' Roseanne scooped up the white ball of fur, cuddling him to her as she walked with Liza to her car parked on the street. "I hope you'll come back and see us soon. How about lunch one day? We can eat on the patio and...''

Roseanne looked up at the sound of a car rapidly approaching. The long white Cadillac came to a screeching halt alongside where they stood, and the driver quickly lowered the passenger window.

"Hi, Dad,'' Roseanne said.

Lester Fleming's face was red with rage as he glared at his daughter. "What's *she* doing here?''

Seemingly oblivious to his unpleasant mood, Roseanne smiled. "Oh, do you know Liza Parker? She brought me a present.'' She held up Max to show him. "Isn't he adorable?''

His angry blue eyes shifted to Liza. "Missy, you go on home and leave us alone. You got no business around here."

She'd had about enough of this bully's tactics. "Mr. Fleming, I can't imagine what quarrel you have with me since we've scarcely met, but I assure you, I mean your family no harm."

Lester shifted his unlit cigar to the other side of his mouth. "The hell you say. You pack up your fancy designer duds and get on out of my town. We don't want you here, you understand?"

My town, indeed. "No, I don't understand. Please explain why I make you so unreasonably angry." J.D. would undoubtedly not approve of her stand, but that was just too bad. She'd never in her life run into someone who'd decided he didn't like her before meeting her.

"Dad," Roseanne said, sounding embarrassed, "Liza's my friend. Why are you being so nasty to her?"

"Never you mind. Go on in the house, Roseanne." He stabbed the air with a thick finger. "And you listen to me, young lady. You be out of here or I'll call the sheriff and tell him you're harassing us."

Liza's chin raised and her eyes never wavered on his. "I wish you would, Mr. Fleming. When he gets here, I can also file a complaint against Clarence Hobbs, who attacked me in front of your home two days ago. I believe Mr. Hobbs works for you, doesn't he?" She hadn't thought the man's face could get any redder, but it did.

Roseanne, visibly upset and not understanding what was happening, touched Liza's arm. "Maybe you'd better go. Dad has a bad temper."

Liza nodded. "I'm going. And I'm sorry if this upset you."

Uneasily, Roseanne glanced at her father, who'd turned off the engine and was getting out of his car. "It wasn't your fault. I don't know what's gotten into him."

"Roseanne, you come with me," Lester said, stomping off toward her side door.

"I'll see you another time, Roseanne," Liza said, getting into her Mazda. "Take good care of Max."

Roseanne hugged the puppy closer to her as if needing the comfort of a living thing. "Yes, I will." Reluctantly, she turned to follow after her father, her footsteps slow and hesitant.

Driving away, Liza couldn't help thinking about the odd relationship between the Fleming father and daughter. She'd figured out that Roseanne was forty-six, long past the age where a woman should be fearful of her father's wrath. But Roseanne was oddly childlike, frequently vague and gave the impression of being fragile. Yet, when she'd witnessed her interacting with the children at the hospital, she'd appeared confident and almost happy.

What hold did Lester have over poor Roseanne? What was she afraid of? Who was it that she'd loved so fiercely, or had her mind been wandering the other day? Liza didn't think so. She'd had such a loving expression on her face, as if, for a moment, she'd gone back in time to visit a remembered lover.

And the biggest question, did this disturbing twosome have something to do with her birth, despite Roseanne's answers?

Liza pulled into the hospital parking lot. She had another someone to track down and, hopefully, this person would have more positive answers for her.

* * *

In her room on the third floor of Bisbee's Bed &
Breakfast, Liza lay on her bed in the dark watching the
moonlight play across her ceiling as it drifted in through
her open window. Evenings were cool now as autumn
approached, but she welcomed the fresh air. It was only
nine and she wasn't sleepy, just emotionally wrung out.

She'd run into another brick wall after leaving Roseanne. Dr. Stanley Rogers had indeed been the Flemings'
personal physician thirty years ago, she'd learned at the
hospital. He'd retired ten years ago to a new condo in
Sedona where he lived with his wife. She'd obtained the
address and driven there with high hopes, only to discover that Dr. Rogers had died last year.

His widow had been very gracious and had spoken to
her at length about the Flemings. A frail eighty-two, Mrs.
Rogers nevertheless clearly remembered them all, including Anna Fleming, Lester's wife, who'd died from
complications of a second pregnancy, the child still-
born. She remembered parties at the Fleming house, what
a lovely girl Roseanne had been and how protective Lester had been of her.

However, when Liza had casually slipped in an in-
quiry about the year Roseanne had been home ill, Mrs.
Rogers had literally dried up. In a suddenly stern voice,
she'd told Liza that she'd never been one to gossip and
that her husband, may he rest in peace, certainly wouldn't
want her discussing any former patient's illness or health
history. At that, she'd picked up her cane, shoved herself upright and shown Liza to the door.

Lester certainly had this town, even its former residents, in his tightfisted grip, Liza thought as she listened
to a car slowly rumble past, interrupting a cricket's song.

Apparently he inspired undying loyalty. Or was it unending fear?

She longed to talk with J.D., to tell him of her encounters. But when she'd called his office after returning from Sedona, she'd been told he was off at the desert range training his new posse members on gun usage. And, of course, his beeper was out of range. She'd left a message with his younger deputy, Richie White, to have J.D. call her when he returned, although the message was not urgent.

He still hadn't called.

Liza listened to her stomach grumble a protest over not having had dinner. She'd missed the evening meal in the Bisbee dining room and, since Ethel had retired to her quarters, she hadn't wanted to bother her with a request for a piece of fruit or something. She hadn't felt like driving to the diner on Main Street, thinking it was probably closed anyway. The only other place in town was Sal's Bar & Barbecue, which was more saloon than restaurant, and held no appeal to her at all. Missing a meal wasn't going to kill her, although she hadn't had dinner the night before last, either. Of course, she'd been too occupied then with J.D. to give food much thought.

J.D. Liza drew up her legs as warmth spread through her at just the thought of him. That evening, in his arms, had been wonderful. She was falling for him, she knew, falling hard. No words of love or talk of the future had been exchanged. Yet the feelings that had exploded between them, that had been building since the day they'd met, were real and difficult to ignore.

Liza let out a long breath. Was she ready for someone—something—permanent in her life? Was J.D. interested in a serious relationship? *I'm nuts about you,*

he'd told her. But that could have been a throwaway remark, pillow talk. Time would tell.

As for herself, what did she want? First and foremost,
she wanted to clear up this whole mess, to solve the puzzle of who her birth parents were and to establish, if
possible, a relationship with one or both of them. Then
she would have more energy to put into working on a relationship with a man. She would . . .

A rocking explosion from just outside her window had
Liza jumping to her feet. Down below, she could see
black, billowing smoke; then another blast shattered the
quiet evening air. Heart pounding, she shoved open the
window wider and leaned out.

Her beautiful, nearly new Mazda was engulfed in
flames shooting skyward.

Chapter Nine

In her bare feet, Liza took the stairs two at a time, racing down, then through the hallway, nearly colliding with Ethel as she rushed out onto the porch. She stopped short as she saw the flames rapidly engulfing her car, the heat from the curbside inferno reaching all the way to them.

"Good Lord," Gloria whispered, clutching at the folds of her long satin robe, as awestruck as the rest of them. "What in the world happened?"

From the corner of her eye, Liza caught a movement and went to the porch's side railing. The shadowy figure of a man could be seen hobbling off. He wasn't running like a young man, but rather straining from the effort.

Clarence Hobbs, she thought immediately.

At the edge of the porch steps, Ethel watched in horrified fascination. "Dear God, what if someone had been inside?" she muttered, almost to herself. Her hair in curlers, she grasped her chenille robe around her small frame.

Just then, a white pickup roared past, spewing up dust as it hurried on by, the driver looking neither right nor left. Liza didn't have to see his face to know who he was. "Clarence Hobbs," she said, her voice low and angry.

Neighbors from across the street and on both sides were out, watching the blaze, talking in low, frightened whispers. Margaret and Maude peered out through the parlor window, apparently afraid to step outside. Henry Grovener stood just inside the screen, mumbling about youthful gangs and rampant crime spreading even to peaceful small towns.

"Not this time, Henry," Ethel said quietly. Slowly she turned to Liza. "You just couldn't let sleeping dogs lie, could you?"

Though Liza didn't think Ethel expected an answer, she gave her one anyway. "No, I couldn't."

A heart-wrenching sigh escaped from Ethel. "This has gone on long enough. I'll go call the fire department, then J.D. You'd best put something on your feet. It's chilly out here." Pushing past Henry, she walked inside, her shoulders sagging as if she carried the weight of the world on them.

It was the first thoughtful thing she'd said to her, Liza thought, then turned to watch the fire die down and the smoke spiral upward, acrid black and smelling of burning paint, plastics and oil. How could someone do this? Maybe J.D. had been right. Maybe finding her parents wasn't worth the trouble, the pain.

But the next moment, as she listened to red-hot metal popping from the extreme heat, she ground her teeth in anger. If she quit, if she let them run her off, they would win. There had to be an ugly secret buried in this town, and she was convinced that Lester Fleming was at the heart of it. And it had to involve more than her illegitimacy. No one would go to such lengths to keep hidden a birth that took place nearly thirty years ago. There had to be more.

But what? She would find out, hopefully with J.D.'s help. But if not, she'd find out on her own. And expose whoever it was for the damnable coward he was.

In the distance, she heard sirens coming closer. With purposeful strides, Liza hurried upstairs to get her shoes and a sweater.

J.D. tossed his hat onto the van's seat through the open window and ran a weary hand through his hair. Damn, but it had been a long day.

He'd been here nearly two hours after an early-morning trip to Prescott, then eight hours spent on the shooting range. The fire trucks had left and people had finally dispersed, going back to the safety of their homes. J.D. wished he could do the same.

He walked over to stand staring at the blackened wreckage of Liza's Mazda, at the gray water from the hoses running down along the curb. Liza hadn't cried, or even ranted and raved in anger, when he'd arrived. She'd only stood hugging herself in the chill night air, watching her car turn into a smoldering frame and ashes. Eyes bleak, she'd told him she'd seen Clarence Hobbs's truck speeding away shortly after the explosion.

Glancing at his notepad, J.D. frowned. He'd talked with Ethel and each of her guests, interviewed the neighbors and listened to Liza recite all she'd seen and heard. It wasn't a pretty story.

But it was a consistent one. Everyone had mentioned seeing the white truck race by. Gloria had even caught the last three numbers on the license plate: 742. Shortly after arriving, he'd radioed in for Eddie Reynolds to run a check on it with the license bureau, though J.D. was fairly certain what he'd find.

He'd also dispatched Richie to locate Clarence Hobbs. The deputy had driven by Clarence's house and all his known haunts and finally located him. His truck was parked in Lester Fleming's drive and both men swore he'd been there since dinner.

J.D. rubbed the back of his neck. He was vacillating between rage and frustration. Liza's arrival in Pine Bluff had surely opened a hornet's nest. He was enormously grateful that she hadn't been hurt. He was also concerned that he might not be able to prevent the next incident, wherever and whenever it might occur. There seemed to be only one answer.

Shoving his notebook in his shirt pocket, J.D. went back into the house and found Liza alone in the kitchen. The clock on the wall told him it was nearly midnight. He declined her offer of coffee with a shake of his head. "Go up and throw some things in a bag. You're coming with me."

Her huge eyes looked up at him. "You're doing it again, ordering me around."

He swallowed his irritation because he could see the residual shock on her face. "All right, *please* go get your bag." He took hold of her arms and pulled her up and into his embrace. "I won't rest unless you're with me tonight where I'm sure you'll be safe."

His last statement weakened what little resolve she had left to tough this out alone. She could argue, but she didn't have the energy for it. Besides, she'd been frightened enough to want to distance herself from this place. J.D. might not agree with what she was trying to do, but she did feel safe with him. Without another word, she rose and went upstairs to pack a bag.

J.D. put the top on the cheeseburger he'd just finished grilling, set it on a plate, then proceeded to fix the other two before hurrying back through the glass doorwall into his kitchen where Liza was seated at the table. "Getting cold out there," he told her.

She was sipping a glass of wine, which he'd insisted she have, thinking it might relax her. But he could see as he placed her plate in front of her that she was still keyed up, her fingers drumming on the tabletop. He sat down opposite her with his own plate, chugged catsup on his burger, then dug in. After the first bite, he sighed with satisfaction. "I haven't eaten in twelve hours," he confessed.

She hadn't, either, yet she wasn't all that hungry. The events of the evening had diminished her appetite. But, so he wouldn't nag her, she took a bite and was surprised to find how good it tasted. She might even enjoy it if only she could forget the events of the past couple of hours. "Did your men pick up Clarence?"

J.D. fished a pickle out of the open jar. "Not exactly." He told her what Eddie had run into at Lester's.

"Damn it, J.D., are you going to accept still another lie from those two conniving crooks? Gloria got most of his license plate numbers, for goodness' sake. Is this how the law operates around here?" She was ready to boil over with the futility of it all.

"Simmer down. I told you on the way over, we'll get them. We have several witnesses willing to testify to what they saw and heard. But I'm not about to go storming into Fleming's home in the middle of the night and arrest him. His lawyer will have him out before we've had our morning coffee. Lester knows every judge in the county."

"Swell." Liza set down her sandwich, no longer interested in eating. "Then how, exactly, are you going to get him and his hired hoodlum, and when?"

He chewed slowly, letting her cool down, before answering. When he finished his burger, he looked at her. "I will go after them when I get all the facts together." He watched her toy with her wineglass and could feel her disappointment. Probably because he shared it. "I warned you things might get rough."

"Yeah, you did. And I didn't have the good sense to go home where, as everyone in town believes, I certainly belong."

"Not everyone."

She glared at him, needing someone to blame. "Oh, no? You've told me repeatedly to let it be. You warned me I might get hurt if I didn't forget my silly search."

"Didn't tonight prove to you that you could have?"

Liza pushed back her chair, getting to her feet. "See what I mean? You're just like all the rest. You want me to go away so you can sweep this town's dirty little secrets under the rug and go merrily along as if nothing were wrong, as if no one here would ever harm a fly. Well, I won't go away."

She grabbed up her purse. "But I will leave here. I don't want your help. I don't *need* your help, or anyone else's." Turning on her heel, she stomped to the front door and was pulling back the dead bolt when he whirled her around.

"Just where in hell do you think you're going?"

"Away from here. Away from you. You don't really believe me, and I'm sick and tired of being with people who don't. I'll find everything out by myself or ... or die trying." Brave words and she wished she felt half as brave as she hoped she sounded. She yanked open the door. Outside on the stoop, a chilling wind blew her hair about her face. Lord, but it was dark just a few yards beyond the circle of light from the house. A coyote howled in the distance and she shivered in reaction. Maybe she'd been a little hasty.

Stubborn little fool. There was no way he was going to let her tromp off, but he wanted to see if words alone could make her stay. "Don't go, Liza," J.D. said from his stand in the doorway.

She turned around to face him. "Give me just one good reason to stay."

"Because I'm not your enemy, Liza, and because I care about you."

The fight drained out of her in that instant. Searching his eyes, she took a step closer. "What did you say?"

"I'm not your enemy."

"No, no. That other part."

"I said that I care about you, more than I'd planned on." He watched her expression, saw that she wanted to believe him, but was afraid to let herself. He couldn't blame her. He'd been as surprised by what he'd said as she.

It had sneaked up on him, his feelings for Liza. Oh, he'd wanted her from the beginning, but somewhere between her stubborn refusal to give up her car on the highway to that same car turning into an inferno as she watched, he'd fallen for her. Hard.

"You're not just saying that to...to quiet me down?"

He smiled. "I rather like you noisy." He took her hand and tugged her back inside, then into his embrace. "I rather like everything about you."

She held on to him, inhaling his wonderfully familiar scent, absorbing his strength. "Oh, J.D., I've been so scared. That dreadful man, the way he hit me that day, so casually, as if I were some pesky bug. And tonight, the explosion. And then I thought . . . I was afraid you were getting tired of me and my troubles, that you didn't really care about me. And here I was so crazy about you and . . ."

He angled back. "Say that again."

She smiled then, her arms going around his neck. "I'm crazy about you, you big lug." And she reached for his kiss. When it ended, she sighed, feeling safe within his arms.

J.D. shoved the door closed and bolted it. "We'll get Fleming and Clarence and anyone else involved, I promise."

Liza couldn't prevent a shudder as she pictured the wreckage of her car in her mind's eye, knowing she'd be ashes if that explosion had occurred when she'd been in it. "Do you think that awful man and whoever sent him were trying to kill me?" The words came out wobbly, which was how she felt.

J.D. reached over and took her hand in his, squeezing it. "No. I think they were trying to scare you into leaving town. And it might have worked, on a lesser woman." She'd told him on the drive to his home about her encounter with Lester at Roseanne's house, about the old man telling her to get out of his town. And she'd also described her visit with Dr. Rogers's widow. "But you don't scare easy, babe, nor give up easily. I want you to trust me, to believe that I'll get to the bottom of this and make whoever's doing this pay."

He saw her eyes fill, watched her struggle to hold back the tears. She'd had one hell of a shock tonight and she was handling it better than most would have. "Do you believe that I'm on your side?"

Her eyes on his shirt buttons, she picked at a loose thread. "Yes, but it's been hard to tell around here who my friends are. I've never encountered so many antagonistic people all in one place. I've never been on the receiving end of so much hate."

He stroked her hair. "It's not hate, it's fear. Someone out there is very afraid that you've discovered some deep, dark secret he's hidden all these years. Something that could do far more than embarrass him. Something that could harm him badly and shake up his world."

Liza looked up. "That's exactly what I thought as I watched my car burn. That's too serious a crime for simply exposing a baby born to someone so long ago. There has to be more to it."

His hands moved up to frame her face. The tears she refused to shed clung to her thick lashes, making them spiky. He looked into the blue depths of those eyes and thought he'd never seen anything more beautiful. Anyone more beautiful. "I agree. We'll get to the truth, I promise you. But you have to trust me, to let me do this my way. I will help you, but I need your promise that you'll follow my plan."

She felt a flare of hope. "You have a plan?"

"Yes." He'd decided on a plan of action as he'd walked around listening to the witnesses tell their stories, and he'd finalized it on their drive home. "Will you trust me?"

Liza nodded, seeing the sincerity in his dark gaze, feeling the weight of having to go it alone drop from her. "Yes, I trust you. Just don't make me sit somewhere quietly while you solve the whole puzzle. I have to be involved."

He gave her his slow grin. "You, sit somewhere quietly? That'll be the day. For your information, I welcome your involvement. I'll need it." He checked his watch and saw it was past one. "We'll talk it over in the morning. For now, we should get to bed. We've both had a long day." He bent his head, kissed the corners of her mouth, then drew her into a kiss that had them both breathing hard in moments.

Her eyes opened lazily as her hand resting on his chest felt his heartbeat increase. She was ready to be distracted, ready to shut down her mind and open the floodgates of feeling. "I thought you wanted to rest?"

"I believe I said we should get to bed. We can rest later." But first, he wanted to make her forget the horror of the last few hours. He wanted to blot out her worries and replace them with pleasure. He wanted to remove the fear from her eyes and instead fill them with desire. "I have some things I want to show you." He nibbled on her ear and saw the pulse in her neck begin to pound.

She was certain there was much he could show her. And she wanted to see, wanted to know. She would let him divert her attention and maybe then they could both rest. "All right, show me."

He carried her upstairs, not setting her down until they were alongside his huge bed, where just days ago, she'd napped. The moon shining in through the wall of windows was the only light in the room. He wanted it that way, wanted to see her body wearing only moonglow.

He saw her tremble as she stepped out of her shoes and wondered if he was pushing her too quickly after her frightening ordeal. "Are you afraid?"

"Of you? No." Of herself perhaps, of disappointing him. She didn't say it aloud, but instead stood before him, waiting.

J.D. couldn't remember the last time he'd slowly, methodically undressed a woman, couldn't recall the last time he'd wanted to. Slowly, teasing them both, he tugged her cotton sweater off over her head and tossed it aside, then watched her hair settle around her shoulders. "So lovely," he said, threading his fingers through the thick waves.

Liza let her head fall back as his strong fingers massaged her scalp slowly, sensuously. Her breath caught as his mouth skimmed along her throat, tasting, arousing. Her fingers fumbled with his shirt buttons, freeing each, following his lead by taking her time. She shoved the shirt from him and splayed her hands on his chest, ruffling the dark hair there, tracing the broad muscles. Then she pressed her lips along the same journey and felt him huff in a breath.

J.D. slipped her cotton slacks from her and she kicked them aside as he gazed down at her small swatches of silk, at the moonlight dappling her skin. He noticed a small parrot embroidered on her panties. "Do you own anything that doesn't have parrots on it?"

"You don't like parrots?"

He pressed his lips to the tiny bird and felt her heat. "I love parrots." With great care, he removed each piece from her, prolonging the delight of discovery. Then he filled his hands with her breasts and saw the heat rise in her cheeks.

Needs clawed at Liza, dark and hot and insistent. When he put his mouth to her, her knees nearly buckled. She let him ease her onto his navy quilt, inhaling the masculine scent clinging to his sheets, then watched him remove all but his briefs before following her down. "You're overdressed," she murmured as her hands slipped to his waistband.

He stopped her, grasping both hands and stretching her arms over her head. "Not just yet." His lips streaked over her heated flesh, learning her at his leisure, since the time before they'd been too rushed to lazily explore. But now he would savor, now he would enjoy, now he would show her all that could be between them.

Still so new, this dizzying descent into fiery feelings, this restless need to have it all. So thrilling, this eager rush to find fulfillment, this irresistible urge to be one with him. So wild and freeing, this escape from self, this journey into sensations just out of reach.

She struggled to free her hands, eager to draw him to her, but he evaded again, his mouth devouring hers until she forgot what she'd intended, until she forgot her own name. Shamelessly, she writhed beneath his clever fingers, his seeking tongue, his skillful mouth. He took her to the edge, then drew back and wouldn't let her fall the rest of the way.

Impatiently, she moaned his name, and he discovered how that small sound fueled his own need. At last he shoved off his briefs and whispered his hot request in her ear. "Touch me now." When her fingers closed around him, he shuddered with the fierce pleasure of it. Her hands loose at last roamed his back, along his ribs and inevitably returned to the source of the heat.

She had him vulnerable now and he knew it. Heady with the power of it, she gently pushed him and they rolled over. Looking into his eyes hazy with passion, she smiled as she straddled him, taking him inside. It was his turn to moan and grip her flesh in hands that shook with a need more powerful than he cared to admit.

Her mouth settled on his as she shifted to take him deeper, her movements driving them both wild. In seconds they tumbled down the hot dark tunnel and found release together.

J.D. hung up the wall phone with a disgusted scowl. Leaning against the kitchen counter, coffee cup in hand, Liza raised a questioning brow as he turned to her. "The last three numbers of Clarence Hobbs's license plate are 742."

"That confirms it, then." She finished her coffee and placed the cup in the sink. "Tell me about your plan." She'd been patient long enough. Not that his distractions all night long hadn't been wonderful. They had, and she felt a glow she couldn't remember feeling any other morning of her life.

But she also felt an impatience to clear up the questions that plagued her. Only then could she and J.D. go on with their lives. She watched him drain his cup, then refill it from the pot she'd made earlier.

He was going to need more than a caffeine jolt to get him through this day, J.D. thought as he sat down at the table. "I have nothing dramatic in mind, but rather a simple series of confrontations." He waited to continue until she'd taken the chair across from him. "I think it's confession time, for everyone involved. We need to go to Ethel. I saw her face last night and so did you. She knows far more than she's told so far, and she's had a good scare witnessing that fire firsthand. I think she's finally realized just how far the people she's been covering for are willing to go. I think she's ready to talk."

Liza agreed. With the two of them facing her, Ethel would cave in. "I'm all for that. What next?"

"Then, because I believe she knows even more, we pay a little visit to Priscilla Sparks. I'm sure Ethel's updated her on last night's happening, if others in town haven't.

She's probably getting worried about now. The little house of cards is about to tumble down.''

Liza's eyes took on a brightness as she realized that J.D. had carefully thought this through. "Good so far. And then?''

J.D. released a troubled breath. Then came the hardest part. "Then we drop in on Lester Fleming. Armed with the evidence—witnesses who put Clarence's truck at the scene and the hopefully corroborating evidence from Ethel and Priscilla—he won't be able to wiggle out of his involvement.''

Thoughtfully, Liza nodded.

Noticing her expression, he leaned forward. "What's wrong? Do you see a flaw in the plan?''

"Not a flaw, exactly. But what if Lester, having had all night to assess the situation, has skipped out by the time we get around to dropping in on him?''

J.D. shook his head. "He won't. He's too entrenched here in Pine Bluff. His capital's all tied up here. Besides, he's come to think of himself as inviolate. He's been powerful so long in this town that he believes himself above the law, as I see it.''

"You're probably right.'' Liza shoved back a fall of her hair, wishing she didn't have so many misgivings. "I still can't believe he'd do all that he's done to cover up the fact that his daughter probably had an illegitimate child so long ago. There has to be more, something we don't know.''

"Yes, I think so, too. But we won't know what until we start getting answers and putting the puzzle together.'' He waited until she met his eyes. "This could get sticky. You may learn things you never wanted to know. Are you still willing to go for it?''

She didn't hesitate. "Yes. We need to get to the truth. I wouldn't dream of stopping now."

He covered her hand with his. "All right, then, we go for it."

She smiled. "Does this mean that you've changed your mind, that you believe I was right in searching out my biological parents?"

He looked down at their joined hands. "You've made me change my mind about several things. Something you said the other day, about people regretting the risks they never take, got to me. Yesterday morning, before I went to the range with the posse, I drove to Prescott and looked up my father."

"That couldn't have been easy. What was he like?"

He'd forced himself to go, sure he'd find a hard-drinking, foul-mouthed bum. Instead, he'd found a tired, lonely man living in a one-bedroom house with only a dog for company. "He's still pugnacious as hell, but there's a beaten look about him. Like life's whipped him, you know?"

"I'm sorry. Did you get a chance to talk?"

He shrugged. "Some. I was surprised he asked so many questions about my mother. He said he wished he'd have swallowed his pride and gone to her before she'd died."

"Maybe he loved her all along and just didn't know how to show her."

"Yeah, maybe." Or maybe his father had learned how to love too late, yet had been afraid to risk being rejected. And maybe there was a lesson in there somewhere.

"Are you planning to see him again? I could go with you."

He'd told Roscoe about Liza, and had wondered all the way home why he had. "Yeah, maybe one day," he answered, then checked his watch.

"So, are we ready to go?" She badly wanted to get started.

"I need to take a side trip first, and I need to go alone." He saw her frown and hurried on. "I want to talk with Gray. I find it odd that Eddie remembered Roseanne going to the dude ranch, yet Roseanne doesn't. If Gray's the man Roseanne was involved with at that ranch, he will remember even if, for whatever reason, she doesn't. And if you're his daughter, I don't want it to come as a complete shock."

She could see the merit in that, and the compassion in his concern for Gray. "That's fine."

He stood, tugging her up to meet his kiss. "Thanks for the vote of confidence."

Gray Eubanks was seated behind his oak desk in his den when he heard heavy footsteps approaching in the hallway. It was early for a visitor. Rudy always came in to let him know someone had come to see him, with one exception. J.D. was the only other man who had a key and the run of the house without preamble. Sitting back, he swung his eyes to the open door.

J.D.'s big frame filled the doorway. As always, Gray felt a rush of pride at the fine man the skinny boy he'd once known had become. His smile was warm and welcoming. "Come in. It's good to see you."

Reaching across the desk to clasp Gray's outstretched hand in both of his, J.D. returned the smile. "You're looking well." Backing up, he sat down in the leather chair facing his mentor, still wondering how a man tells another that it's possible he has a daughter he'd never suspected he had. On the drive over, he'd wrestled with finding the right words and finally decided he'd have to play this one by ear, following Gray's lead. The trouble with rehearsed dialogues, he'd discovered, was that the other guy never knew his lines.

"I see you're going over the books. How are things shaping up?" He would go slowly, unable to just plunge right in.

"Comfortably in black ink, even after all the renovations we did this spring, I'm happy to report." Gray picked up his pen, needing something to occupy his hands. He had an odd feeling that J.D. hadn't driven out today to discuss his business or the ranch or the weather.

He had something else on his mind, Gray was sure. Years of watching the boy had taught him the signs. He saw J.D. shift in his chair, juggling his hat on his lap. Could his hint of nerves have something to do with that lovely woman he'd brought to the ranch days ago? He would give him time, let him sort out his thoughts. "How are things in the sheriff's office?"

J.D. shrugged. "Moving along. Pretty quiet most days." Except for yesterday. J.D. cleared his throat. "We did have an incident last night that has me concerned."

"What was that?"

"Someone set Liza Parker's car on fire in front of Bisbee's."

"Good Lord. She wasn't in it, I hope."

"No, fortunately she was upstairs in her room at the time. But that's only the last of several things that have happened to Liza since her arrival in Pine Bluff. On close examination of these incidents, I believe there's someone who wants her to leave. Very badly wants her to leave."

Interested now, Gray propped his elbows on his desk and leaned forward. "Does this have something to do with her search for her parents?"

"Yes, I'm sure it does."

"I see." J.D. often came to him to talk over his tougher cases. This one concerned him especially since Gray felt that he cared a great deal for Liza Parker. "So, what do you make of it?"

"I'll get to that in a minute." J.D. set his hat down on the carpeted floor, placed his left ankle on his right knee and studied Gray. How to even begin. He drew in a steadying breath. "Let's take a walk down memory lane, Gray, you and I."

Gray frowned. "Whatever does all this have to do with me?"

"Bear with me, please."

"All right, but when you get to be my age, that road gets longer every year. How far back do you want to go?"

"To the summer you worked at Wilson's Dude Ranch in Wickenburg." He saw the quick flicker of nerves in Gray's blue eyes. Funny how he'd never noticed how deep a blue they were. As blue as the ones he'd kissed closed last night. "You've told me the story often, about the summer you were twenty and met that beautiful girl with the strawberry blond hair."

A muscle in Gray's jaw flexed before he dropped his gaze to the pen he held in his hand. "What about that summer?"

"You confided to me some time ago that you had an affair with that blonde, remember?"

Gray's voice was suddenly sharp. "Yes, I remember, and I asked you to never repeat what I told you."

"And I never have. But I need to tell you something I've only recently learned."

He set down the pen when he found his hands weren't quite steady. "What would that be?"

"Though you never mentioned her name, I believe you knew who that girl was at the time she walked away from you. I think you worked hard to get ahead and that you were planning to go to her when you felt you had something to offer her. But then the accident happened."

J.D. watched Gray's normally ruddy face lose some color and wished he hadn't had to shock him. But perhaps in this case, the end justified the means, for if all went well, Gray would have a daughter he didn't know existed. "Am I right?"

Gray Eubanks was a man unused to lying, most especially to the man he cared about more than any other. He'd been worrying that he'd given himself away when he'd seen that dried rose and read the lone entry in the green diary. "What if you are? Even if you've discovered her identity, you should know that I would never go to her as . . . as I am now."

"Do you still care about her, Gray? I wouldn't have asked so personal a question a month ago even. But I've recently fallen in love myself and I know how it feels now." J.D. heard the echo of his words and realized that he very much meant them. "Do you still love her?"

Gray turned to gaze out the window at the nearest corral where a chestnut mare pranced along the fence line. But he saw instead another fenced corral nearly thirty years ago in another town, and a gray-eyed girl he'd helped up into the saddle, a girl with a laugh that had sent shivers up his spine. "I've never stopped loving her, but I'm not the man she once knew." His pride kept him from saying more.

"That's where you're wrong. After Liza and I left here that night, she guessed from your conversation that you'd once loved someone very much. Yet you hadn't gone after her. I explained to Liza that it was because the accident incapacitated you that you didn't go. And she said something that made a lot of sense to me later, as I thought it over. She said that the only things in life we regret as we grow older are the risks we didn't take. She said that a woman doesn't fall in love with a pair of legs. She falls in love with a man, a whole man, not individual parts of him."

Gray couldn't prevent the bitterness from seeping through. "But I'm not a whole man. I can't walk, can't dance, can't…do a lot of things. Who would want a man like that?"

"Roseanne Fleming would."

Gray's head shot up. "How did you find out her name?"

"I didn't. Liza put it together. She's talked with Roseanne and she's told me how lonely she seems, so much so that she nearly wept when Liza gave her a puppy."

Gray's face turned stormy. "She talked to Roseanne about me? She had no right to…."

"No. She didn't mention you to her because she didn't know for sure."

"Know what for sure?"

J.D. decided to take the chance. "That you might be her father and Roseanne her mother."

Chapter Ten

For only the second time since Bisbee's Bed & Breakfast had opened thirty-eight years ago, the guests were served juice, sweet rolls and coffee for the morning meal instead of the elaborate breakfasts Ethel usually prepared. Seated at her kitchen table with a cup of coffee after everyone had finished and gone their separate ways, Ethel was amazed she'd had the energy to put together that much.

She had slept hardly a wink during the endless night. Who could have after watching that cute little car burn down to rubble, after seeing the look of horror and loss on Liza Parker's face, after catching sight of Clarence Hobbs running from the scene? Shakily, Ethel picked up her mug and took another sip of strong coffee.

It was nearly noon and she knew J.D. would be paying her a visit soon. She'd seen the questions in his eyes last night, the ones he'd been too considerate to ask in deference perhaps to her age and her state of mind then. But the sheriff had a job to do and she would cooperate. Because things had gone on long enough.

She hadn't meant any harm, hadn't dreamed the baby girl she'd held in her arms so long ago would one day return and upset everyone involved, hadn't ever thought things would turn violent. But they had and, although no one had actually gotten physically hurt yet, Ethel feared it could come to that. Powerful men get so used to having things their way that they forget to consider the consequences of their acts after a while, certain they'll continue to get away with things.

She would have to put things to right, or she'd never sleep another peaceful night again.

Ethel heard the front door open and knew instantly who was entering. Liza Parker was with him, she guessed. Well, why not? She had a right to hear the truth, as well. Wearily, feeling every day of her sixty-eight years, Ethel rose to get two more mugs down from the cupboard.

J.D. stepped through the swinging door into the kitchen. His first thought was that Ethel appeared to have aged between last night and this morning. Her dark hair already liberally sprinkled with gray seemed limp and lifeless and her eyes as she swung them to him looked defeated, as if they'd lost their sparkle. "Hello, Ethel," he said as Liza walked in behind him.

Ethel made a stab at a welcoming smile. These two weren't here to crucify her, she reminded herself, but rather to gather information that perhaps only she could give. She owed that much to Liza. "Sit down, please," she said, indicating the empty chairs around her table. "I've got fresh coffee." She'd already had too many cups; nevertheless, she poured herself another.

Although she'd wanted this confrontation, Liza's nerves had her hands clammy and her throat dry. Her heart went out to the older woman, knowing this wouldn't be easy for her. Whoever she'd been protecting for so long must mean a lot to her. Or have a lot on her. Seating herself in the chair by the window, she decided to let J.D. do the questioning.

He took a taste of coffee he didn't want as Ethel sat down. The dress she was wearing featured a field of tiny wildflowers in a background of navy, the dark color causing her complexion to look even paler. Over it she wore her usual white apron with Bisbee's embroidered in a red slash across the bib, as if to give herself courage. There seemed no point in waiting. "Ethel, I'm sure you know why we're here."

"Yes, I know I owe you both an explanation." Dark freckles dotted the backs of the hands Ethel gripped together on the table as she began. "Twenty-eight years ago last April, I took a baby girl to Phoenix to an attorney's office. My cousin, Abby Thatcher, worked for Winthrop Ames, and I knew that, together, they'd handle the adoption." She raised her eyes to Liza. "That baby was you."

Unable to speak, Liza struggled with a rush of emotion. All these years later and finally, she was going to learn her background.

"You were so sweet," Ethel went on, her eyes misting as her mind flooded with memories. "Even then, your eyes were the same extraordinary shade of blue and you had this reddish blond hair. I'd lost a baby just a few years before that, and then I lost my husband. I wished with all my heart I could have kept you myself and raised you right here." Sniffling, she reached into her pocket for a tissue.

Liza wanted to take her hand, to help her through this hard time, but she hardly knew the woman and, until now, Ethel hadn't shown her much friendliness. So she kept still and waited.

Dabbing at her eyes, Ethel continued. "I felt bad for you, even though Abby told me the couple taking you were kind and wonderful people. The Parkers, she told me, both Phoenix schoolteachers, were unable to have their own child. I placed a tiny gold chain with a dainty heart on it in the box that came with you, for luck. It had been mine as a youngster and I'd hoped to pass it on to a daughter. But I knew that, for me, there'd be no more babies."

Opening her bag, Liza found the lacquered box and removed the gold chain. "This?" she asked.

Lips pressed together, Ethel nodded.

J.D. thought to get Ethel past the emotional part and on to the heart of the story. "Where did you get the baby, Ethel?"

Drawing in a deep breath, Ethel regained control of herself. "Priscilla called me one day, asking if I could help with a problem. She worked for Lester Fleming, J.D., as you know. The whole thing had to be very hush-hush."

She looked down at the tissue nearly shredded in her hands. "I'm not proud of this part, but Priscilla told me that Lester would pay me for my trouble, pay me enough to discharge the mortgage on this place. I was just scraping by and there were repairs needing to be done. The money was a godsend, I can tell you." Again she looked at Liza. "But the real reason I called Abby and made the arrangements was because I felt in my heart that you'd have a better life with the Parkers than if you stayed here. Lord only knows what might have happened if you'd remained in Pine Bluff." Her voice faltered. "Maybe I did wrong."

Liza did reach out then and cover Ethel's hands with her own. "I did have a good life with the Parkers. They were wonderful to me."

Ethel's eyes were swimming in tears. "I'm glad. I'm truly glad."

J.D. wanted to hear more. "Then the baby, Liza here, was born to Roseanne Fleming?"

Liza held her breath, waiting for the answer as she gripped J.D.'s hand.

"Yes," Ethel answered. "Before she married Reid. Roseanne was only seventeen or eighteen."

"Who's the father?" J.D. asked.

Ethel shook her head. "I don't know. Maybe Priscilla does."

J.D. turned to Liza and squeezed her fingers. After his conversation with Gray, he felt strongly that he knew who Liza's father was, but he realized she still had her doubts. "Roseanne will be able to tell us."

"I doubt that she will," Ethel said, then went on. "I don't know what happened to Roseanne, but something bad took place that summer, because to this day, the poor soul doesn't seem to remember a thing, including that she's had a child."

"You mean something traumatized her into a memory loss?" J.D. asked.

Ethel nodded. "It would seem so."

Liza's forehead wrinkled. "That explains why, when I asked her some questions about her past, her answers were so vague. I could tell she wasn't lying, yet she didn't know."

J.D. sat back. "I ran across a case several years ago that was similar. There's something known as psychogenic amnesia. The person knows their name, the year, who's the current president and can function in the everyday world. But they completely block out a period of time where a traumatizing event took place in their lives."

"I've heard of that," Liza said, her spirits deflating. To finally learn who her mother was and then not have her know her would be a terrible irony.

"In the case I worked on in conjunction with the sheriff up in Kingman, a young girl had witnessed her sister's brutal murder as she lay in the other twin bed, pretending to be asleep. That event so badly traumatized her that, much later, she still couldn't recall that entire year of her life."

"Do you think that's what happened to Roseanne?" Liza asked him, unable to keep the dread from her voice.

"It could be." J.D. touched her cheek lightly. "But don't give up hope. She could snap out of it. The girl I mentioned did. Years later, she went to a gas station with her father and recognized the killer who was working there. The floodgates opened and she began to remember everything."

"I don't know what might snap Roseanne out of this," Ethel said. "Ever since your birth, she's been very fragile healthwise, which is why Lester's always been so protective of her. That's another reason I agreed to help him." She hoped she didn't sound as if she was alibiing her way out of her fair share of responsibility.

"I can understand a father protecting a fragile daughter," Liza commented. "But he gave away his own flesh and blood. I have trouble with that."

"Lester wasn't thinking along those lines, I'm sure," Ethel went on, trying to explain what she herself never quite understood. "For years, since Roseanne's mother died, it had been just the two of them. Lester never let her go anywhere alone, driving her to school and picking her up daily. He was always hovering in the background. I often told Priscilla that that was why, once Roseanne got into high school and discovered fun and boys, she got a little wild. Lord, she'd been all but chained to Lester's side all her life.''

"Did she ever date any one particular young man here in town?'' Liza asked, unable to make up her mind about Gray until all the facts were in. She didn't want to be disappointed again. This was too important.

"I don't recall her with any special young man. She went out with all of them. I'm not saying she slept around, you understand. Only she knows that, I'm sure. But the crowd she ran with, they liked to party, liked a good time. Lester had a fit trying to keep her home.''

"Would you happen to know if Roseanne ever spent a summer working on Wilson's Dude Ranch in Wickenburg?'' J.D. asked.

"I remember that she spent two summers working up there. To tell you the truth, I think she went to get away from Lester. Except Lester and Charley Wilson were friends since boyhood and Lester had Charley watching over Roseanne like a mother hen circling the chicks in the barnyard. Priscilla told me that Roseanne complained that she could scarcely take a walk after hours without Charley dogging her footsteps.''

Apparently she managed to avoid Charley some nights, to hear Gray tell it, J.D. thought. They'd talked for nearly an hour this morning, Gray handling the news he'd given him very well. He'd told J.D. how instantly and fiercely he and Roseanne had fallen in love, making a game of eluding Charley and his watchdogs to steal some time together. The longer they talked, the more convinced J.D. had become that Gray was Liza's father.

Gray believed it, too, and was nervously awaiting news of what J.D. could discover in his confrontations today.

Liza's thoughts were still on Lester Fleming. "Do you remember, several years after my adoption, when Ralph Parker came here and tried to find my birth parents?" she asked Ethel.

Embarrassed again, she nodded. "Lester hired some people to get rid of him. See, I'd made the mistake of telling him after I'd returned from Phoenix that Ralph and Blair Parker had adopted you and named you Liza, after Blair's mother. I thought he'd feel good knowing you'd be well taken care of." She shook her head. "Lester didn't want to hear it. His only concern was Roseanne. She was married to Reid then, and they weren't getting along. He didn't want anyone to make things worse. He warned me not to talk to Ralph Parker." She dabbed at more tears. "I've always felt bad about being so rude to that poor man."

"Ethel," J.D. said, "I need to know something. Was the man hired to get Ralph Parker out of town, to search Liza's rooms and to set her car on fire, Clarence Hobbs?"

Ashamed now, Ethel nodded. "I didn't know about all Clarence did to get Ralph out of here until one day when he'd had too much to drink and let it slip." She turned her troubled gaze on Liza. "And I want you to know, I didn't know he'd searched your room until afterward. I was here all day, but I never saw him come in or leave. But when you mentioned what had happened, I guessed that Clarence had been here. He's real sneaky and he'd do anything for Lester." Her mouth tightened. "But I never thought either of them would go so far as to set your car on fire. Temper or no temper, I can't protect Lester anymore." Her voice faltered. "I'm an old woman and I want to live in peace. I can't take this violence. Lester's just going to have to face the music."

"I'm not blaming you, Ethel," Liza said softly. "You thought you were doing the right thing."

"Yes, but things got out of hand. I'm sorry, Liza. So very sorry." Tears rolled down her wrinkled cheeks as she pulled out another tissue.

Liza struggled with a multitude of conflicting emotions. J.D. had said this wouldn't be easy, and he'd surely been right. "I guess what I'm having the most trouble handling is knowing that my own grandfather ordered that terrible man to set my car on fire. He must want to get rid of me very badly."

"He did it to scare you away, to make you go back home, not to hurt you physically, I'm sure," Ethel explained tearfully. "Underneath, he's a good man, Liza."

It must be very well hidden. "But why would he hate me so much?"

Ethel shook her head. "I don't think he does. It's just that he's been protecting Roseanne so long that he can't stop."

J.D. wasn't sure he bought that explanation. He'd certainly witnessed overly protective parents before, but there was something more here with Lester, as both he and Liza had suspected last night. Roseanne no longer needed such fierce protection. Why was Lester still at it?

"I...I hope I've cleared things up for you, Liza." Ethel looked beseechingly at J.D. "If it's any consolation, I'm truly sorry for the part I played in all this."

J.D. patted her hands, then stood. "I appreciate your frankness. I think we'll go talk with Priscilla. She might be able to fill in some of the blanks." He reached for Liza's hand.

After they left, Ethel dried her eyes and blew her nose. She wished she felt better having told it all. Sighing heavily, she went to the phone to call Priscilla Sparks.

"If Roseanne was as wild in her teens as we've heard, we may never find out who my father is," Liza commented as she sat beside J.D. on the short drive to Priscilla's. "Maybe even she doesn't know."

"Maybe she doesn't remember that summer," J.D. said, "but Gray does. He remembers every detail as if it were yesterday."

She hadn't asked him much about his visit with Gray and all he'd said so far was that everything was okay at that end. Now, in light of what she'd just heard, she wanted to know more. "What did he say?"

He told her what Gray had told him about the clandestine meetings in the hayloft of the barn and down by the stream under a big oak tree where he and Roseanne had first made love. "That's why he carved the acorn ring for her, because they'd found it together that night. And as to Roseanne's wildness, it didn't include sleeping around. She was a virgin when she came to Gray."

Liza felt a rush of relief. She reached to touch J.D. "Thank you for that. Everything we've heard so far points to Gray. But I need to hear it from someone who knows for sure to actually believe it."

"Liza, we may never get Roseanne past her trauma enough to remember, but Gray very much wants to get to know you. That night I took you there, he was shaken by your resemblance to the Roseanne he remembered. And, of course, there's the fact that your eyes are *his* eyes." He pulled the van to a stop in front of the modern stucco ranch house on Marshall, shut the motor and turned to her. "I don't know how I missed that myself."

"Because you weren't looking to find a similarity to Gray, I guess. Neither was I."

He leaned across the console and slipped his arm around her. "Are you okay with all this so far?"

She nodded. "It's nice to know we're on the right track. I could have done a lot worse than learning that that lovely woman is my mother, even if she doesn't remember me."

"She will. I'm sure of it. And, Liza, Gray's the best. I've told you I've looked on him as a father for years now."

"I look forward to getting to know him." She fiddled with the collar of his shirt, straightening it, wishing she could hear from her mother's own lips the verification of Gray's paternity. "How do you feel about sharing Gray with me, if he is my father?"

"I can't think of anyone I'd rather share him with." He gathered her to him, with difficulty since the console intruded, and kissed her thoroughly and lengthily, wishing they were parked in front of his house instead of Priscilla's. "If we continue this much longer out here, we're going to be arrested."

"I'm not worried. I'm with Pine Bluff's top cop." But they had something important to finish, so she moved back and straightened her clothes. "I hope Priscilla wasn't watching out her window."

"I just hope we find her in a talkative mood," J.D. said as he stepped out of the vehicle.

Priscilla Sparks sat on her apricot-colored couch and rubbed her left thumb with her right hand as she looked over the two young people across from her, seated on twin pale green chairs. She'd been expecting their visit, thanks to Ethel's call. Forewarned should have meant forearmed. Yet she was still nervous.

"You have a lovely home," Liza commented, looking around at the living room obviously scarcely used. Above the couch was a soft watercolor in pastel shades by an artist whose work she now recognized instantly.

"I redecorated recently after my retirement." And after today, when Lester learned what she was about to do, her generous retirement income would probably end, Priscilla thought. No matter, for she had a goodly amount set aside. Some things you had to do, no matter the consequences. She'd agreed with Ethel that things had definitely gotten out of hand with that car fire. "I'm so sorry about what happened to your car," she told Liza.

Before Liza could acknowledge the woman's comment, J.D. jumped in. "You know who's responsible, don't you, Ms. Sparks?"

She cleared her throat before answering. "I understand that Ethel Bisbee and several neighbors have identified seeing Clarence Hobbs in the neighborhood around the time of the explosion."

"And you also know who hired Clarence to do his dirty work for him." It was not a question.

Priscilla rubbed at her painfully swollen joints and wished this day would never have come. But it had and she had to deal with it. "Lester isn't an evil man, I want you to know. I worked for him for over forty years, hired on right after his wife died and Roseanne was still a child. I practically raised her myself. Such a pretty thing, so full of joy, always laughing. She was the light of Lester's life. He was very protective of her, unable to stand the thought of her getting hurt." She sighed softly. "I used to tell him that no one could escape getting hurt occasionally, that that was how a person learned. But he wouldn't listen.''

J.D. decided the best way to get Priscilla's story out was not by direct questioning but by gently leading her. ''And Roseanne began rebelling against his protective ways as a teenager?''

''Yes, she certainly did. Lester wanted to keep her under lock and key, but he couldn't. She was young, pretty and eager to taste life. She began sneaking out at night to attend parties when she was only sixteen. I caught her several times and warned her that her father would punish her if he found out. She just laughed and went on doing it.''

''Headstrong, was she?'' he asked, glancing at Liza pointedly. But he saw she was watching Priscilla so closely that she hadn't caught his glance.

''Indeed, very headstrong.''

''She worked at a dude ranch in Wickenburg, I understand.''

''Yes. After the first summer, she came home enthralled with horses. But when she returned that last summer, she came back changed. She was quieter and very moody. I could tell something was wrong. She was due to start college in the fall, and Lester was pushing her to date Reid Mitchell, his close friend's son. He considered Reid suitable for his daughter, a studious boy who was planning to be an attorney like his father. I think he wanted her safely married to his first choice before she got into trouble.''

''What did Roseanne think of Reid?''

Priscilla smiled. ''He wasn't nearly exciting enough for her. A boring bookworm, she called him.''

''Did you find out what was bothering Roseanne that summer?''

The older woman stared out the window, lost in the past now. "She'd returned early, the first part of August instead of the end, as she had the year before. Suddenly she didn't go out anymore—just stayed home brooding, staring out the window, going for walks with her dog in the woods behind the house. Then one morning, I found her sick in the bathroom. I guessed that she was pregnant, and she confessed to me that she was. She was very afraid to tell her father."

"Did she ask for your help?"

"No. She just asked me not to tell Lester, that she'd work something out."

"Did you ask her who the father was?"

"Yes, but she wouldn't tell me his name. Only that she'd fallen very much in love with a handsome young man who'd also worked at the ranch."

Listening, Liza drew in a sharp breath. Could that man have been Gray Eubanks?

Priscilla looked over at the young woman. "You're the spitting image of Roseanne when she was young. I knew who you were the moment I saw you, even before I heard your name."

"Why didn't you tell me then?" Liza asked. Maybe things wouldn't have gotten so out of hand if she had.

"You have to understand, my loyalty's been with Lester and Roseanne for so long, and I didn't know you." She shook her head sadly. "I should have known better. Should have seen that one day this would all come out. But I didn't think Lester would go off the deep end as he apparently has."

J.D. wanted to lead her back to that fateful summer. "How did Roseanne finally tell Lester about her pregnancy?"

"She never did. Something happened that changed things. One evening, Roseanne went for a walk in the woods with her dog. I was at the house, but I didn't think anything was unusual since she often went there when she needed to think. It wasn't until later, when I heard someone at the back door and found Roseanne hurt and bleeding, that I knew something terrible had happened."

Both J.D. and Liza leaned forward, listening intently at this new twist. "Go on," J.D. urged.

"As I was helping Roseanne up to her room, Lester came home. Roseanne had us both upset with her clothes all torn, blood coming from a cut on her head, all dirty and crying. Lester called Dr. Rogers who came right over. He and Lester'd been friends for years. The doctor examined Roseanne and finally she told us what happened."

Liza could see that Priscilla had to gear herself up for this part as she adjusted her rimless glasses on her small face.

"There was a man named Jack Guthrie who worked for Lester. He was a good carpenter, I guess, because Lester had him do work at the house, shelves and the like, storeroom cupboards. He rented a small cabin Lester used to have on the back of the property. I never cared for the man myself. He had small, mean eyes and he always smelled so bad." She cleared her throat. "Anyhow, the evening that Roseanne went walking into the woods, so her story went, she ran into Jack. He made advances to her and she rebuffed him. She tried to run away, but he caught her. There was a struggle and quite a fight. I could well believe that Roseanne would have fought like a tiger. But he was much stronger. He raped her."

"Oh, no," Liza said softly. "How terrible."

"Yes, it was terrible," Priscilla agreed. "When we finally got the story out of Roseanne, you should have seen Lester. He was beet red and fighting mad. He stormed out and was gone for a long time, looking for Jack, we assumed."

Priscilla found a handkerchief with a crocheted edge in her pocket and dabbed at her eyes, visibly upset by the retelling. But she hurried on, anxious to be done. "The next afternoon, Roseanne and I were sitting by her upstairs bedroom window when we saw Jack come out of his rented cabin. We both wondered out loud how the man dared to show his face, but we saw that he had a suitcase with him. He was apparently about to leave town. Lester's temper was no secret to anyone in Pine Bluff."

"So he got away?" J.D. asked, wondering why he'd never heard anyone even hint at this story, not even the older residents.

"He must have. No one ever saw him again. The next thing we knew, his cabin burned to the ground." Priscilla drew in a shaky breath.

The older woman looked so pale that Liza felt a rush of compassion for her. She rose and went to sit beside her. "This is difficult for you, I know."

From behind her glasses, Priscilla's blue eyes blinked as if to keep the tears at bay. "It's difficult for you, too, dear." She glanced at J.D. who was trying to appear patient.

"Did anything else happen after you saw Jack Guthrie leave with his suitcase?"

"I'm not sure. I convinced Roseanne to lie down and I went out for about three hours. It was my canasta club meeting. When I returned that evening, the doctor was again examining Roseanne and Lester was pacing the floor. I couldn't blame him. Roseanne lay in bed looking paler than the sheets and just gazing off into space."

"What had happened to her?" Liza wanted to know.

"Dr. Rogers said she'd retreated to a place where no one could hurt her again, a place where we couldn't reach her. She wouldn't answer when we spoke to her, seemed scarcely aware of her surroundings and just stared vacantly. Lester was beside himself with worry."

"And you say she didn't have this reaction until a full day and night *after* she was raped?" J.D. asked.

"Yes, that's right. The doctor called it a delayed reaction."

Frowning, J.D. considered that.

"Finally, after several weeks with no noticeable change in Roseanne, I decided to tell Lester that Roseanne was pregnant. That really sent him into a rage. I tried repeatedly to explain that she'd been pregnant *before* the rape and she'd been afraid to tell him. Nothing I said registered. He ranted and raved like a madman that his daughter would bear the child of a rapist. He was beyond reason."

"Didn't Roseanne tell him the truth when she got better?" Liza asked gently.

"Ah, but she didn't get better for a very long time. She would just sit in the garden and stare for hours on end, not moving. The doctor would come and go, checking on her and telling us that the pregnancy was proceeding normally, but Roseanne seemed unaware of the changes in her body. I had to coax her to eat and help her to bathe. She was so pitiful."

"And Jack Guthrie never returned?" J.D. asked, needing her to verify that point.

"Not that I heard about. I always thought that Lester set a match to that cabin to erase the memories of that man. Frankly, I was glad to see Jack go, and his cabin, too." Priscilla's tight-lipped expression showed what she thought of a man who would rape.

Maybe Guthrie had left town and was long gone, J.D. thought. Then again, maybe not. He made a mental note to check back in the files for a report on the cabin fire.

"Naturally, Lester and Dr. Rogers and I were all worried about Roseanne's grip on reality as her time came due. Only the three of us knew about the pregnancy because Roseanne never left the house and grounds. When she went into labor, Dr. Rogers delivered the baby right there in her bedroom. Lester ordered him to make out the birth certificate but not to record it. He wanted no one in Pine Bluff to discover that his daughter had had a rapist's child."

So that was why Mrs. Rogers had clammed up, Liza thought. She didn't want to sully her husband's memory by admitting that he'd done something underhanded.

Priscilla smiled at Liza. "I was the first to hold you. You were so small and pink, a perfect baby. I cleaned you up and dressed you in a white gown and booties I'd crocheted, then wrapped you in a pink blanket." Her face grew distressed. "But Lester wouldn't even look at you. He'd convinced himself you were the daughter of a man who'd ruined *his* daughter. I hope you'll try to understand that, dear, and not hate him too much."

"I can try," Liza answered, knowing it would take time. A great deal of time. To blame an innocent child was beyond her comprehension.

"Was it Lester's idea that you call Ethel and hand the baby over for adoption?" J.D. asked.

"Yes. Of course, Lester knew Ethel well and knew that her cousin worked for an attorney in Phoenix. He arranged the whole thing with Ethel. I took the baby to the boardinghouse the morning she was to drive you to Mr. Ames's office."

Priscilla reached for something she'd left on the end table and offered it to Liza. "I took this picture of you with my new Polaroid camera, maybe an hour after you were born. And I tucked another into this black lacquered box that Roseanne used to sit and hold as she sat staring off into space. I knew what it contained—reminders of her summer in Wickenburg. I thought it best that, when she started feeling better, those reminders wouldn't be around. So I gave the box to Ethel when I took you to her."

Liza picked up her bag and produced the box as well as the duplicate picture. "You mean this box?"

Priscilla nodded. "Yes, that's it."

"I'm still puzzled about something," Liza said. "Obviously, Roseanne did recover in time. Didn't she remember anything that happened?"

Sadly, the older woman shook her head. "To this day, she has no memory of the two summers in Wickenburg, the baby she had or the rape. The whole experience just faded from her mind. I suppose it's all there somewhere, but after all this time, I doubt she'll ever recall it. If seeing you with your obvious resemblance to her didn't do it, I don't imagine anything will."

"You can never tell," J.D. added, not wanting to destroy Liza's hope that one day her mother would know her.

"How long after I was born did she begin to improve?"

"Months. Six or more. Slowly she became aware of her surroundings, to take an interest again in her appearance, to drive into town occasionally. Volunteering at the hospital with the little ones helped. And she used her painting, which she'd always enjoyed, as an outlet for her bottled-up feelings."

"I bought one of her paintings," Liza said.

Priscilla glanced over her shoulder at the framed watercolor. "She's very good, isn't she?" Again she shook her head sadly. "If you'd only known her before. Afterward, the change in her was enormous. The laughing, fun-loving girl I'd raised was gone, replaced by a somber and sad woman with eyes so troubled that at times she almost broke my heart."

"Did Reid Mitchell start coming around about then?" J.D. asked.

"Lester prompted him to, I'm sure, but yes, he did. Roseanne didn't seem terribly interested, but as much as she'd defied her father before all this, she now bent over backward to please him. So when Lester told her he wanted her to marry Reid, she said yes. She couldn't conceive with Reid and he blamed her, then left her, which was probably just as well. I don't believe she ever loved the man. How could she when I *know* in my heart that she still loves the man who fathered you."

"Did you ever learn that man's name?" Liza wanted to know.

For the first time, Priscilla hesitated. "I believe I figured it out," she said finally, "but since I'm not certain, I'd rather not conjecture. I felt I had to tell you about Lester and Roseanne, but I can't justify interfering in still another person's life."

"It's all right, Priscilla," J.D. said. "We're fairly certain that Gray Eubanks is Liza's father."

"Oh, my," Priscilla whispered, confirming their information.

"When the truth starts tumbling out, everyone just has to take it in stride," J.D. told her. "I talked with Gray this morning and he's thrilled to learn about Liza."

Priscilla, her cheeks damp, reached for Liza's hand. "Of course, it's the eyes. Anyone can see that. I'm so glad you'll at least have him, my dear. I don't know if you'll ever be able to get through to your poor mother. I don't even know if Lester will let you see her."

J.D. stood. "Lester's no longer calling the shots. It's time he learned that the law applies to him as much as to any man." He shifted his gaze to Liza who was still struggling to absorb all she'd learned. He was impressed with her strength, learning so many new things about her parentage in one day.

They said their goodbyes and he led her out to the van. At this point, he decided to let her choose. "Where do you want to go next, to visit Lester or to drop in on Roseanne?"

"I think to Roseanne's," she said. It was time. Perhaps way past time.

Chapter Eleven

The afternoon had turned cool with gray clouds milling about overhead threatening rain as J.D. stopped the van in front of Roseanne's home. He'd tried to talk Liza into stopping in town for a bite of lunch, thinking some food might counteract what too much coffee had done to their systems. But Liza was too intent on facing her mother to consider eating.

She turned to him as he shifted into Park. "If she gets too upset by our questions, we should back off and try another day."

"I agree. Then we'll track down Lester." That was the one he was looking forward to, the confrontation that would hopefully reveal whatever dark secret the old man was hiding. "Are you sure you're up to this?" he asked her.

Liza nodded. "I think I've been waiting for this most of my life." She shoved open the passenger door.

They heard Max's puppy yips even before they rang Roseanne's front doorbell.

"Looks like he'll grow into a good little watchdog," Liza commented over the pounding of her heart. Please let her be having a good day, she prayed.

Roseanne's pale face moved into a gentle smile when she saw Liza. "Have you come to check on the puppy?" she asked.

"That, too. And to talk with you." Liza drew J.D. closer. "May we come in?"

"Sure." Betraying no curiosity, Roseanne opened the door wide and ushered them into a lovely glassed-in room off the back. They settled into white wicker furniture with yellow-and-green floral cushions as Roseanne turned on a table lamp. "It's gloomy today, isn't it?"

"Fall is here, I guess," J.D. commented, in an attempt at small talk. He'd decided to let Liza take the lead this time.

"Can I get you something—coffee or a cold drink?" Roseanne asked.

J.D. glanced at Liza, then shook his head. "I don't think so, but thanks."

Max scampered all over the room, sniffing first one visitor, then the next, his stubby tail wagging. Roseanne sat down on a large ottoman and smiled at his puppy antics. "Isn't he cute?"

"I'm so glad you're enjoying him," Liza said. She noticed that Roseanne looked the same as always, though there were faint fatigue patches beneath her eyes, indicating a loss of sleep. Rain began to fall in earnest, running down the windows, the sound not unpleasant. If only their visit were for a happier reason.

"Did you come to pick out a picture?" Roseanne asked Liza. "I did promise you one." Her glance slid to J.D. "Or is there some problem?"

"Not really a problem." Liza jumped in before J.D. could answer. "We've been talking with Priscilla Sparks and Ethel Bisbee and I wanted to share with you what we learned."

Pulling her attention from Max, Roseanne turned to Liza. "Does this concern me?"

"Yes." Liza gathered up her courage and plunged in. "The reason I'm in Pine Bluff is not just to vacation, but because I was born here twenty-eight years ago this last April fifteenth."

Roseanne frowned. "I don't recall any Parkers living here."

"Parker is the name of my adoptive parents who lived in Phoenix. They died and recently I came into some papers regarding my adoption that led me to believe that both my parents live around here."

"Really? Who are they?"

Liza was saddened to see not an iota of recognition in Roseanne's politely interested but largely unconcerned expression. Feeling shaken, she looked to J.D. who took her hand and took over.

"Roseanne," he began, "we've learned that Liza's mother, when she was about seventeen, worked at Wilson's Dude Ranch in Wickenburg, where she fell in love with a young man that summer. He was tall, with dark hair and blue eyes. She became pregnant, but when she returned to Pine Bluff, she was afraid to tell her father. He was very protective of her since her mother had died years before."

Halfway through his recitation, Roseanne began to look agitated, rubbing her hands together repeatedly, her eyes darting around the room as if looking for an escape. "I...I can understand that. My father was like that, always watching me." Suddenly her face moved into a cunning smile. "But I fooled him. I'd sneak out and meet my friends at night. Poor Priscilla worried all the time. But I had to get away from him. I couldn't breathe." She looked at Liza imploringly. "You understand, don't you?"

"Yes, I do," Liza answered, swallowing around a lump in her throat. "That last summer, at the dude ranch, you managed to fool your father and Mr. Wilson, didn't you? You snuck off to meet someone, right?"

Roseanne's eyes were focused on the past. "He was afraid we'd get caught, but I wasn't. I'd have done anything to be with him. I wanted us to run away and never come back. But he was so sensible. He said we had to wait until he had more to offer me." She shook her head, her expression anguished. "Didn't he know all I wanted was him, to be with him?"

Liza took a deep breath. "Who was he, Roseanne?"

Her face became stormy. "I should have known it wouldn't last. That fat Mr. Wilson called me in one afternoon, told me he knew I'd been sneaking around behind his back and meeting someone. He told me he was going to call the police and have the man I loved with all my heart arrested. For what? I screamed at him. Wilson sneered as he told me. Corrupting a minor. Statutory rape. He'd call my father, he said, and they'd see to it that the sentence would be long and harsh." Tears slid down her cheeks, but she was unaware. "I couldn't let that happen, not to him. He was so good. The best thing that ever happened to me."

Liza had thought something serious must have happened, that Roseanne hadn't just simply taken off on a whim. "So instead you left the ranch."

Roseanne stared into middle distance, her voice a chilling monotone. "I had to, don't you see? I couldn't let them hurt him. I knew my father wouldn't hesitate to have him arrested. I sent him a message through one of the grooms, told him I had to leave and he mustn't try to find me." She was shaking now, the sobs hiccuping from her. "I didn't want to leave him. Oh, God, I didn't want to do it."

Liza moved to sit alongside her on the wide hassock, sliding an arm along her shoulders. "It's all right. Please don't cry."

But Roseanne couldn't stop, her breath hitching out, the sounds mournful. She bent nearly double, reliving it all, in obvious pain.

"We didn't mean to upset you like this," J.D. said softly.

With visible effort, Roseanne straightened. "I'm all right. Just give me a minute." She patted Liza's hand and rose somewhat unsteadily, then walked over to stand gazing out at the rain.

Liza watched Max run to Roseanne, press his front paws to the door and begin to whine. She stood as Roseanne let the dog out. "Can I get you something, perhaps a cup of tea?" Liza asked her.

"Yes, that would be nice," Roseanne answered without turning around.

"May I use your phone?" J.D. asked and saw Roseanne nod absently. He followed Liza to the kitchen where she was putting water on to boil.

"What do you make of it?" Liza asked him. "God, I hope we didn't send her over the edge."

"She's stronger than you think," J.D. said. "There's a couple of puzzle pieces still missing. For instance, Jack Guthrie's disappearance worries me."

"You mean about his cabin burning down? I suppose Lester might have done it, in the state he apparently was in."

J.D. was more inclined to think it went beyond that. Like maybe Lester setting fire to the cabin with Guthrie in it. He didn't like to think of Lester as a killer, but even a mild-mannered man dealing with the rapist who ruined his daughter could lose it. He picked up the wall phone.

Liza poured boiling water onto the tea bag she'd placed in a mug she'd taken from the cupboard. Perhaps tonight she'd call Dawn and ask her to look up psychogenic amnesia so she'd know how to handle Roseanne.

As she pondered that, she carried the tea back to the enclosed porch. To her surprise, the room was empty and the door ajar. Hurrying over, she saw Roseanne shrugging into a red sweater and following Max. "Roseanne," she called out. "You'll catch cold. Come back."

J.D. came up behind her. "What happened?"

"I think she's trying to get Max to come in and he's playing hard to get." Liza heard her calling the puppy, but the little dickens paid no attention and shot into the trees. Roseanne stopped at the edge of the woods, looking hesitant. Suddenly she squared her shoulders and followed after the dog. "J.D., I think we'd better go after them. Roseanne said she never went in there anymore."

Ignoring the rain, Liza hurried across the lawn and stepped past the first row of trees with J.D. close behind her. She could hear Roseanne not far ahead, calling out for her dog, could see her red sweater as she dodged in and out among the pines. "They're running parallel to the road, heading toward the woods in back of Lester's home," she told J.D.

"Is this where you went searching for that pine tree?"

"A little farther on, I think. But I never did find it." She slowed, not wanting to startle Roseanne by calling out to her.

J.D. saw the puppy sniff at the base of a tree and Roseanne come up behind him. She nearly had him, but he took off like a shot as her shoes slipped on the damp grass. She went down and all the fight seemed to go out of her. Overtaking Liza, J.D. rushed to her side. "Let me help you up, Roseanne," he said as Liza came up to them.

"I've got to get my dog," Roseanne muttered, getting to her knees and trying to stand. "Scrappy, where are you?" she yelled out.

Confused, Liza watched her take off after Max. "Scrappy? That was the name of her dog when she was young. What is she doing?"

J.D.'s mouth was a grim line as he set out after Roseanne. He thought he knew what had happened. "She must be back in the past."

Abruptly Roseanne stopped, her hands flying to clutch at her chest. "No, Daddy, please, no. Stop. You're killing him." She stood frozen, rooted to the ground, staring wide-eyed as Max busily dug at the base of a pine tree.

Liza caught up to J.D. and stopped alongside. "That's it, the bent tree in her painting. Oh, God. What's happened to her?" she whispered.

"She's back there," J.D. told her quietly, "back when she was seventeen and witnessing something she's buried inside her mind all these years."

"Daddy, don't hit him anymore, please. Oh, God, please make him stop." Roseanne fell to her knees in front of the puppy as he kept on digging frantically. Bending over in her private agony, Roseanne made a low keening noise, the sound heartbreaking in its anguish.

Liza could stand it no longer. Moving to her mother, she put her arms around the thin shoulders and leaned down to her. "It's all right now. Everything's going to be all right."

Max was still digging, but J.D. didn't need to see what was buried there to know what it was. Jack Guthrie hadn't been in the burning cabin after all. He'd be willing to wager that his remains had been under that bent pine for all these years, that Lester had killed the rapist and buried him there. That had been the horror that Roseanne had seen that day while Priscilla had gone to her meeting, the thing that had traumatized the young woman so badly that it had taken her over a year to regain some sense of self.

"Take the puppy, Liza," he instructed. "I'll take Roseanne." As Liza, obeying for a change, moved to pick up Max, he leaned down and gathered Roseanne Fleming to him. "Just hold on to me, Roseanne. You're going to be fine." Carrying her, he set out through the woods to her house.

The light autumn rain had dampened their clothes, the wet ground muddied their shoes. Unmindful of her own messy state, Liza helped Roseanne to clean up and change, then accepted a towel to dry off her own hair. By the time they went back to the living room where J.D. had a blazing fire going in the hearth, Roseanne had finally stopped shaking, and her gray eyes were clear.

Accepting the cup of tea from J.D., Roseanne took a hearty sip and seemingly waited for the warmth to invade her. She closed her eyes, perhaps trying to absorb it all.

"Are you all right?" Liza asked, moving to her side on the couch.

Slowly Roseanne turned her head toward Liza and opened her eyes. "Thanks to you, and to J.D., I think I'm better than I have been in a long while. I'm remembering so much, though some of it isn't clear."

J.D. edged his chair closer. "Maybe we can help clarify things. Can you tell us about what happened back then?"

She pulled in a tremulous breath, unsure if she could say the words aloud. "There was a man named Jack Guthrie," she began. She spoke softly, but they heard every word as she detailed that frightening night when she'd been raped. Roseanne became aware that Liza had reached to grip her hand as she went on to explain how later the next afternoon, she'd been resting in bed and heard noises outside her window. She looked out and saw Jack by the cabin loading boxes into a truck. Then her father appeared and the two disappeared into the woods.

"You followed them?" J.D. asked.

"I had to. I was afraid Dad would do something terrible." She closed her eyes a moment, then went on. "It was raining, like today," she said, her voice surprisingly firm. "Scrappy and I ran in, and I had trouble spotting Dad. But Scrappy didn't, rushing after him on his short little legs. When I finally reached them, I stopped in my tracks.

"Dad had Jack cornered by that crooked pine tree. He'd picked up a thick stick and was beating him about the head and shoulders with it." Roseanne swallowed hard as the scene replayed itself on the screen of her mind while she held Liza's hand in a fierce grip. "Blood was flying onto Dad's white shirt, I remember, but he still didn't stop. Jack fell to the ground and didn't move, but Dad kept on hitting him. Scrappy was barking hard and finally he ran up to Dad and began tugging with his teeth on his pant leg. Dad stopped long enough to...to kick my dog hard enough to send him hurtling into the trunk of the tree. Then he turned back and continued beating Jack. I crawled over to Scrappy and picked him up in my arms. I held him close, but I could tell his heart had stopped beating."

Liza smoothed back her mother's hair, unaware that her cheeks were damp with tears as she shared Roseanne's pain.

"I sat on the wet ground, holding my dead dog and begging my father to stop, telling him that he was killing another human being. He wouldn't listen. Finally he stepped back and turned to me. I think he'd forgotten I was there because he seemed sort of dazed. He helped me up, took Scrappy away from me and laid him next to Jack, then put his arm around me and we walked back to the house. I remember he helped me into bed and then he left again. I must have fallen asleep because the next thing I knew, Dr. Rogers was there and so was Priscilla." She ran a shaky hand over her face. "But everything after that is sort of hazy."

J.D. waited a moment, letting Liza soothe Roseanne and hand her a tissue to wipe her face. Not knowing if she remembered anything prior to that night, he decided to move slowly, fearful she might regress again. "Were you and your father getting along before this thing with Jack happened?"

"About the same as always," Roseanne remarked. "We got along when I did as he wished. But I remember I'd gone walking in the woods that day trying to think of a way to tell my father that... that I was pregnant." Her brow wrinkled as parts of the memory refused to click in. "I don't remember ever getting around to telling him even later."

"Do you recall what did happen after you and your father came out of the woods that night?" J.D. asked. "Were the police called? Did anyone come around asking about Jack Guthrie?"

She searched her mind. "I don't remember seeing the police. I think I asked Priscilla once what had happened to Jack, and she told me he'd moved away. I knew that wasn't right, but I couldn't grasp what actually had taken place. I think I made myself forget because... because if I let myself remember, then I'd have to admit that my father murdered a man."

She'd come to the right conclusion on her own. "But he did murder Jack Guthrie right in front of your eyes, didn't he, Roseanne?" J.D. asked quietly.

She looked down at her hand still held in Liza's. "Yes, he did." She raised her other hand to her forehead. "Oh, God, what's going to happen to him now?"

J.D. wanted to lead her away from that for now, to hear what else she could recall. "What happened about your pregnancy? Do you remember?"

Roseanne's head came up, her expression serious as she wrestled with fragments of memory. "I...I think they told me I lost the baby. I asked Dad once when he'd come into my room late at night and I couldn't sleep. He said that we were better off because the baby's father had been a rapist." Her eyes cleared and she looked at J.D. "Only, that wasn't true. Jack wasn't my baby's father."

"Who was?" Liza asked, hoping desperately that she would remember this part.

Roseanne's face softened and her eyes warmed. "A man I met earlier that summer. We were so much in love. But I had to leave him or Dad would have sent him to prison."

"What's his name, Roseanne?" J.D. pressed.

"Gray Eubanks," she said, her voice strong. "I wonder whatever happened to him."

J.D. smiled at her. Finally, out of all this, comes something good. "He lives about twenty miles from here, and he very much would like to see you, Roseanne."

Shock and disbelief mingled in her expression. "Are you sure? Twenty miles. Why hasn't he ever come to see me then? Because of my father? Because I—"

"It's a long story," J.D. interrupted. "Trust me and you'll soon know everything. When this is over, I'll take you to Gray."

Her hand flew to her mouth. "I can't believe Gray's nearby." Then her expressive face fell. "I don't imagine he'd want me after all this time. I'm much older, much . . ."

"He's never stopped loving you," Liza said, brushing away her tears as a smile finally broke through. "Are you up to another piece of startling news?"

"I guess so." She looked from one to the other. "I don't know why you two have shown up like this, to help me remember and to help me get past all this. But I'm so grateful you have."

"You were traumatized by witnessing your father's act, Roseanne," J.D. went on to explain. "It was too terrible for your mind to absorb, so you blocked out that whole year. Even now, it's painful to remember, but you're strong enough to handle it or you probably wouldn't have."

"A whole year?" She appeared momentarily confused. "I lost a whole year?" ·

"Perhaps you really didn't lose it," Liza said. "Nor did you lose your baby. You had a healthy little girl."

Roseanne's eyes widened, then filled. "How do you know that?"

"Because I was that baby, the one born to you twenty-eight years ago this past April 15." She blinked at another rush of tears and found her throat tight. "I'm your daughter, Roseanne."

"Oh my God." She held out her arms, gathering Liza close. "I can't believe this."

Watching, J.D. found himself moved far more than he'd suspected he would be. This was what Liza had meant, what she'd dreamed of all these years. He'd been wrong to discourage her. His father had turned out to be a disappointment, but that didn't mean others couldn't be luckier. He found himself smiling like an idiot as the two women pulled back to examine one another in the light of this new knowledge.

"The eyes. You have Gray's eyes, of course." Roseanne was smiling around her tears. "I remember his wonderful eyes."

"But I have your hair and your build and your artistic talent. Not to the degree you have it, but..."

"You design clothes. I remember." She choked back another emotional outburst. "Let me hug you again. You have no idea what this moment means to me. I've...I've felt so alone."

Liza clutched her mother to her, their tears mingling. "It means every bit as much to me. You don't have to be alone anymore."

Little niggling questions were working their way into Roseanne's consciousness as she drew back again. "But who raised you? Where have you been?"

Swiping at her eyes with a tissue, Liza explained about her adoption, about Priscilla and Ethel and their involvement. Liza picked up her purse and withdrew the black box. "Do you remember this?"

Roseanne pressed her lips together, struggling to hold back more tears. "My box. I kept the ring Gray carved for me in there. And my diary and . . ."

"The dried rose." Liza removed the things she'd carried with her since finding it. "They're all here."

Roseanne looked over each item, pausing over the dried flower. "He used to call me his wild rose." Carefully she replaced everything, then held the box close to her heart. She had to know something. "Did my father do this? Did he take you from me and make those two ladies give you away to strangers?"

They were finished with lies and half truths. "I'm afraid he did. But, in all fairness, I think he believed that Jack Guthrie was my father, and he couldn't handle that."

"But was he aware that I'd sunk into this...this what? A deep depression or whatever?"

"It's called psychogenic amnesia," J.D. explained. "The mind shuts out events it can't handle. And yes, I believe he did know. He chose to ignore your needs, thinking only of his own. After all, if you'd have remembered, then you might have told someone that he'd killed a man."

Roseanne sank back into the corner of the couch. "I can't believe he did this to me. I thought he cared about me."

"Don't dwell on it now," Liza told her. "Perhaps he'll have a reasonable explanation for what he did." Although she couldn't imagine what it could be.

Roseanne turned to J.D., having thought of something else. "Are you going after my father now that you know?"

As if in answer, the front doorbell rang, followed by a hard pounding. "Roseanne, open this door," Lester Fleming shouted.

But before she could rise to let him in, he used his key, swung the door wide and stomped in. His face red with fury as he clamped down on his cigar, Lester glared at all three of them. "I saw your van out there, J.D. What are you doing bothering my daughter? How dare you bring that woman in here? You'd better have some good answers for me, son."

J.D. rose and walked over to Lester. "No, sir, I think you've got this turned around. *You* better have some good answers for *me*."

Chapter Twelve

"I can't help feeling sorry for him," Roseanne said as she walked through the double doors at the back of the courtroom. She was comfortably aware of Liza's hand at her elbow and of J.D. flanking her other side. She'd insisted on going to her father's arraignment and they'd insisted on accompanying her.

Roseanne was awfully glad they'd been there with her.

"I feel the same," Liza said, walking toward a row of chairs in the hallway outside Courtroom C in the high-ceilinged county courthouse. Lester had been booked and arraigned within the prescribed twenty-four hours as required, which was good since they needed to get all this behind them. Her mother had remained strong throughout the brief hearing, but Liza sensed the tension in her through the thin material of the jacket she wore. "Let's sit down over here for a minute."

As the lawman who'd arrested Lester Fleming, J.D. had mixed emotions. Certainly a man who'd brutally murdered another, as Lester apparently had according to his daughter's eyewitness account, and showed not a bit of remorse, deserved to be punished. Yet if he were to consider his personal feelings, J.D. could understand the rage that could cause a father to want to kill his daughter's rapist. The basic difference, as J.D. saw it, was that though most men in that situation might *want* to kill, they wouldn't carry out the deed.

Lester had.

Watching the two women, mother and daughter, who'd been inseparable during this trying time, he felt a rush of warmth at how quickly they'd begun a relationship. "I think it's commendable of both of you to be so forgiving," he said. After all, Lester had kept his daughter a prisoner of her own fears and had hired a man to run his granddaughter out of town using some violent tactics. He knew he wouldn't have been quite so quick to offer absolution, even though Lester and Clarence were now being held in adjoining cells.

Roseanne sat down and looked up at J.D. "Carrying grudges doesn't work for me, J.D.," she told him quite honestly. "It's a real waste of energy and hurts me more than the person I'm annoyed with."

Annoyed with. Her father had taken years from her and yet, Roseanne was merely annoyed with him, Liza realized. Over the past couple of days, she'd been continually amazed at her mother's capacity for love and forgiveness. She could learn from her, she decided as she smiled at Roseanne. "He's paying the price now for what he's done," she said, picturing the white-haired old man who'd walked into the courtroom in handcuffs, scarcely looking up during the proceedings. His close friend and

Roseanne's former father-in-law, Owen Mitchell, would be defending him. "Not just in public humiliation and a probable prison sentence, but because he's all but lost contact with you, the one person he was trying to protect at the expense of others."

J.D. shook his head. "Actually, Lester was trying to protect himself more than Roseanne," he pointed out.

"In the end, yes," Roseanne acknowledged. "But in the beginning, he was trying to shield me, to keep me out of harm's way. Perhaps because my mother died and he felt the responsibility of raising a little girl all alone."

"That happened to me, too," Liza reminded her. "But Ralph Parker was very different from Lester Fleming. He encouraged me to try my wings, to experience new things. He taught me right from wrong, then trusted me to live up to his expectations."

Roseanne crossed her long legs as she angled toward Liza. "There's something else here that I think is important. Apparently Ralph Parker was confident of your love for him and not afraid that if you stepped out into the world, you'd no longer care about him. My father didn't have that kind of faith in me. He always made me feel that I'd choose wrongly if left alone to do the choosing without his guidance. Heavens, he even handpicked my husband." She shook her head in wonder. "And I went along with everything, like a fool. Poor Reid. I'm sure he never had a happy day with me."

Liza touched her mother's hand reassuringly. "You went along because you were so traumatized by earlier events that you were vulnerable to your father's manipulations. But no one was pushing Reid, so apparently he went into the marriage with both eyes open."

Roseanne looked thoughtful. "Perhaps, but he was as much a victim as I. Owen Mitchell and my father, being such good friends, had wanted the two of us to marry since we were children. Reid wasn't strong enough to stand up to his father until he became so unhappy that he finally found the courage.''

Squeezing her mother's hand, Liza smiled. ''And you found the courage the other day when you told the truth about what happened that night so long ago, even if it meant risking your relationship with Lester.''

J.D. agreed. ''That was a tough call. When he started yelling that day in your living room, I wasn't sure you'd stand firm. I was very impressed when you did.''

Roseanne waved off the compliments. ''Oh, don't slip a halo on my head just yet. I'm very human with many failings, I assure you.'' She glanced toward the closed courtroom doors. ''Human enough to worry about what will become of him.''

J.D. stepped closer as two attorneys deep in conversation passed by. ''He'll get a fair trial by his peers, Roseanne. And Owen Mitchell's a man with an outstanding record as a criminal defense attorney.''

''I guess you're right.'' Roseanne stifled a yawn. She still wasn't sleeping well nights. ''What happens now?'' she asked J.D.

Shoving his hands in his pockets, J.D. explained. ''Well, today, we've had the first step, the arraignment where the charges were spelled out and you heard Owen Mitchell put in a plea of not guilty. Now the investigating team from the prosecutor's office goes to work gathering evidence, hoping for a conviction, while the defense prepares their case.''

''Why do you suppose Mr. Mitchell is pleading Lester not guilty when he knows the prosecution has an eyewitness?'' Liza asked.

"There are often extenuating circumstances. A man driven to kill by shock over his raped daughter. And there's temporary insanity."

Liza frowned. "Do you think he'll get off?"

"That's up to the jury, and ultimately the judge."

Liza turned to Roseanne. "When I drove over to pick you up today, I spotted a crew moving into the woods behind Lester's home. I would imagine they're digging around the base of that pine tree, right?" she asked J.D.

"I'm sure they are." He didn't think it necessary to tell them that he'd received a call earlier from his deputy informing him that they'd located several bones belonging to an adult male, and also the skeleton of what appeared to be a small dog, plus the frame of a rotted suitcase.

"It isn't going to be easy finding twelve impartial people in a case against the most powerful man in town, now, is it?" Liza asked.

The likelihood of a request for a change of venue was strong, but J.D. again decided there was no point in jumping the gun until and if that became fact.

"It's going to take weeks, maybe months, isn't it?" Roseanne asked. The prospect of the whole ordeal going on endlessly was enough to stagger her. She'd already asked J.D. if she'd have to testify and he'd explained that she was the prosecutor's main witness.

"It's definitely going to go on for a long while," J.D. answered, unable to sugarcoat the truth.

Roseanne pressed her lips together briefly, then turned to Liza. "I have this irrational wish to go away, to just not show up." She shook her head, dismissing the thought. "Of course, I won't do that, but I'd sure like to."

"I'll be here with you, if you want me to be." Liza had already decided that she couldn't let Roseanne go through this alone. Her mother was definitely stronger than days ago, but she was still more fragile than she should be.

"Of course I want you here." Roseanne's eyes were overly bright with unshed tears, something that happened frequently these days. "I've only just found you. We have so many years to make up for."

"And we will, too," Liza assured her. "And once the trial is over, we'll go away somewhere, a trip to take your mind off everything unpleasant where we can just relax and have fun."

Roseanne looked suddenly wistful. "Fun. I can't honestly remember the last time I had fun or felt really happy."

Liza found her statement a heartbreaker. She glanced at J.D. as he crouched down in front of them, his gaze on Roseanne.

"I have a suggestion that might make you happy."

"What might that be?" Roseanne asked.

"A visit to the Flying D Ranch in Palo Verde. There's a man there who'd very much like to see you." He noticed the quick concern leap into her eyes. "I've been keeping Gray updated by phone, but he wants to know when I'm going to take you to see him." He looked over at Liza. "And he wants to see his daughter, too."

Roseanne closed her eyes briefly before turning to Liza. "Does he really want to see me after all that's happened?"

Liza smiled. "I *know* he does."

"I know it, too," J.D. added.

Glancing down at her beige suit and pink blouse, Roseanne frowned. "I should probably get something new to wear."

As J.D. stood, Liza laughed. If Roseanne was concerned about looking good, she was going to be all right.

Rising, she picked up her leather bag. "Well, then, come on. Let's go shopping."

Gray Eubanks sat in the big leather chair behind his desk in his den and repressed the urge to run a hand over his hair to check it out. He hadn't felt this nervous since he was sixteen. Maybe not even then. At that age, he'd owned the world, or thought he had. But now, he had a lot riding on this meeting.

What if she turned from him? he asked himself, for perhaps the tenth time in the past hour. *She won't.* J.D.'s words echoed in his head. *She's as nervous as you are,* he'd informed Gray this morning when they'd talked. Impossible, he thought. Roseanne wasn't in a wheelchair. What did she have to be nervous about?

With Rudy's help, he'd dressed carefully, then agonized over where to be when she arrived. He knew that J.D. had told her about his accident, about why he hadn't gone to her all these years, about the wheelchair. And he'd decided he didn't want her to see him in that damn chair, not this first time after nearly thirty years.

Astride his stallion would have been best. Gray was vain enough to know that he looked good, damn good, like any other man on his horse. They could have gone for a ride together, gotten reacquainted that way. He remembered how she'd loved to ride like the wind, often bareback, defying orders at the dude ranch. She'd loved the feeling of freedom as much as he. But what would he do when it was time to dismount?

So he'd decided on his den, the room he liked best, seated behind the desk that offered some measure of protection. He was already vulnerable to her by the fact that he loved her so much. He couldn't afford to be totally vulnerable. No man could.

Recalling his last few conversations with J.D., Gray thought again about all Roseanne had gone through during the years they'd spent near one another, yet vastly separated. He'd suffered the loss of the use of his legs, but she'd lived her own private hell.

The news that Lester Fleming had been arrested on murder charges didn't come as a great shock to Gray. He'd always thought the man was power drunk with a hair-trigger temper—a bad combination. Yet a part of him understood the urge to kill the man who'd raped Roseanne. His heart turned over at the thought of what she'd had to endure. Small wonder her mind had blocked out the events of that night, and much that had come after. He was amazed that she'd survived intact, that she'd finally remembered and wasn't bitter.

Nor did their daughter hold any grudges over the way circumstances had kept her from knowing her parents until now. J.D. had brought Liza to him last night, and they'd had a wonderful evening. She was everything he could have wanted in a grown child, and more. She was beautiful, the picture of her mother years ago, with that quick, musical laugh and the same impatient gestures. And her eyes—it had been like gazing into a mirror, only hers were far lovelier.

They'd had dinner and talked, about her years growing up, her adoptive parents, her life in Tucson. And she'd wanted to know all about him—his work, the ranch, everything. Never once did she make him feel less than a man, not by word or gesture, because of his being confined to a wheelchair. Instead, she'd been openly affectionate, hugging him, reaching to touch his hand, sitting alongside him. He'd felt warmed and humbled by her unconditional love, a bonus he hadn't dared hope for.

She'd answered his questions about Roseanne and re-
cited the story she'd told them, and he'd hung on her
every word. And then he'd asked about her feelings for
J.D., who'd let her do most of the talking but whose
hand she held on to in a gesture as natural as breathing.
She'd looked into J.D.'s eyes and smiled and that had
said it all, for he could see that J.D. felt the same. It was
all he could have wished for both of them.

His thoughts drifted again to Roseanne, and a smile
came to him unbidden as he recalled the way she'd looked
that long-ago summer, her zest for life, the way she'd
opened to him like a flower unfolding. J.D. had told him
she was fretting over how he'd view her now, nearly thirty
years later. If only she knew how often he'd dreamed of
this day, she wouldn't waste another moment worrying.

He heard the sound of an engine and swiveled around
in his chair. J.D.'s van pulled up near the front door.
Peering through the wooden slats of the blinds on his
window, Gray felt his heart pick up its rhythm. Then she
stepped out and his pulse began to pound.

She was as slender as he remembered, her hair darker
and shorter now, shimmering in the afternoon sun with
the streaks of red he'd always admired. She was wearing
yellow, his favorite color, and he wondered if she also had
been remembering. He watched his daughter reach out a
hand to Roseanne, as if to encourage her, and saw that
slow smile that had haunted his dreams. Gray swung
back to face the desk, nervously clearing his throat.

In the hallway, J.D. walked alongside Roseanne as Liza
trailed behind. "He's in his study, that open doorway on
the right. What would you prefer, that we go in with you
or wait outside?" he asked.

She'd spent a restless night and a jittery morning. But on the ride over, suddenly Roseanne had felt a sense of calm she hadn't known in a while. She wasn't coming to Gray the way she would have wished, young and unmarked and full of vision as she'd once been. But she was coming with love in her heart and the hope that together they could wipe out the past and think about a future. She was no longer afraid, but rather excited.

Roseanne stopped, turning to smile at both of them. "I'll be fine. Please don't worry. Go out and enjoy yourselves."

Liza kissed her cheek and J.D. gave her a hug. Then, hand in hand, they retraced their steps and went outside.

Roseanne took a deep breath and walked into the den.

She saw him immediately, seated behind his desk, sunlight from the windows pouring in on his dark head. Slowly she moved toward him, noticing the touches of gray on his sideburns, sprinkled there by time. She saw his big hands, the first that had ever touched her, the only ones that had ignited her, folded now atop his desk. She saw his mouth and remembered, as if it were yesterday, the pleasure it had given her. She saw those incredible blue eyes, the ones he'd passed on to their daughter. And she saw the hint of nerves as a muscle in his jaw twitched.

The silence stretched on as they looked their fill, but it wasn't an uncomfortable stillness. Finally she smiled at him. "Hello, Gray."

"Roseanne." He was pleased that his voice hadn't wavered, but he didn't trust himself to say more just yet. He was content just looking at her, hardly able to believe she was really here where he'd pictured her so often in his restive dreams. She was here and suddenly, the clock was rolling backward and he was twenty again, and in love for the first time. In love forever.

Because her knees were none too steady, Roseanne slipped onto the chair facing his desk. "You look so good, so very good." She had to blink as her eyes filled, triggered by a myriad of emotions.

He shrugged, trying for nonchalance. "A little older, a lot wiser." His eyes met hers. "You're as lovely as I remember," Gray told her, meaning every word.

She gave a short laugh. "Your memory's a bit rusty, but I thank you."

"There's nothing wrong with my memory. However, my legs are another story." He'd decided to get the subject out in the open right off so he could gauge her reaction. Because, despite J.D.'s reassurances, if Roseanne couldn't get past this hurdle, he needed to know up front.

"I know about your accident. How could you have thought that would matter to me, Gray?" Going on instinct, she rose and walked around the desk. She waited until he swiveled his chair around, then crouched alongside, taking his hand. "How could you ever have thought I'd stop loving you, no matter what happened to either of us?"

Gray's other hand reached to stroke her hair. "I couldn't be sure. There's so much I can't do these days."

"And so much you *can* do." Her fingers laced with his and she hung on, as if to a lifeline. "Did J.D. tell you why I left Wilson's that night?"

His jaw tightened. "Yes. He threatened to have me jailed."

"I couldn't risk that. But you have no idea what I went through afterward, the tears I shed over having to give you up."

"I wish you'd have come to me. We'd have found a way somehow. You wouldn't have had to go through . . . all that happened later."

"I wish I'd run back to you, too." She smiled and reached up to lay a hand along his cheek. "If wishes were horses, right?"

"Yes, beggars would ride." He leaned closer to her, his eyes burning with an intensity she remembered from years ago. "Not one day has gone by that I haven't thought of you. It was as if someone ripped out my heart. I left Wilson's, determined to make a ton of money and then march to your father's door to claim you."

"I never wanted money."

"No, but I felt I had to impress him."

"You would have."

"He didn't know about us, about that summer?"

"No. I understand that our housekeeper tried to explain, but Dad wouldn't listen. That's why he went out of control. He thought that the man who'd raped me was the baby's father."

"I'd do anything if I could turn back the clock and spare you that terrible attack."

She looked down at their tightly clasped hands. "Fortunately, I can't remember most of it." Determined to make things positive, she brightened. "What do you think of Liza?"

His smile came instantly. "I think she's every bit as lovely and intelligent as her mother."

"She is beautiful, isn't she?" Roseanne straightened, leaning against the desk's edge, studying his face. His wonderful face. "There's so much I want to ask you, so much I want to tell you."

He took her hand in both of his. "We have time now, don't we? Nothing but time."

Her eyes drifted to his mouth. "I want to kiss you."

Gray smiled. "You always were the bold one. Come here." His strong hands scooted her onto his lap.

"Oh, are you sure it's all right?"

"It's very much all right." His mouth touched hers and, in seconds, the years fell away. He was back in his youth, kissing the only woman who could make his blood race through his veins.

Roseanne's arms went around his neck and she kissed him just as fervently as she had as a young virgin. Memories flooded her as she felt his hands at her back, pressing her closer. No other man had ever made her feel this way, no one ever could.

Her breathing unsteady, she eased back from him, linked her arms around his neck and touched her forehead to his. "So, where do we go from here, Gray Eubanks?"

"We follow the path we should have followed the first time."

"We're not the same people we were back then, Gray."

"I know that. So we'll take some time to sort things out, to get reacquainted. I no longer expect miracles, Roseanne. I'll settle for a generous helping of happiness."

"You think being with me is settling?"

"I think being with you would be a dream come true."

She sighed. "There's my father's trial to get through."

"I'll be at your side, if you want me there."

She smoothed back his hair, a loving gesture. "I want you there. I want to be with you. I would give anything if we could all be a family, the three of us, now that our daughter has reunited us."

"I think that'll have to be the four of us." His hand on the desk's edge, Gray swiveled his chair around so they could look out the window. Through the blinds, they could see Liza sitting on the grass with her back against a tall oak tree. J.D. lay with his head in her lap. As they watched, she bent to kiss him, long and lingeringly. "Do they remind you of anyone?"

Roseanne smiled at him. "Do you think they'll find a special acorn under that tree?"

Gray reached into his shirt pocket. "Like this one, you mean?" He slipped the ring on her finger. "Liza gave me this last night. Now it's finally where it was meant to be." He knew there were hurdles yet for them to overcome. But now at last, he had hope. "Together we can do anything, have everything."

She was content with what they already had. If this was all there would be, she would take it, for it was already more than she'd dared hope for. "What was it that Bette Davis said in that movie? Don't let's ask for the moon. We already have the stars." And she kissed him.

Liza lay with J.D. wrapped around her, waiting for her heartbeat to slow, waiting for the room to right itself. Dizzy. He made her dizzy and frenzied and wilder than she'd ever been. And she loved every second of it. Loved him.

J.D. rolled from her, taking her along for the ride, then settling her against his body, still heated from their lovemaking. He drew in a breath and inhaled the special scent that he'd forever recognize as hers alone. "I can't get over it," he said, more to himself than to her.

Stretching, Liza slid her bare foot along the length of his calf, sighing at the delicious contact. "Can't get over what?"

"The fact that the more I have you, the more I want you. That's never happened to me before, not with anyone. I have a history of getting bored easily."

She raised her head, propped it on her hand as she bent her elbow. "Is that a warning?"

"Yeah." He stretched to kiss her again. "Your last warning. You'd better run from me because this is it."

"It? What?"

"Escape now or you're stuck forever."

Liza stifled a yawn. She'd driven up from Tucson nonstop after a full day's work and perhaps her mind was foggy, Liza thought. Tomorrow, the trial started and, as she'd promised Roscanne, she'd come to be with her. During the weeks it had taken both sides to prepare the case, she'd been driving up on weekends, or J.D. had been driving down. Their need to be together hadn't diminished. Their rest time had.

"What am I escaping from and what will I be stuck with if I don't? The condemned woman needs to know these things." Her hand toyed with the hair on his chest.

"The answer to both questions is the same. Me."

She frowned, trying to follow him. "Forgive me, I'm tired. What do you mean?"

"That I'm tired of all this, driving three or four hours so we can be together a fast twenty-four. I'm through with it. Kaput. Finished."

"Oh. Well, okay then." Pulling the sheet around her, she sat up. The hurt was swift and sharp, but she wouldn't let him see. "Don't think it hasn't been fun." She stuck one foot onto the floor.

He yanked her back, two strong hands dragging her up close to his frowning face. "I might have known you'd misunderstand."

"I don't think so. When it's over, it's over, right?"

"Wrong. I don't want to spend another hour on the road or another minute waiting for you to arrive. I want us to live together, right here, in my house."

"Live together." Liza eased back again. "I don't know, J.D. I . . ."

Again, he hauled her up within a whisper of his mouth. "As husband and wife, silly. I'm asking you to marry me." He closed the gap between them and kissed her.

The kiss was wonderful, but she still had questions. "Just so you can get off the road?"

J.D. shifted to a sitting position, laying her across his lap. "Yeah. Not because I want your sexy little body next to mine as we go to sleep each night, and still there every morning. Not because I want to be the father of your children. Not because I'm nuts about you. Only so I won't have to drive so much."

"Oh. Put that way, so charmingly, how can I refuse?"

He kissed her again but he saw that she still wasn't smiling. "All right, what is it? What else is wrong?"

"Nothing, really." She ran a finger along his strong jawline. "It's just that, this little phrase *nuts about you*. It's so... so incomplete. What exactly does it mean?"

She wanted the words, those three little words he'd never said to any woman. "Just like a woman. You want it all, don't you?"

"Yes, Sheriff, I guess I do."

"Like I said before, I didn't plan on falling in love. But it happened." His arms drew her nearer as his eyes darkened. "It sure happened, lady. I love you. I sure do love you."

She smiled up at him. "That wasn't so hard, was it?"

"Yeah, it was."

"It'll get easier."

"What about you?"

She wasn't going to make it easy for him, either. "What about me?"

"How do you feel? I think I ought to know."

She traced his ear with a finger. "I'm fond of you."

"Fond?"

"All right, I'm crazy about you."

"Which translates to?"

Her smile turned sensual as she pressed closer. "That I love you, Sheriff. Now, what are you going to do about it?"

"Kiss me and find out."

"Is that an order? What did I tell you about giving me orders all—"

He shut her up the best way he knew how, by kissing her quiet.

Abby Thatcher stood in the doorway and gazed at the empty office that once had housed the thriving law practice of Winthrop Ames, Esquire. She felt a mixture of relief and regret.

Over. It was all over. More than forty years working in this small place, literally hundreds of clients who'd paced these polished wood floors, and now no more.

Since Winthrop's death months ago, she'd taken her time, disbursing his remaining cases, dispensing the mounds of paperwork to their proper recipients and finally selling off the furniture, the file cabinets, the law books. She brushed at a strand of her salt-and-pepper hair as she took a final look around.

This room had seen its share of tears and heard muted laughter, as well. There'd been the sadness of divorces, of the reading of wills, and the joy of new home purchases and of happy adoptions. She'd been a part of it all, as she'd been a part of Winthrop's life. A good part, though she'd thought he hadn't noticed.

But he had.

He'd remembered her in his will, leaving her a comfortable sum which, along with the generous salary he'd paid her through the years, would allow her to live without worries. Monetary worries, that is.

She would still have to learn to fill her hours each day, since she'd no longer be coming here. She'd have to learn to get along without Winthrop's comforting presence, too, which she hadn't quite managed to do yet. But she would. She was strong. Winthrop had told her that on many occasions.

Abby was also comforted by the fact that she'd personally handled each and every file that had been special to Winthrop. The babies, the adoptions, that he'd so enjoyed. She hoped and prayed that the receipt of the adoption packets had gone well.

Switching off the light, she sighed deeply, then closed and locked the door for the final time. Her work here was finished. Walking briskly, not looking back, Abby Thatcher left the building.

*   *   *   *   *

Silhouette®

SPECIAL EDITION

COMING NEXT MONTH

#979 SUNSHINE AND THE SHADOWMASTER—
Christine Rimmer
That Special Woman!/The Jones Gang

From the moment they were thrown together, Heather Conley and
Lucas Drury were instantly drawn to each other. Giving in to that
passion made them expectant parents—but would Heather believe in
Lucas's love and stick around for the wedding?

#980 A HOME FOR ADAM—Gina Ferris Wilkins
The Family Way

Dr. Adam Stone never expected to make a house call at his own
secluded vacation cabin. But then the very pregnant Jenny Newcomb
showed up on his doorstep. And one baby later, they were on their way to
an instant family!

#981 KISSES AND KIDS—Andrea Edwards
Congratulations!

Confusion over his name unexpectedly placed practical businessman
Patrick Stuart amongst Trisha Stewart and her cute kids. Pat *swore* he
was not the daddy type, but he couldn't resist sweet Trisha and her
brood for long....

#982 JOYRIDE—Patricia Coughlin
Congratulations!

Being thrown together on a cross-country drive was *not* the best way
to find a mate, Cat Bandini soon discovered. Bolton Hunter was her
complete opposite in every way—but with every passing mile, they
couldn't slow down their attraction!

#983 A DATE WITH DR. FRANKENSTEIN—Leanne Banks
Congratulations!

Andie Reynolds had spent her life taking care of others, and she'd
had it. Then sexy Eli Masters moved in next door. The neighbors
were convinced he was some sort of mad scientist. But Andie sensed
he was a single dad in need....

#984 THE AVENGER—Diana Whitney
The Blackthorn Brotherhood

Federal prosecutor Robert Arroya had time for little else but the pursuit
of justice. Then Erica Mallory and her adorable children showed him
how to trust again. But could their love survive a severe test?

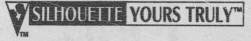